SUMMER FLING

JILL SANDERS

GRAYTON

This is a work of fiction. Names, characters, organizations, places, events, and incidents are either products of the author's imagination or are used fictitiously.

Text copyright © 2020 Jill Sanders

Printed in the United States of America

All rights reserved.

No part of this book may be reproduced, stored in a retrieval system, or transmitted in any form or by any means, electronic, mechanical, photocopying, recording, or otherwise, without express written permission of the publisher.

Published by Grayton Press

ISBN-13: 978-1-945100-14-7

Paperback: 9798639252976

SUMMARY

Scarlett had learned to keep her head down early in life. Zoey, her older sister, had always taken the reins in life, even when it came to helping their mother get back up after their father stole everything and ran off with a woman half his age, leaving the three of them with only the clothes on their backs and Zoey and Scarlett's inheritance. She'd been behind her sister one hundred percent in investing into River Camps. It had only taken one look at the sexy Levi to convince her that this was where she wanted to be.

After Levi had been raised by his grandmother, he'd searched high and low for the best job around. When he'd heard that River Camps was reopening, he'd jumped at the chance to stick close to his ailing grandmother. He hadn't expected to fall so hard for the beautiful Scarlett.

PROLOGUE

Scarlett stood on the banks of the river, looking out over the tall sea grass. She could see the small boat moving closer and walked to the end of the old dock to wait. She was fourteen, two years younger than all the other Wildflowers, but already she'd found the boy she wanted to be with for the rest of her life.

Levi Grant was the nicest, hottest boy she'd ever laid eyes on. He had beautiful blond curly hair that always seemed to fall in front of his sky-blue eyes. His skin was flawless, unlike her own, and he was tan and perfect. His smile, in her opinion, was his best feature and made her knees go weak.

She'd met Levi a week earlier, when he'd visited the camp with his grandmother, a personal friend of Elle Saunders' grandfather. The man ran River Camps, the only place Scarlett and her older sister, Zoey, had ever felt truly accepted.

Scarlett and Zoey, along with Elle Saunders, Hannah Rodgers, and Aubrey Smith, their best friends, had called themselves the Wildflowers ever since they'd met four summers ago. They were now as close as sisters. They looked forward to spending their summers together and, when possible, talked on the phone with one another during school season.

Zoey and Scar, as everyone called her, were the only sisters in the group. Elle's grandfather owned the camp, and Elle had been the one who had brought the five of them together that first summer. She was tall, blond, and the most outgoing and organized of the group.

Hannah, with her perfect style, hair, and makeup, had been the envy of most of them. Even though she was soft spoken, Hannah was the one who coordinated their activities.

Aubrey was the shiest out of them all, even more than Scarlett. Her fiery red hair and haunting blue eyes usually got her attention she didn't want or ask for.

Scar was the youngest of the five of them and just a step behind them in most things—except for this one thing.

Being the first one to fall in love somewhat embarrassed Scarlett. The others could never understand how her heart hurt when Levi wasn't around or when she looked at him. At this point, her heart hurt all the time.

Just watching the way that he moved and talked did funny things to her insides.

As the small boat bumped into the dock, she raced forward to catch the rope he tossed towards her.

"How was it?" she asked, eagerly.

Levi looked up at her with those sexy blue eyes, his blond hair, curls and all, tucked under a New York Yankee's ball cap.

"Good." He shrugged, then turned and helped his grandmother out of the boat. His grandmother smiled up at her through a large sun hat.

Levi was the complete opposite of his grandmother. The woman had straight dark hair, darker skin, and deep brown eyes that showed the woman had seen a few things in her life. Including sadness.

"Hi, Scarlett. My, you've grown so much since the last time I saw you." The older woman looked much younger than Elle's grandfather. If Scarlett hadn't known, she would have thought that she was Levi's mother instead of his grandmother. She'd met Mrs. Grant a few times before since coming to River Camps, an elite summer camp for privileged girls. The camp was tucked onto acres and acres of private land between Pelican Bay and the emerald waters of the Gulf of Mexico on Florida's Panhandle.

Scarlett had been coming here since she was nine and hoped to continue coming back for the rest of her life.

"Thanks." She smiled as she finished tying off the boat, her eyes skirting to Levi every chance she got.

"Wow, you've gotten taller too. You're almost as tall as my Levi." Her arm went around Levi as the boy rolled his eyes.

"Gran, everyone's taller than me," he complained.

"You'll hit your growing spurt soon," she said, patting him on the shoulder. Then she leaned forward and whispered to Scarlett, "Boys mature later than girls."

Scar would have been embarrassed at that comment, but just then, a bunch of other girls from the summer camp came rushing up to talk to the only boy on campus.

News of his visits spread throughout the cabins. Stories of how cute he was had reached every single one of the almost hundred girls in attendance that summer.

Somehow, Scarlett ended up being pushed to the back of the group of admirers as Jenny Carpenter and her cronies, as the Wildflowers called them, surrounded Levi and his grandmother.

All of the girls threw questions at them as if they were celebrities.

She didn't know who was responsible—after all, she was too busy watching Levi's reaction to something one of them had said—but before she could grab hold of anything, hands shoved her from behind.

Falling sideways into the water was one thing—she'd taken plenty of jumps off this very dock on purpose. But this time it was in front of Levi and the others. She was completely mortified when she surfaced. Her long mousy hair blocked her view of everyone laughing at her. She may not have seen them, but the sound would stick in her memory for years to come.

Pushing her hair out of her eyes, she swam towards the ladder as tears stung her eyes.

"Here." A hand appeared before her face. "Let me help you up."

All the laughter died away as Scarlett looked up into the bluest eyes she'd ever seen. Her heart quickened at the feel of his warm skin against her own.

If she'd thought she'd lost her heart before, having Levi shower attention on her for the rest of his visit that day sealed the deal.

To her complete joy, he was back the following day. The fact that he went out of his way to hunt her down caused her heart to skip a beat for the first time. She'd read about people falling in love in some books and had often wondered how it would feel to have her heart react like that to someone. Now she knew.

"Hey." Levi caught up with her the following day, jogging over to her until he fell into step next to her. "Where are you heading?" Today, he hadn't worn a ball cap, leaving his hair loose, allowing her to enjoy all those blond curls. He kept shoving it out of his eyes, a move that made her knees go weak again.

"I..." She stopped and glanced around. They were alone on the pathway. She was supposed to meet her friends at the pool for a swim, but now, she didn't want to share Levi with anyone else. "Nowhere." She shrugged.

"How about going to the beach with me?" he asked, shoving his hands deep into his short's pockets. "Gran and Joe are having a meeting."

"Sure," she answered a little too quickly.

When he started walking towards the camp's private beach, she fell into step next to him.

"You don't think Joe and my grandmother are…" he asked as he glanced over at her.

Her dark eyebrows shot up. She hadn't thought of the older couple in that way. Elle had mentioned that they were old friends, not romantic.

"I don't think so," she answered slowly. "Why? Would it be so bad?" she asked as they turned down the path that opened to the beach.

"No, I guess not." His eyes scanned the beach. She glanced around and groaned when she saw Jenny and her cronies.

"Hey." He took her hand and pulled her back a step before the group could see them. "We can go somewhere else?"

She thought quickly. "I know a place." She tugged on his arm until they rushed through the trees together.

"Gosh, slow down," he said, laughing. "Your legs are so long."

She stopped, frowning down at herself. It was true. She'd grown freakishly tall in the last year. She'd let his grandmother's comment the day before sliding off her, but hearing Levi say it today… stung.

"Hey," he said, stepping closer. "That's a good thing." He nudged her chin up until she met his blue eyes. "I like girls with long legs." He moved closer. "And hazel eyes." He took another step towards her. "And soft hair the color of dark honey." His hand reached up and brushed a strand of her hair out of her eyes, causing her breath to catch.

She'd never been this close to a boy before. Had never been kissed. Was Levi going to kiss her?

Just then, they both heard laughter nearby as a group of girls approached the pathway. Without thinking, she grabbed his hand again and pulled him towards Elle's secret hideout.

Elle's grandfather had built the small tree house a year ago.

The Wildflowers used it every chance they could. They had even snuck out and slept up there a couple nights. But since her friends were all at the pool waiting for her, she knew it was a place they could be alone.

Pulling on the rope, she tugged the hidden ladder towards the ground.

"Geez, that's cool," Levi said, helping her pull it down so they could climb up. She climbed up first with him following close behind her. "Wow," he said, stepping inside the small one-room tree house. There weren't any windows yet, but Elle's grandfather promised to install some later that winter.

For the next few minutes, Levi walked around the space, looking at all the things the Wildflowers had dragged up there—a couple of chairs, an old futon, and a bunch of books and magazines along with a camping lamp.

"Do you want some water?" she asked suddenly, unsure what to do or say. She walked over to the cooler where they kept bottles of water and warm soda.

"Sure," he said, moving closer to her to take it from her. When their hands met, she felt her skin spark.

"Scarlett." Levi set the bottle down. "I like you."

She swallowed. "I like you too." She smiled.

"Can I kiss you?" he asked as his eyes went to her mouth.

Her heart rate spiked, and she felt her palms go sweaty. She didn't think she could talk, since her throat had closed suddenly.

Instead of answering, she nodded and closed her eyes. The moment Levi's lips touched hers, she knew she would never love anyone else, ever.

CHAPTER ONE

*E*ight years later...

Scarlett would never hate anyone as much as she hated Levi Grant. The man infuriated her. Who did he think he was? God's gift sent down to woo every woman and sweep them off their feet?

She held in a growl as she marched towards the main building. Her fists were clenched tight as she pushed open the back door, which opened to a long hallway leading towards her office.

When she saw Dylan come out of her sister's office, she rolled her eyes.

"Men," she said as she changed direction from her office to her sister's and pushed by him.

"What did we do?" Dylan asked with a laugh.

Normally, she would have ignored him. After all, she liked her sister's fiancé. Really, she did. But she wasn't in the mood. Instead, she faced him, hands on her hips as she narrowed her eyes and assessed him. Sure enough, there were signs he and her sister had just been making out. His dark hair was ruffled and, was that a hickie on his chin?

"You only want one thing," she finally said, causing Dylan to laugh again.

"I can assure you, there's more to life than just sex," he replied with a smug smile.

"Right," she spat out.

"Cookies," he said, shocking her. It was then that she noticed he held out a plate towards her. The pile of double chocolate chip brownie cookies sat there like a peace offering. No doubt the lot was missing from the kitchen where Isaac Andrew, the camp's celebrity chef, controlled everything. She knew that if she was caught as an accessory… She glanced up and down the hallway before taking two of them.

"If Isaac catches you…" she warned.

Dylan's smile grew. "I have his blessing." He nodded and started to pull the plate away.

"In that case." She grabbed another two cookies. When Dylan started to complain, she stepped inside her sister's office and shut the door on his face.

"What happened now?" Zoey asked from across the room.

Scarlett's eyes zoned in on her sister. Yup, she was right. Zoey's hair was coming out of its long braid as if someone's fingers had been messing with it. Her shirt was almost sideways, and her chin was red from Dylan's stubbly chin.

Taking a bite of her first cookie, she plopped down on the chair opposite Zoey's desk and rolled her eyes for good measure.

"Men," she said again.

"Let's be honest. You don't have an issue with all men. Just one man." Zoey leaned forward and handed Scarlett a bottle of water. "For the cookies. Tell me what Levi did now."

"He…" She took a drink of the water and somehow the mix of the coolness and the chocolate helped dissipate some of her anger. "I caught him flirting with Andrea."

Zoey laughed. "Everyone flirts with Andrea. Actually,

scratch that. Andrea flirts with everyone. Elle even mentioned that Andrea came on to her once," Zoey said, sitting down and glancing at her computer screen.

"Duh, Elle's hot." Scarlett shrugged. "I'd come on to her too if I wasn't…"

"Totally infatuated with Levi?" Zoey supplied, glancing up at her and earning a glare from Scarlett.

"I am not…" She started to deny it.

"Oh please." Zoey stood up and moved around the desk to stand in front of Scarlett. "Go ahead, deny it." Her sister leaned closer until they were eye to eye. "You have been totally infatuated with him since that summer he swaggered into the camp with his grandmother."

She wanted to deny that Levi swaggered but bit her lip instead. He did have a sexy way about him when he walked. Sigh.

"I thought so." Zoey chuckled and reached back to take another cookie from a smaller plate sitting on the desk. Scarlett watched her sister bite solidly into it.

"So, it's less than three months before you and Dylan tie the knot." Scarlett figured that changing the subject was the best way to combat her sister.

Zoey's smile tripled, if there was such a thing. Her eyes sparkled and she did a little booty dance Scarlett had grown up making fun of.

"I'm getting married," she sang as she danced around the room, munching on her cookie.

"And you won't fit into your wedding dress if you keep eating that." She stood up and snagged the cookie from her sister.

"Hey." Zoey grabbed it back. "I'm filling in for Elle later today in her evening yoga class." She took a huge bite, sending half the cookie to the floor. "So, leave me alone," she added through a full mouth. "Besides..." She motioned to the cookies Scarlett had grabbed from Dylan. "You have more than I do."

"These are for later," she lied. She hadn't gotten around to eating lunch that day. Come to think of it, she hadn't eaten breakfast either.

Zoey walked back around and sat down at her desk. "What did he do now?" she finally asked.

Scarlett took a deep breath, after finishing off her second cookie and drinking some water. What she wanted was a huge glass of chocolate milk, but figured the calorie-free water was a good thing since she was having a gazillion calories with the four cookies.

"I caught him with Andrea," she reminded her sister.

Zoey rolled her eyes. "Caught him just flirting or something more?"

"I walked in..." Scarlett started. "He was flirting..."

"Ugh!" Zoey groaned. "What was he actually doing?" she ground out.

Now that Scarlett had calmed down, thanks to the talk and the chocolate, she realized just what a fool she'd been.

"It doesn't matter," she mumbled.

Zoey's laughter had her back on edge. "You always mumble when you realize you were wrong."

"Shut up." She stood up and marched towards the office door. For good measure, as she left, she stuck her tongue out at her sister and slammed the door.

She hadn't calculated that there would be a person standing on the other side of the door. And, just her luck, that person was the one she'd been avoiding.

Levi stood just on the other side of the door; his hand poised to knock on her sister's office door.

Scarlett's forward motion about took him out, but he grabbed her with his strong arms and steadied them both. She heard her remaining cookies crumble against his chest as their bodies collided.

His chuckle sent waves of anger and desire through her at the same time. Still, just remembering their past together, she felt her spine straighten.

"You are such a klutz. You've crushed my cookies," she accused him.

His chuckle deepened. "Darlin', it wouldn't be the first time."

Her back teeth clenched as she jerked out of his arms. What remained of her breakfast and lunch fell to the floor.

His eyes followed hers to the floor. "Did you steal those from Isaac?"

"No," she ground out as she bent down to pick up the pieces so she could throw them in the trash. Of course, he chose that exact moment to do the same. Their foreheads collided and for a split second, she saw stars.

"Damn it," she growled out, falling backwards and landing on her butt in the middle of the hallway.

"If you'd let me..." he started, his hands going under her arms as he lifted her back to her feet.

At some point, years after that first kiss, he'd shot up to his current six-three height. Just the fact that he'd outdone her in even this area had her on edge. She would never admit it to even herself, let alone anyone else, but she kind of missed the days when they were close to the same height.

Scarlett opened her mouth to argue, but he was already kneeling before her, scraping up the remains of some of the best cookies she'd ever eaten.

It took him two trips to the trash can at the end of the hallway before the floor was clean. When all the crumbs were gone, she was still standing there with her arms crossed over her chest, watching him.

"You owe me," she said.

His blond eyebrows shot up. "Still?" His smile was intoxicating. How was any woman supposed to not fall hard and fast for that sexy smile?

She jerked around and started walking away, only to have him fall in step with her.

"Don't you have a meeting with my sister?" She motioned behind her to the door he'd been just about to knock on.

"No, just a quick question." He smiled and held open the outer door for her. "One that you can answer for me instead." He followed her down the pathway. She had about an hour before she was due to show some new guests around the grounds. She and her friends had spent the last two years rebuilding the camp and turning it from a run-down elite summer camp for privileged girls into an exclusive year-round snowbird retreat.

It had taken almost a full year to revamp the cabins, which used to house at least a dozen young ladies from wealthy families, into private cabins for singles or couples. Once all the original cabins had been refurbished, the task of building more unique cabins had started.

The new cabins spread all over the one-hundred-acres of land on the beautiful emerald coast of the Florida Panhandle. Currently, there were thirty-five cabins, most of which were booked solid for the next year. Thankfully, there were five more cabins in the works that would be finished being built by the end of the year.

The rest of the old buildings on the campgrounds had taken a lot of work to get ready as well. When Elle's grandfather had died and left the five friends the property, it hadn't taken them long to decide to pool together and open the place again. Now, they were determined to stick it out through thick and thin.

The first year, before the doors opened, there were a lot of thin times. Even after guests started flooding in, they had to stretch their money to make things work. But sometime after that first season, everything had just fallen into place.

She knew it was in part thanks to Dylan and his brothers. The Costas came from an elite family in Destin. Their family's large empire had gained them the reputation of being one of the top families in the area. Everything they touched turned to gold.

When the camp had been low on potential employees, Owen, the oldest of the three brothers, had sent over a group of people looking for jobs. It had helped greatly, since there was a serious shortage of good full-time employees in the area.

The fact that Owen and Hannah Rodgers were now a solid item and engaged had of course helped the cause. Actually, all three brothers were now roped in with her friends. Dylan and Zoey had been the first to make their relationship public after a nasty bout with an ex-worker, Ryan Kinsley, who had pulled a gun on Dylan.

But since her sister Zoey was such a bad ass, she'd tackled the woman, who had been quickly arrested. Months later, after posting bail, Ryan had snuck onto the campgrounds and stabbed Elle at one of the camp's dinner parties. The woman had served a couple months behind bars and had been released early on good behavior.

Again, they had lucked out that it hadn't been life threatening. The woman had tried to sue the camp after that, but with the help of the Costa's lawyers, the case had been closed quickly enough. Ryan had seemed to slink away into the darkness. Rumors had it that she'd moved to California, but everyone kept their eyes peeled for her on a daily basis.

Now, as she walked down the wide pathways, through the thick underbrush that surrounded the campgrounds, she couldn't imagine herself being or working anywhere else.

"What's your question?" She finally stopped and turned to Levi when he didn't ask his question.

"Are you always going to walk as if you're late for a fire?" He was smiling at her again. The kind of smile that always made her knees weak.

"Yes." She turned and started walking again. "I'm glad I could clear that up for you. Now, if you don't mind—"

She stopped when he put his hand on her arm.

"Sassy, I don't know what I ever did to make you hate me..." Her eyes narrowed at the use of his old nickname for her. "Well, maybe I do, but nothing that would warrant such..."—he shook his head— "disdain."

Her eyebrows shot up. "Think it over." She glanced down at his hand on her arm and smirked when his hand dropped away. "I'm sure you'll figure it out, someday." She turned to go again.

"Whatever it was, I'm sorry," he called out to her.

"Save your apologies until you know what it is exactly that you are apologizing for," she said over her shoulder.

As she stepped out of the clearing near the dock area, she realized she'd headed the wrong way. She had needed to go towards the front of the main building to greet the new guests. That man totally infuriated her and turned her around.

She glanced down at her watch. Luckily, she still had time before she was supposed to meet the newcomers.

"Lost?"

She glanced up and growled at Levi, who was leaning against the trunk of a tree.

"Go away," she hissed, and started marching down the pathway in the right direction. Of course, he fell in step with her.

"I can't, I work here." He smiled. "Remember?"

"Don't you have...work?" She glanced around.

He chuckled. "Actually, it's what I was coming to ask you or your sister about."

"Well?" She sighed. "What is it?" She had totally lost her patience with the man.

Damn, why did his camp T-shirt have to stretch over his chest so tightly? She forced her eyes back up to his blue ones. Damn, they were just as sexy as ever. Deep pools of blue that she could get lost in. She remembered the first time he'd kissed her. The first time he'd touched her, really touched her.

Her body instantly reacted. Crossing her arms over her chest to hide the fact that her nipples had puckered at the memory, she waited.

"Liam needed my help setting up a few new bench swings around the grounds later today. I have a group I was supposed to go hiking with at four." He glanced down at his watch. "Elle mentioned that you or Zoey might..."

"Zoey's got a yoga class. I'll take the group." She made a mental note to rush up and change into her hiking boots after she finished with the newcomers.

"Thanks." Levi smiled and then surprised her by reaching up and tugging a strand of her hair in a playful move he used to do all the time. "I really will owe you after this."

This time, he was the one who turned and disappeared down the pathway, leaving her to watch that impressive body disappear—his tight ass in the shorts, his tanned and toned legs. Suddenly, she wanted to lick every part of him. It was probably due to her hunger. After all, she'd only managed to eat two of those cookies. She felt her stomach growl.

"Damn," she mumbled as she made her way towards the front of the camp.

She pasted on her welcoming smile as she met the Clines on the front steps of the main building. Falling into her well-planned tour guide script helped calm her down after her run-in with Levi.

She happened to catch a glimpse of Liam and Levi installing one of the massive log swings along the path near the beach. She knew it was a perfect spot for couples to enjoy the sunset, since she had at one point, had a magical night with Levi in that very spot.

Feeling her face flush at the memory, she avoided his gaze and turned the opposite direction down the pathway, showing the couple the boathouse instead, telling them all about the sunset sails, kayaks, and canoes available to them during their stay.

There was so much to do around the camp that, even after an hour of showing them around, she knew there were plenty of things that she'd missed. But since they had flyers of all the activities in each cabin, she doubted they would miss out.

After leaving the couple with drinks at the pool bar, she rushed upstairs and changed into a pair of khaki pants and hiking boots. She even made sure to grab a light jacket, since the evening weather report called for rain.

She'd left a message for the group she was supposed to take out to bring appropriate gear as well. Each of the cabins was outfitted with state-of-the-art touch screens that had their own messaging system for announcements.

Guests could schedule fun activities or massages, order food and drinks, or learn about planned events during their stay.

She headed off down the chosen hiking path with five guests—the wife of one of the gentlemen had preferred to get a massage instead of hiking in nature. She told the group about the local vegetation and wildlife as they went.

When the light rain started, two of the guests decided to head back to their cabin. She was going to escort them, but they waved her off and disappeared down the pathway alone. Since they had headed in the right direction, she relaxed.

"Shall we go on?" she asked the rest through the light rain.

"I'm game," the single man said eagerly.

The last couple glanced at one another. "I think we'll stroll down to the pool bar and have a hot toddy instead," the man said.

After telling them which direction to go, she turned back to the last guest. "Would you like to continue?" she asked.

He motioned for her to lead the way.

They walked for a few minutes as she filled him in on everything she knew about the area.

When she stopped by a large magnolia tree and started talking about when the flowers would be blooming, she realized just how alone she and the older man were.

Not that she couldn't take care of herself, but she'd never been left alone with a guest like this.

Each time she stopped to talk about something, the man seemed to get closer to her. She decided to start making their way back towards civilization. They were less than half a mile from the nearest campground pathway when she realized just how dark it had grown. The clouds had completely closed out any sunlight as the light rain continued to fall.

"Do you do this often?" the guest asked.

"Um, no, I'm filling in for someone," she said, a little uneasy now, since he'd brushed his arm against hers a few times. She could tell it was on purpose. There was enough space between the trees for a truck.

"Oh, that's too bad." He smiled at her. "I really do enjoy walking with you." His eyes ran over her top and she realized that she hadn't zipped her jacket all the way up, leaving her white camp shirt clinging to her and almost completely see-through from the rain.

Reaching down, she tried to zip up her jacket, but the zipper stuck. Deciding quickly on a different tactic, she crossed her arms over her chest to hide the fact that the wind and rain were chilly.

"I'm sure your wife will enjoy going on the next walk with you." She moved faster through the brush.

"Oh, she's not the outdoorsy type." He kept up with her easily enough and reached out to take her arm. "Why don't we slow down, enjoy ourselves some?"

She was just about to open her mouth to discourage the man when Levi stepped out of the darkness.

"There you are." His eyes took in the man's hand on her arm. She was pretty sure that there was a panicked look in her eyes, since she watched Levi's blue eyes heat and turn towards the man.

"Carl, I think Barbara was looking for you. She was leaving the pool bar when I saw her last and was heading back to your cabin when the rain started."

The man's hand dropped away from Scarlett's arm and he took a step back.

"I'll go…" He started to turn around.

"That way." Levi pointed in the right direction.

"Thanks," Carl said, rushing down the pathway.

Even though she'd been relieved to see Levi, just as she would have been to see anyone else, she knew she could have handled the unwanted attention all by herself.

It wasn't as if she hadn't been hit on by other guests since they'd opened their doors.

"Hey." Levi smiled at her and stepped closer. "You doing okay?" He'd changed into khaki pants and boots but was still wearing that damn sexy camp T-shirt that showed off his muscular arms and chest. Especially since it was now soaking wet and sticking to his body. His blond hair had been cut recently, shorter than she liked it, since all his curls were gone now.

She'd dreamed often of what he looked like under his cotton camp shirt ever since she'd seen him playing volleyball once with the other employees, before the camp was officially opened. He'd pulled off his shirt to play in the sun. Just seeing all that tan, toned skin had almost sent her system into overload.

She tried to avoid his eyes and shrugged. "I could have handled myself." She motioned behind her, where the man had disappeared.

"Right," he said, taking her hand and leading her out of the thickest part of the brush. When they stepped into an opening, she jerked her hand free.

"I could have." She stopped herself from stomping her foot, only because she was standing in about an inch of mud at the moment and didn't want to splash it all over her pants.

"I don't doubt it." His eyes ran over her, and she noticed a change in them. Glancing down, she realized that her camp shirt was just as glued to her skin as his was.

Pulling her jacket closed, she jerked her chin up.

"I made a mistake," he said in a low tone.

"What?" She crossed her arms over her chest again. "I've taken groups out on hikes before. I can take care of myself."

He shook his head. "No, that's not what I meant." His eyes moved to hers as he stepped closer to her, as close as Carl had been moments ago, yet it felt worlds different.

"Me. Touching you. Ever," he said softly. "I shouldn't have ever allowed myself to."

She swallowed and held her breath as he moved even closer to her. What was he saying? Why was he telling her this now? How could she focus on what he was saying when all she could see was the blueness of his eyes boring into her soul, stealing her heart once more.

CHAPTER TWO

He knew that he would pay for his sins someday. He just hoped it was a lot later in life. He was right, he had made a mistake all those years ago. Touching Scarlett had been the most grievous sin he'd ever committed.

Yet he couldn't stop the pull towards her now. Her long dark hair was matted to her face, those big hazel eyes of hers scanning his as if searching for answers to life, the universe, and, well, everything.

It was her lush lips that called to him now. The memory of their plump softness under his own was an addiction he'd denied himself of for years. His dreams were filled with once more enjoying them, taking what he wanted, letting them fill his every need.

He realized he'd reached out and touched her, pulled her close, when their wet shirts collided, sending a zip of heat throughout his skin.

He'd marveled at the sight of her erect nipples poking through her thin camp shirt. Then he'd heated at the thought of Carl hitting on Scarlett, seeing everything he had. He should have knocked the man on his ass.

"Levi?" Scarlett's sultry voice drew him back to the now. He felt her shiver against his body as she raised her chin, bringing her sexy lips closer to his.

"Sassy," he said, calling her the old nickname he'd given her all those summers ago when he'd first dared to kiss her.

That was all it took. She arched up on her toes as he closed the distance between them. It was like returning home after years of being left to wander the desert.

She was everything he'd ever wanted. Everything he'd ever needed. She tasted like heaven and when he arched to get a better hold on her, he felt her tense. It was like a bucket of cold water fell over his head. His arms dropped to his sides as she stepped back from him.

Her hand went to cover her mouth, and her eyes widened as they scanned his. The pain in them was heartbreaking, as was the shocked look she gave him.

"How could you?" she asked, shaking her head as she backed up even further.

"Sassy." He reached for her, to explain, to tell her something, but she turned and darted through the darkness, leaving him wondering just what in hell he'd done to cause her so much pain.

Why couldn't she talk to him? Each time he'd asked her, she'd told him that he had to figure it out on his own. But the truth was, he honestly didn't know what he could have done to cause her so much pain.

Walking back to the main building, he dried himself off and then jumped into his old Jeep and drove home.

The fact that he lived less than ten minutes from the camp was one of the main reasons he'd taken the job. That, and Scarlett.

His Gran had needed a little more help in the past few years, which meant going away to college had not been one of his options.

The woman had given up everything for her only grandchild after her daughter had fallen into addiction and died shortly after Levi's seventh birthday. His mother had taken the secret of who Levi's father was to the grave, and this haunted him daily. It was like a part of him was missing, a part that he would never find.

He felt the same about Scarlett.

He parked next to his Gran's sedan and dashed through the rain to the front porch. He stomped the mud off his boots and hung them on the hooks to dry. He pulled off his soaking camp clothes just inside the mud room and pulled on an extra pair of sweats he kept in the room for such occasions.

"Gran," he called out, hearing the television running in the TV room in the back of the older house.

"Back here," she called out. "I have dinner ready for you."

He sometimes helped out at the camp in the evening with the elaborate dinners in the huge dining hall but, a while back, they had hired enough help that he was only needed on special occasions. Tonight, wasn't one of those nights, which meant he was going to enjoy dinner with his grandmother. The woman's meals could easily go head to head with Isaac's best meals. It was one of the reasons he'd been a chubby child, and the main reason he worked with the old weights in the garage at least twice a week.

"What'd you cook up for me?" he asked, moving over and planting a kiss on the paper-thin skin of her cheek.

"Meatloaf." She smiled up at him, then waved her hands. "Help me up."

He pulled her easily from the recliner and wrapped his arms around her, holding onto her for a moment. "How was your day, beautiful?" he asked, feeling saddened by the way she was shrinking before his very eyes.

His entire life, the woman had been bigger than life. Now,

she was so frail and thin he was concerned he'd break her every time he wrapped his arms around her.

"The same." She sighed and patted him on the back. "You?"

"I kissed Scarlett," he blurted out. He'd never kept anything from his Gran.

"It's about time," she said, chuckling as he let her go. "Come on, you can tell me everything over dinner. I bet you're starving."

"I am," he agreed and followed her back into the kitchen.

She chuckled and he felt part of his heart settle at the sound. "When aren't you hungry?"

It was like a reboot. Sitting at the old table, talking with his grandmother about his day. About kissing Scarlett, the woman he'd been infatuated with since the first time he'd laid eyes on her so many summers ago.

Still, he couldn't bring himself to tell his Gran about Scarlett's disdain for him. He hadn't been lying. He really didn't know what he'd done to her to cause all the animosity. Still, he had a clue.

After all, when she'd left to go home after their magical summer together, he hadn't called, texted, or written to her like he'd promised he would. Not that he hadn't tried initially.

Four months after promising his heart to her, he'd gone to the school dance with Emma Willis. A year later, he'd dated Robin Stephens, only breaking things off with her when she'd moved away with her family half a year later.

He'd been a rake. It hadn't been until he'd heard the five friends had moved back into the camp full time almost two years ago that he'd remembered how he'd felt for her.

Then he'd seen her strolling across the grounds in short cutoffs and a tight red tank top, her long dark hair flowing around her face as she laughed at something her sister had said.

When her hazel eyes had found him, he'd recognized the instant return of attraction and had felt like he'd been knocked over the head. Then her smile had faded, and he'd sworn to himself that he would happily spend the rest of his life trying to get it back.

He'd had plenty of practice, as class clown, at getting girls to laugh at him. It wasn't hard. Normally. He purposely bumped into them, spilled things on himself, or cracked a few well-timed jokes.

But with Scarlett, things had gotten... muddled.

Instead, he'd usually caused the drinks to land on her. Bumping into her was almost a given, since he had practically followed her around that year before the camp had officially opened.

Then, when guests were running around the place, he'd only seemed to irritate her. Still, he'd caught her almost cracking a smile a few times.

Remembering how he'd found her alone with Carl earlier that evening had him reassessing his plans. He knew it wasn't the first time she'd been hit on. Hell, several of the camp employees talked about who was going to crack her tough outer shell first. There was even a pool going on who was going to be the conqueror of Scarlett.

After he'd eaten his fill of his grandmother's food and had helped to clean up the mess in the kitchen, his gran returned to watching her evening shows. He headed out to the garage to lift weights, since he was going stir crazy thinking about that kiss.

At the end of his workout, he was still restless. The rain had continued as the wind picked up, sending the tall pine trees that surrounded their house swaying and creaking in the dark night.

He showered and decided a quick drive would help clear his mind. When he parked at the camp and saw the lights surrounding the dining room, he realized the only thing that could soothe his mind was talking to her again.

Stepping into the loud dining room, he glanced around until he spotted her standing at the bar near the back of the room.

He was halfway across the room when he realized the theme for the evening must be neon, since most of the guests were dressed in brightly colored clothes.

Guests frequently went out of their way for the themed dinners at the camp. Over the last year, they'd had everything from masquerade balls to fifties parties. Their website was updated often and allowed guests to coordinate for parties during their visits. Most guests totally got into the nights, but some just came dressed in normal summer attire.

Tonight, it seemed, the entire room was flooded with bright colors, accented by the black lights placed around the massive room.

Scarlett was no exception. Her tight bright-pink dress clung to her body and glowed in the black light that hug over the bar. When he stepped closer to her, he realized even her lip and eye makeup glowed pink.

When she spotted him, her eyebrows shot up.

"I didn't think you were working tonight," she said smoothly. The smile that had been there moments before slipped.

"I'm not." He leaned against the bar and watched her sip from the drink she had.

"Then?" She waited, her head tilting slightly. She'd tied her long hair back in an intricate braid that wrapped around her head. Bright glowing ribbons intertwined with the braids. Large hooped earrings dangled from her ears, catching the light every time she moved her head. She was a magnet to his desire.

His eyes traveled down her, over the impressive cleavage exposed by her skintight dress.

"You went all out tonight." He motioned to her dress.

She glanced down and shrugged as she leaned back against the bar. "It's Elle's." She shifted as if suddenly uncomfortable. "It's too small."

He smiled. "Yes, it is."

Her eyes narrowed and he watched annoyance cross her face. "What are you doing here?"

Instead of answering, he waved Britt, the head bartender, over. "Rum and Coke." She glanced over at Scarlett.

"He's off the clock," she answered with a shrug. "I'll have another." She motioned to her own drink.

"What are you drinking?" he asked, moving a little closer to her.

"Ginger ale." She glanced around, as if looking for something to interrupt the conversation. Then, upon finding nothing, she turned back to him. "You didn't answer my question."

"I came to see you," he answered, "and I'm thankful I did." His eyes ran over her dress again.

"Listen." She straightened suddenly, but Britt moved back over and set the drink in front of him.

"You're underdressed," Britt joked.

He glanced down at his white T-shirt and jeans. "I hadn't planned to stop by." He shrugged.

She started to respond, but Scarlett glanced at her and the woman disappeared instead.

"You scared her." He shook his head. "I didn't think anything could scare Britt."

He'd meant it as a joke, but Scarlett frowned and took up her new drink. "Go away." She started across the room, and he grabbed his drink and followed her.

"Why?" he asked, falling in step with her.

She glanced over at him, then stopped in the middle of the dance floor.

"Because I'm working."

"When aren't you working?" he asked, taking her drink and setting it down with his on an empty table. Then he surprised her and himself by taking her hand and moving around the dance floor.

"Purple Rain" was playing and, even though the dance floor

was filled with couples grinding against one another, he pulled her into his arms and started moving slowly.

"What are you doing?" she asked, moving in his arms.

"I would think it was obvious." He smiled down at her. "We're doing it together, after all."

She shook her head. "Why do you keep persisting?"

"I would think that was obvious too," he said smoothly.

Her eyes moved to his lips, and he couldn't stop the smile as he glanced down at her own pink glossed lips.

"Your lips are glowing," he said.

She frowned. "It's the gloss Elle gave me. It glows under the black light."

"Makes me want to kiss you again," he said smoothly. She stiffened instantly.

"Don't," she warned.

"Why not?" He nudged her a little closer. His hand spanned her narrow lower back. The softness of her body was causing his own to harden uncomfortably.

"I don't want you to," she responded, her eyes once again going to his lips.

"Something tells me that's not the truth." He moved across the floor. Her hand bunched against his shoulder, yet he felt her relax slightly.

"It is." She bit her bottom lip, a sure sign she was lying.

"How long have we known each other?" he asked, suddenly.

"Too long," she admitted.

He chuckled. "Then you should know by now, you can't fool me."

She was silent as the music changed to a slower tune. "Forever Young" filled the room as the bodies around them slowed and started swaying to the melody.

"What would you do if I kissed you?" His eyes moved back to her lips, then up to her hazel eyes. He could see the change, the desire that flashed there. "What would you do if I took you, made love to you?"

He felt his heart skip at the thought of being with her.

"No," she said under her breath. He could see the fear, then the anger started to build in her eyes. Taking a step away, he dropped his hands from her, instantly missing the softness of her body next to his.

"Soon," he promised. "Soon you'll want... me again." Then without giving her time to respond to him, he turned and left.

He'd thought it had been hard to get his mind off of her before he'd driven to the camp that evening, but lying in bed thinking of her in the tight pink dress was pure hell.

Why did he continue to torture himself with Scarlett? It was obvious she hated him. But he had seen sparks of interest in her and there was no faking the desire that had radiated from her when she'd kissed him.

No, passion had never been a problem between them before.

CHAPTER THREE

Scarlett's week was filled with so much fun and activities that she didn't have time to stop and think about what Levi had told her or about that kiss. Or so she told herself over and over again. But the truth was, every time she found herself alone, she thought of him. Of that amazing kiss. The kiss that made all others she'd experienced pale in comparison.

Since the five friends had reopened River Camps, they'd strictly abided by certain rules. One of those rules was that each of them had two days off a week. She'd agreed to the rules mainly because she knew Elle wouldn't ever take time off if they all didn't consent.

She normally spent her two days in town, where Elle's grandfather's house was their home away from camp.

So much had changed since they'd first decided to reopen the camp after Elle's grandfather had passed away, leaving the property to the five friends. That first few months, they'd lived in the big house in town together. Then, after Aiden Smith, Elle's cousin of sorts, had had the electric and plumbing inspected and had signed off on the apartment Elle's grandfather had lived in on the campgrounds, they had all moved over there instead. Being close had made it easier for them to work daily on turning the camp into what it was now.

Things had changed when Zoey and Dylan had moved into one of the newly built cabins together. It was just a temporary move while they built a house on the outskirts of the grounds.

Elle and Liam were living in the old treehouse, which had been freshly remodeled with new additions, doubling the space. They had all worked on upgrading the small place shortly after Elle had fallen ill with meningitis, and now it was more like a home instead of a child's hideaway.

Since Owen still had his work in Destin at their family's business, Pelican Investments, he and Hannah spent their time split between the camp and his place across the bay in the larger town. He had recently purchased an older house in town, even thought it was currently being remodeled.

It was strange. The three-bedroom apartment had never felt crowded, even when all the friends had been living in it.

Now, however, with only Scarlett and Aubrey left in the space on a daily basis, the apartment felt empty.

Just like the big house in Pelican Point always felt empty when she spent her days off there.

The small town of Pelican Point was a delight to stay in, but she couldn't help but be lonely without her friends. She tried to fill her time by checking books out at the local library, making shopping runs, or spending time at the beach.

With her next days off quickly approaching, she wasn't surprised that she wanted to delay her loneliness. After all, it meant that she would have more time to think about Levi, who was already filling her mind and driving her crazy.

The man kept bumping into her. Everywhere she went around the grounds, he seemed to be there. Sometimes, like that night, he even tagged along on her evening group horse rides.

The more he joked with the two couples along for the sunset

ride, the more she thought that spending two days away from seeing his sexy butt in tight jeans as he rode smoothly in the saddle would be helpful. How had she never noticed what a perfect horse rider he was before this? His smooth motions were almost hypnotic to watch.

God, she needed time away from him, if only to forget how perfect his muscular arms looked in a tight T-shirt and how wonderful they'd felt wrapped around her as they'd danced together. Not to mention how his smile melted her knees and made her insides quiver.

In all the years since Levi had first kissed her, no one had ever made her feel like he had. Trust her, she'd tried to find someone, anyone, who could make her knees feel like Jell-O and turn her insides into the vibrating mess it was now as she tried to focus on the evening ride.

"Carol, honey, look! Manatees," one of the guests said and pointed to the small inlet they were riding by.

Sure enough, the manatees that often hung out in the clear water were grazing on the fresh grass near the edge of the inlet.

"Why don't we stop here?" she suggested to the group as she pulled her horse, Lady, to a stop. "It's a perfect spot to watch the sunset before we head back for the night."

When the group all agreed, she helped Carol and her husband, Bob, dismount from their horses.

Levi made sure all the horses were secured while the guests made their way to the edge of the water to take photos of the gentle grazing water giants.

"I bet you're glad you came along tonight," she said sarcastically to Levi when he stopped beside her.

When he chuckled, she felt her body betray her once more as a warm shiver washed over her at the sexy sound.

"It's a perfect night for a ride." He glanced sideways at her. "I think this is one of my favorite jobs on the grounds."

"Oh?" She turned slightly towards him. "I don't know, you

seemed to be enjoying refereeing the water volleyball game the other day."

She'd seen several of the guests paw him during the game, no doubt trying to score in other ways.

It had become clear to the friends, shortly after they had opened the gates of the camp, that a certain... voyeuristic clientele mixed in with the happily married couples.

They didn't have anything against couples who liked extra sexual activities, not if they kept to the rules of the camp. After the destruction caused by a big swingers' pool party early on, strict rules were printed clearly on small metal signs and displayed for all to see.

Destruction of any kind meant a hefty fine. The signs and the extra line their lawyer had added in all the rental agreements seemed to be doing the trick to discourage the wreckage.

But the warnings didn't stop some private parties. The fact that men and women flirted with their staff didn't bother most of the employees. Scarlett knew the benefits of allowing it to continue, since most of the staff enjoyed the heavy tips that flowed from the wealthy guests after a little flirting.

After her parents had divorced, Scarlett had taken a few waitressing jobs to help with the bills. She knew that flirting often greased the wheels and payed the bills.

"Yes, I always enjoy refereeing games," he answered her as she glanced over the water.

The sun was slowly setting, turning the sky an almost neon pink. The white clouds were turning purple and the pastel colors mixed together, lighting up the sky.

"It's a perfect unicorn sunset," she said with a sigh.

He chuckled. "I'd forgotten you called it that." He turned towards her, his blue eyes scanning her face. "There's a lot I'd forgotten about you." His eyes moved to her lips and he took a step closer. "Like how wonderful your lips feel and taste. How your sexy scent stays with me for days after I kiss you."

His voice was so low now that if they hadn't been standing so close, she wouldn't have been able to hear his words. Words that caused her mind to blank from anything and everything else except for what he was saying to her.

For just a moment, she lost herself in the memories, in the want. Her body even remembered how wonderful he felt next to her, holding her—his strong arms wrapped around her, how his lips felt on her skin, his tongue against her own. Then she shook her head and remembered the pain he'd caused. The deceit.

"Levi." She took a step back.

"Why do you do that?" he asked, his smile falling away.

"What?" She watched those sexy dimples of his disappear on the sides of his mouth and instantly missed them.

"Pull away like that?" He took her hand in his. It was warm, callused, and much bigger than her own.

"I'm not the one who pulled away."

"What does that mean?" He frowned slightly.

She opened her mouth to answer him, but just then a guest approached them with a question, and she spent the next fifteen minutes, as the sun continued to set, telling the couple about how warm the winters were around these parts.

Riding back towards the barn, she made a point to let Levi take up the rear position in the group. The less she had to look at that sexy butt in his worn jeans, the better off she was.

She was able to focus more on her job, making a point to tell the guests every detail she knew about the area as they went, even adding in an old story she'd heard as a kid at the camp long ago about pirates using the area for their buried treasure.

"You've been coming here a long time?" Carol asked as they dismounted just outside the barn.

"Yes." She smiled. "The first time I came here I was nine."

"It must have been nice." The older woman glanced around

as she stretched and rubbed her back side. "I can only imagine this place in its heyday."

Scarlett looked around, realizing that not much had changed here at the barn. Still, so much of the camp was better off now than it had been under Elle's grandfather. Not that Joe hadn't known how to run a camp. But only having privileged girls fill the space had been... well, boring.

The woman, who had obviously been around horses before, followed Scarlett and Levi into the barn and helped her get the animals settled for the night.

When Carol's husband came to collect her after smoking his cigarette by the dock in the designated smoking area, Scarlett was left alone to finish the rest of her tasks for the evening. She'd assumed Levi was somewhere in the barn, doing some task that needed to be done. She could hear him talking to an animal, chuckling at one of his own jokes, something she knew he did often.

Hell, she talked to the animals herself as she brushed them down and fed them. She got along better with them than she did most people.

She was in the process of telling Stormy, an older gelding, about her plans for her days off when she heard a chuckle behind her.

"You know, there are apps for people who are so lonely that they ask a horse to hang out with them on their days off."

She glared at Levi over her shoulder. "I wasn't asking him..." She sighed. "Go away."

"Make me," he joked. He took the brush from her hands then continued to rub the horse down himself.

"I can do that myself," she said, trying to take the brush back.

"I know, but if I do it, we can be done in time to head over and grab some snacks from the kitchen. I'm always hungry after a ride." He smiled over his shoulder at her and she lost her breath.

She stood back as he finished the job, talking to her or the horse as he went. She was too preoccupied with watching the way he moved to really focus on his words.

"Ready?" he asked when he'd finished the task.

"Sure." She moved out of the stall and secured the latch after he'd stepped outside.

She'd seen him in his worn jeans and boots plenty of times, but since that kiss... things were different.

"What?" he asked her when she stood there, looking at him.

She'd been thinking about that kiss again. The recent one. The one that had caused her toes to curl up in her hiking boots. How was she supposed to get any work done around him?

"Nothing." She jerked her chin high and stepped past him only to have him reach out and take her wrist gently in his hand. His long fingers circled around her arm easily.

"Sassy."

"Don't call me that." Her eyes narrowed and she felt the old pain surface.

"Why?" He smiled as he tilted his head to the side.

"You know why."

When she tried to jerk her hand free, he held on easily, making her realize just how much stronger he'd gotten.

"I thought I knew," he continued as his smile fell. "Why don't you tell me again."

She glanced down at their joined hands and realized their fingers were locked now. She hadn't even realized he'd shifted the hold. Damn it, her body was betraying her once again.

"It's what they used to call me," she blurted out. If she'd been more in control of herself, she wouldn't have even given him that bit of information, but she wasn't thinking clearly. Who could when he was slowly running a thumb over the inside of her palm? "Stop that," she said, her voice breathless from the thought of what he was doing to her.

"What?" His smile was back as he took a step towards her.

"That," she said, motioning to their joined hands.

"Why?" he asked as his other hand moved to the lower part of her back. When he nudged her closer, she moved as if he was in control of her body. "Don't you like it?"

"No," she lied. The way his smile doubled told her he hadn't bought it.

"Your hands are soft," he said as his eyes once more danced down to her lips. "As are other parts of you." He sighed. "It's been driving me crazy."

"Hm?" She didn't think she could take in enough oxygen to make a full sentence.

"I've been wanting to kiss you again." He bent his head down and touched her lips gently.

When his lips slanted over hers, their bodies melted together, which allowed her to feel his pulse through his thin T-shirt. Maybe that was her own pulse? It had to be, because it was racing as fast as a thoroughbred.

She hadn't realized he was basically holding her up until his hand moved higher on her back, forcing her to shift on those weak knees of hers.

"Sassy, I've wanted to do that for years," he said next to her lips. "I've been so desperate to feel you against me again."

She closed her eyes as his lips ran down her neck, sending trails of goose bumps all over her exposed skin.

"Yes," she sighed, agreeing with him.

"God, you don't know how crazy you make me, walking around in these." His hands moved to cup her butt, then he pulled her closer to him and she could feel him hard against her through his jeans. "Riding pants are sexier than any tight dresses and heels you have," he said, nibbling on her earlobe. He took it between his teeth and sucked on it gently as his hands ran over her curves, moving up until he cupped her breast.

She arched into his fingers, enjoying the feeling of being

touched again. It had been too long and, if she was going to tell the truth, no one had made her feel the way Levi could.

His name in her mind was like a bucket of ice being poured over her head. Her entire body froze.

Levi. This was Levi. The man who had hurt her, betrayed her. The man she could no longer trust with her heart.

Gripping his wrists, she jerked them away from her body. Without explanation, she bolted for the door, leaving him leaning against the wall of the barn, breathless and confused.

CHAPTER FOUR

What the hell? It took several moments before Levi understood that Scarlett had just run out of the barn. Ran out on him without any answers.

Sometime while they'd been kissing, the lights had dimmed to the point that the place was bathed in shadows. All the animals were quietly tucked in their stalls.

Deciding he needed a long walk; he took off across the grounds. He heard the loud noises inside the main dining hall, knowing that yet another party was raging inside its walls.

He wondered if it would ever get old—being able to spend his workdays outside, meeting new people, attending fun activities.

Then he stumbled upon a couple strolling hand in hand under the soft moonlight and watched them embrace and kiss under the stars.

His heart ached and swelled at the same time. Was it too much to ask to have someone he could grow old with? His grandfather had passed away long before he'd been born, leaving his gran to raise their daughter, Levi's mother, by herself. Gran claims it was all her fault that his mother, Mary, had gotten pregnant at sixteen, then addicted to drugs shortly after her senior year. It would go on to kill her days after Levi had turned seven.

To this day, he was still unsure who his father was. If the man was still around Pelican Point, he'd never stepped up to claim Levi, a fact that stung, no matter how much he denied it to his grandmother.

He knew that Scarlett had the next few days off from work. It was a nice perk to working at the camp, getting two days off a week of your choosing. Initially, he'd chosen the weekends, but since the camp had opened, he'd changed his days off to land in the middle of the week so he could enjoy some of the weekend events at the camp.

His days off were usually filled with chores or errands for his gran. The old house they lived in needed repairs often. He'd been planning to spend his next few days off up on the roof replacing some shingles that had blown off during the last windstorm.

He knew Scarlett and Aubrey spent their free days in the big house in town, just a block away from his place.

By the time he made it to the back door of the kitchen, he was desperately hoping there was some dessert left over. Isaac often allowed him to take leftovers home to his gran. The man was normally very strict about his kitchen supplies. But his gran had visited the camp a few times and Levi was pretty sure that Isaac had fallen for his gran's charms, so the man allowed him to take whatever he wanted home.

Stepping in, he found Isaac yelling at one of his employees. He was no Chef Ramsay, but the man demanded his way as far as kitchen staff went.

Levi thought about retracing his steps, but Isaac caught sight of him and waved him over.

"How is your grandmother?" he asked, after waving the employee away.

"She's…"

Isaac watched the young man he'd dismissed disappear. The guy's head was down, his shoulders slumped. As he exited the room, he glanced back at Isaac, no doubt to make sure the man was done.

"She's good," Levi finished. "Everything alright in here?" He nodded towards the doorway.

Isaac smiled and leaned closer. "Yes. I think that's the last time Tim is going to sneak out for a smoke break during the busy hour."

Levi chuckled. "That's all he did? I thought he'd burned something."

Isaac laughed and slapped him on the shoulder. "I have something…" He moved around the counter and came up with a tall brown paper bag. "For your grandmother. To thank her for her minestrone soup recipe." He set the bag down in front of him. Levi spotted a plate of brownies cooling a few feet away and felt his mouth water.

Betty, the pastry chef, was busy pulling more from the oven.

"Sure." Levi took the bag, but Isaac stopped him.

"I don't think Betty will mind if a few of those go missing." Isaac winked. "Just don't tell her I told you so if you get caught." The man turned and went back to work.

Betty was one of the nicest workers in the kitchen, so he figured the best way was to approach the older woman and ask.

Five minutes later, he left with the bag of soup, fresh bread, and a container of hot brownies.

As he got behind the wheel of his Jeep, he finished off the first brownie. He'd skipped lunch that day, spending his time hunting down Scarlett instead of eating. He often got too busy to eat full meals and usually just took a protein bar or shake instead.

Even though the staff had access to a full buffet during all three meals in the staff's dining area, he more than often skipped out. He knew Scarlett and her Wildflowers held meetings first thing every morning sitting around a booth in the back of the staff's dining room.

He'd been asked to join those meetings a few times, when they'd needed his help planning events or working on repairs.

He'd spent his first six months at the camp helping Aiden and his crew make repairs on all the cabins. He still often helped when the man asked but, for the most part, his job title was events counselor, the same as for most of the staff. He helped oversee events, helped guests check in and get settled, and even filled in to deliver meals out to the cabins. Since Aiden had hired a full-time crew to build all the new cabins, he'd done less and less of the construction portion of the job.

The following day around the camp was boring, since Scarlett was nowhere to be found. He thought about changing his work schedule to match hers perfectly but didn't want to come off as too stalker-ish.

Still, one day without her around was okay. He filled his time with helping guests out and tended to get more done. Since he was working the dinner shift, he pulled on the black suit required for the formal dinner, changing in the locker room that sat off the gym and workout rooms where they hosted everything from yoga classes to Aubrey's tai chi and judo classes.

He stepped into the dining room and jumped to help Elle complete the finishing touches on the decorations for the night.

"A night under the stars," her sign read. "You know…" He leaned closer to her. She was wearing a sparkling deep blue dress, one of many she had that showcased her perfectness. He'd known Elle his entire life. His gran had pictures of the two of them sitting in an old bathtub at the local library filled with huge brightly colored pillows, heads together as they read a book. "We could have saved a lot of work and just eaten outside."

She laughed and slapped him on the shoulder. A sisterly move. Which is exactly how he thought of her. "Wow." Her eyebrows shot up. "You've been working out," she joked and reached up to pinch his biceps, hard.

"Ouch." He pulled back. "You could use a little time with the weights as well." He took her thin forearm in his and squeezed.

"Are you getting fresh with my woman?" Liam crossed the room in a suit that matched Levi's. Instantly, Levi felt small and homely next to the youngest of the Costa men. Levi laughed and wrapped his arms around Elle.

"I saw her first." He hugged her. "We go so far back that I think we shared diapers."

Elle laughed and reached up to kiss him on the cheek. "If you want to live," she whispered, "make sure he knows you're joking."

He shrugged and glanced over at Liam Costa. He wasn't a fighter. The man knew that Elle was head over heels for him. "Trust me," he replied, "he knows." He dropped his arms and stepped away. He slapped Liam on the shoulder and realized the man's arms were just as impressive as his own. "Now that you're here, you can do all your woman's heavy lifting." He quickly headed across the room towards the bar. He was scheduled to help Britt out for the night.

He and a few others knew how to mix drinks and often rotated the position. Seeing Scarlett's sister Zoey standing at the end of the bar, he stopped off to talk to her.

Zoey Rowlett was two years older than Scarlett. They had matching hair and feisty spunk. Where they differed the most was the eyes and the attitude towards him. Zoey thought Levi was funny and showed it often.

"Hey there." She turned to him with a big smile.

"Hey." He pulled her hand out and made a show of glancing up and down her pretty black sparkly dress, which matched Elle's. "Do you five buy in bulk?"

She laughed. "It's easier for us to coordinate." She shrugged. "Mine's black, Elle's is blue. Hannah has silver. Aubrey looks stunning in pink, while Scarlett wears red and knocks…"—her eyes narrowed— "everyone's socks off."

He'd known for a while that his infatuation with her sister was no secret to her.

"Damn straight," he agreed. "Red is her color.".

"We have a few outfits like this." She took a sip of her water, and he caught sight of the rock on her finger.

"Wow, is that new?" He took her hand in his. He knew, as did everyone on the campgrounds, that Zoey and Dylan had made their engagement official, but he hadn't seen the new ring she was wearing yet.

"Yes." Her smile doubled as she looked down at the rock.

Seeing the size of the diamond made his heart sink a little. If this was the standard, there was no way he could afford to purpose to anyone. Ever.

"Wow," he said and stepped back. "When's the big date again?"

"September twenty-second. The first day of fall." She smiled. "We figured it would be the perfect time since there should be a lull in guests."

He chuckled and glanced around the filling dining room. "You've been open for almost two years, and there hasn't once been a lull in guests."

She sighed and sagged her shoulders. "True, but at least we won't be in the middle of summer. The weather should be perfect for a beach wedding."

An image flashed quickly in his mind. A barefoot dark-haired bride in a white flowing dress walked across the white sugar sand towards him as the crystal blue waters of the Gulf sat behind her.

The fact that he was imagining Scarlett in the dress instead of Zoey had him shifting and glancing away. "Where's the rest of your crew?" he asked.

He spotted Hannah welcoming guests at the front door with Brent standing beside her acting as maître d'.

"Aubrey's setting up the band." She motioned to the stage area where the gorgeous redhead was talking to a guy holding a guitar. Her pink sparkly dress caught the spotlights as she moved around. "Hannah's being Hannah," She laughed and motioned to where she was moving a potted plant around. "Elle..." She motioned to where Elle was chatting with guests. "Scarlett has the day off. I'm sure she's enjoying her time away from all this." She motioned around them.

Seeing the four friends, how perfect they were together, and knowing that Scarlett was one of them, had him suddenly realizing that he was in the wrong place. An intruder in a perfect world.

The five of them had met and grown up together because they'd attended the camp reserved for elite families.

He lived with his grandmother still, had never even thought about going away to college. He drove a Jeep that was older than the hills and often broke down. Hell, he didn't even know who his father was.

"I'd better..." He glanced around and, seeing Britt watching them, nodded towards her. "I have to go help out," he said and quickly disappeared behind the bar.

For the next two hours, he worked behind the bar, trying to get into his job and be as fun and lighthearted as he normally was. However, the thought of not belonging loomed over him.

Even Britt noticed something was off with him that evening. During his break, he stepped out the back door. The only way to clear his mood was a quick walk. The pathways around the grounds were perfectly lit and, if you knew your way, took you in a large circle.

By the time he'd made two full circles, he was back to feeling like his old self.

He hadn't yet reached the light of the lantern pathway when he heard Zoey arguing with someone. Glancing up towards the back door, he watched as she paced on the small landing, holding her phone to her ear. He didn't want to bother her and had turned to head towards the front door when he heard her say his name.

"You should see him. Something's off. Levi isn't himself tonight."

Normally, he wouldn't have eavesdropped, but curiosity won out and he found himself straining to hear every word.

Less than a minute later, he figured out that she was talking to Scarlett. It wasn't difficult. He knew how the sisters talked to one another. It was either going to be Scarlett or their mother Kimberly.

"I don't know what's between the two of you, but every time I mention your name..." She was silent for a while. "I still don't think it was him that did that." She waited. "How do you know? Do you have proof?" She waited again. "So, you're going to hold something he did many years ago as a teenage boy against him? How many stupid things did you do in your youth?"

Levi wondered just what stupid thing he'd done to Scarlett? He'd been asking himself that question for a few years now.

He just couldn't remember anything. The last time he'd seen her, when they'd been teenagers, they'd gone their separate ways, promising to keep in touch.

Sure, he hadn't, but... he'd been sixteen. He'd even apologized to her about it when he'd seen her that first week after not seeing her for years.

"I know it's your day off tomorrow, but... maybe you could swing by and... I don't know." Zoey sighed and glanced around. "Think of his gran. She's such a sweet woman and she was so close to Joe."

Great, Zoey made him sound like a charity case. Without wanting to hear the rest, he turned and made his way in through the front door, bypassing her all together.

For the rest of the evening, he was in a foul mood. So much so that Britt told him to clock off early, since he was scaring the guests.

He didn't mind. Not even the plate of cookies his gran had left him on the stove cheered him up. He put them in the fridge and fell into bed, his mind refusing to shut down.

He knew that his time off would be hell. He'd have two full days to think about his position in life. He doubted Scarlett would go out of her way to see him. After all, in the past two years, she'd gotten efficient at avoiding him.

The next morning, he woke with a splitting headache. He knew the only cure for it was arduous work.

Pulling out his gran's list of rainy-day to-do items, he got to work. By noon, he had half of the list done and had worked off most of the foul mood.

His gran had her book club meeting down at the library, and he helped her load up the treats she'd baked for the other ladies in the group, snagging a snickerdoodle as a reward.

Since he knew the meeting would go a few hours, he cranked up his speakers and climbed the ladder to take care of those missing shingles.

He'd just replaced a whole row at the top where the wind had pulled all of them off when he felt a tap on his shoulder.

He jumped, not expecting anyone to climb up on the roof with him. He felt his foot slip on the shingles and reached out to grab whoever it was. Feeling the soft body, he knew instantly it was Scarlett, but he was too late to save them as he fell backwards and started sliding down the pitch of the roof with Scarlett in his arms.

CHAPTER FIVE

Scarlett listened to her sister giving her a guilt trip. It ate at her a little that her bubble bath had been interrupted by the call. She'd told herself to turn the darn phone off, but no, she'd just had to keep playing a stupid game on it. After all, she had won two hours of free lives and wanted to win the hard level.

"You should have seen it. The moment I mentioned your name, his eyes... darkened."

"They're blue. They can't get dark." She rolled her eyes and thought about how, if anything, they lightened when he was in a dark mood.

"They did. Tell me you'll go see if he's okay tomorrow. I just don't have the time tonight to..."

"Nope." She sighed and rested her head back, closing her eyes. She didn't know what she was going to do on her day off, but there was no way she was going to see Levi. She'd just gotten the sexy man out of her mind as it was.

"Fine, I'll call Mom and..."

"Don't you dare." Scarlett sat up, splashing some of the water out of the old claw-foot tub.

Their mother was on a month-long sabbatical with her new boyfriend, Reed Cooper, the sexiest man over fifty that Scarlett had ever seen. He was ex-forces and most likely a secret agent and this mysteriousness made him even hotter.

Of course, the sisters had signed off on the relationship after the man had helped save Hannah's life.

"You are not going to interrupt their trip to Montana," Scarlett warned.

"I might, if you won't at least check up on Levi. After all, he is a friend first and foremost."

Scarlett sighed and relaxed back again.

"Not to mention an employee. And an employee's well-being is part of our concern," Zoey added.

"Fine." Scarlett had had enough of the guilt trip. Besides, her sister was making sense. The last few times she'd talked to him, he had seemed... off. But she'd just chalked it up to the spark of attraction between them. Spark? Hell, it was more like a full-fledged lightning bolt.

"You'll go see him tomorrow? It's his day off," Zoey asked, sounding a little excited.

"Yes," she agreed. She hung up before her sister could say anything else.

Tossing her phone down on the towel, she sunk below the bubbles and tried not to think about Levi. But memories of the summer they'd spent together as teenagers played over in her mind. That first kiss in the tree house, the many kisses they'd shared that summer. The last day of summer, she'd snuck out of the cabin and had met him in the tree house for her first wonderful sexual experience with Levi. Not that it was full sex, just a bunch of heavy petting and kissing. But in her young mind, she'd given him everything.

She'd dreamed of that night so many times since, no doubt building it up in her mind to be something it hadn't been. The way he'd touched her as if he knew exactly where she needed it.

Looking back at that time, she realized she'd been a selfish lover, allowing him to take control, to take what he'd wanted, and not really giving him anything. She'd been young and stupid.

She knew that if they ever got together again, she'd do things differently. After all, she was more... skilled. Not that she'd had a lot of conquests, only three, in addition to Levi.

Still, she'd learned how to make things more comfortable for her partner and herself.

It was strange that, even though they hadn't really gone all the way, it didn't dim the wonder of that night. Instead, Levi was now built up to almost god-like in her mind. Over the years, she'd dreamed that being with him would be better than any other experience she'd had thus far. Better than all of the romance novels she'd read and movies she'd drooled over.

After her bath, she crawled into bed with her Kindle and fell asleep halfway through the last chapter of a book. When she woke, she stayed in bed to finish the book and start a new one. After all, it was her day off and she could lounge around as long as she wanted.

After showering, she ate a quick brunch. Well, a small bagel with cream cheese, anyway. Then she took the stack of books that she'd borrowed the week before back to the library and grabbed a few more for the coming week.

By the time she drove by Levi's grandmother's place, it was past noon and she was hungry again. She thought about stopping off to get a burger at the local diner after she'd checked in on him.

She hadn't expected to see him shirtless on the roof of the house, hammering away as he replaced some shingles.

He had an old radio, the kind she'd seen at Goodwill that no one used any longer, blasting eighties tunes right next to him.

She called out to him, trying to get his attention. When that didn't work, she climbed halfway up the ladder and yelled again.

He started singing along with the song, and she held in a chuckle as his voice rose over the music. He was good, but just something about hearing him sing and move to the music made her smile.

She thought about turning around and leaving, telling her sister that she'd checked in on him, but then she saw his butt sway to the beat of the song. The old denim rode low on his hips, showing off the perfect arch above his hips. Her mouth watered and her body moved forward on its own.

By the time she'd twisted herself around the top of the ladder and climbed up the roof, she'd almost lost her nerve again.

Her eyes ran over his broad shoulders, the muscles that bunched and flexed as he hammered shingles into place. Damn he was pretty.

Just remembering how many times in the past few months he'd interrupted her work or bumped into her had her reaching out her hand towards him.

She hadn't expected him to jerk around, his eyes going wide as he lost his footing on the new shingles. She reached out to steady him and felt him wrap his arms around her as she too started to slide on the slope.

Her breath was whooshed from her as she landed on his sweaty chest, his arms wrapped around her and they slid towards the edge of the roof.

She screamed and closed her eyes, waiting for the impact of the ground and the sound of breaking bones. Instead, all movement stopped and then Levi's sexy chuckle sounded right next to her ear.

"That was fun," he said when she opened her eyes.

She glanced around and realized that he'd stopped them from falling using his feet less than a foot from the edge of the roof.

She jerked free and scooted on her butt higher up on the roof.

"Why'd you do that?" she asked, her heart racing still.

He groaned as he sat up. "Me? I wasn't the one sneaking up on someone working on a roof."

She narrowed her eyes at him, then reached up and tucked her hair back in place. She'd left it down that morning and now, thanks to their little slide, it was all over the place.

Levi was silent for a while and, when she glanced over at him, he was moving slowly. Then he turned slightly away from her, and she noticed the damage he'd done to his back.

"Oh!" She jumped up and took his shoulders, pushing him until he turned away from her. The skin on his back was raw and bloody. "You're bleeding."

"That'll happen when you try to use shingles as a slide." He winced when she touched his shoulder.

"I'll help you clean it." She nudged him towards the ladder, but he pulled away.

"I can deal with it myself." He walked over and winced as he put on his shirt. "What are you doing here?"

"No, you can't." She ignored his question. "It's on your back. You can't even see the damage, let alone clean it up."

"Scarlett." His voice was low, almost a warning. "What are you doing here?" he asked, punctuating each word slowly.

"I came to check up on you." She crossed her arms over her chest. "But now I realize it was a mistake." She started making her way carefully towards the ladder, only to have him stop her.

"I'll go down first and help you," he warned.

She'd been wondering how she was going to move around it and climb down herself, so she waited and watched him.

He moved as if he'd done it a hundred times before, easily swinging his legs and body around the edge of the house while holding onto the ladder. He went down a few steps, then waved her forward.

"Okay, do what I just did," he said. "I'm right here."

She moved a lot slower than he had, gripping the rungs of the ladder in a death grip as she scooted on her butt closer towards the edge of the house. It was hard, since there were gutters on the house she had to move around. Turning her body around, she gasped as her feet dangled. Then, finally, her foot connected to a rung as strong arms wrapped around her hips.

"I've got you," he said next to her ear.

Her body was tucked between his and the ladder as they made their way slowly down to the ground.

She breathed a sigh of relief when she stood on the grass in his grandmother's front yard.

"Let me at least help you clean up. You're bleeding through your shirt." She motioned towards the white T-shirt he'd put on.

He sighed and glanced around as if looking for someone else, anyone else to help him instead. He nodded and walked towards the front porch, and she fell in step next to him.

She hadn't been in his grandmother's place before. She didn't know what she expected. It was probably old and had outdated furniture like the place they were staying at in town. The place had belonged to Elle's grandfather and now belonged equally to the five friends, just as the camp did. They had chosen to spend their money on the camp instead of on remodeling the old house.

As she stepped into the very modern living room, she got the impression that his grandmother knew how to decorate.

"Wow," she said under her breath. He stopped and glanced over his shoulder at her.

"What?" He frowned at her, causing a small crease to form between his eyebrows.

"I like your place," she answered easily. "I guess I just wasn't expecting... it."

"I've been helping my gran redecorate." He shrugged. "Come on back to the kitchen. I'll get the first aid kit."

She followed him down a narrow hallway and stepped into the kitchen. Here she could see that there was still some work that needed to be done. The old cabinets needed a fresh coat of paint or to be replaced. The flooring looked new, but the baseboards hadn't been replaced yet.

"I'm still working in here," he admitted before disappearing back down the hallway into the bathroom they'd passed.

He came back with a small black box. He set it down on the kitchen table and opened it.

She moved closer as he removed some Band-Aids and a bottle of hydrogen peroxide.

"Sit." She motioned to the chair. He flipped it around and straddled it after removing his ruined shirt.

She hissed at the mess. Several long scrapes marred his back, running up and down his normally perfect skin. She could see dark spots of debris left from the shingles and dug into the box. Finding a pair of tweezers, she got to work.

He held still while she cleaned him up. When she was done, he was left with four large clean scrapes down his back. She was thankful that it had looked much worse than it had actually been.

"This might sting," she said before pouring some peroxide down his back, catching most of it at the base of his back with a hand towel he'd given her.

He hissed and arched slightly, and she couldn't help watching as his muscles flexed again.

Leaning forward, she blew softly on the areas where the liquid bubbled, and he stilled completely.

Her eyes traveled lower, to where his jeans rode low. Desperate to touch him there, she tried to focus on the task at hand, drying the liquid from his back using short little dabs so as not to hurt him further.

"How does it feel?" she asked after straightening up.

He was silent for a while, then answered in a husky voice,

"Fine." He stood suddenly and reached for his shirt. Noticing the dried blood, he walked towards the back door and tossed it in the washing machine in the small laundry area. Then he grabbed a black T-shirt and pulled it on over his head. "Thanks," he said as he rolled his shoulders. She watched the movement like her life depended on it.

"I… was going to grab some lunch," she said out loud before she could stop herself. "Let me buy you a burger… to make up for…" She motioned towards his back.

"Turning me into shredded meat?" he said with a slight smile. The fact that he could laugh about the ordeal told her that he wasn't hurt that badly. "I was going to just have a sandwich alone but enjoying a burger with you… sounds much more appealing."

CHAPTER SIX

Sitting across from Scarlett at the Sunset Café, one of the best places in town to grab a burger, excluding the camp, he tried to ignore the sting on his back. The pain kept him from leaning back in the booth. He didn't mind, since it brought him closer to Scarlett.

Still, since overhearing her sister on the phone last night, he'd come to a decision. After their drinks had been delivered and their meals ordered, he told her of it.

"I've decided to take a job in Destin," he said, and watched her reaction. It was instant, the hurt that crossed her eyes. She tried to hide it, but he knew that look too well.

"Why?" she asked with a slight frown.

"I think you know why," he answered after taking a sip of his drink. Since she'd driven, and he needed something to dull the pain, he'd ordered a rum and Coke. She'd stuck to drinking her standard drink, a club soda.

"Where?" she asked after a moment.

He shrugged, a move he told himself he had to avoid until his back could heal after feeling his skin tug and open again.

Thankfully, he'd pulled on a black T-shirt, which would hide any more bleeding.

"I haven't decided yet," he admitted.

"You have offers?"

"No." He sighed. "Haven't even applied anywhere else." He thought about the possibilities and what it would take for him to make the drive into town on a daily basis. Mainly, he'd need a new car. Something more reliable.

Scarlett relaxed slightly.

"Don't leave River Camps," she said easily. "Not on my account."

"There are other reasons." He thought about his future and knew that if he didn't get away from her, he'd never be able to move on. Hell, who was he kidding? No matter what, he'd have a hard time moving on from her. Especially after that kiss.

She leaned back and watched him. "Name one other reason."

Since he couldn't come up with anything, he took a slow drink and tried to shrug casually.

"Everyone knows there's more money across the bridge." It was true. Jobs in Destin or other popular tourist areas usually paid more than ones across the bay, further away from public beaches.

"I'm not buying it." She shook her head.

"It's my choice," he added, then waited until their food was delivered. "What about you?"

"Me?"

"Sure." He waved a fry in her direction before dipping it in the spicy mustard sauce. "You can't seriously be planning on living the rest of your life sharing an apartment with your friends."

"Friend," she corrected, before taking one of her own fries. "It's just me an Aub in the apartment now."

"Right," he said between bites. "Still..." He let the question of her future hang between them.

"For now, I'm completely happy," she answered, yet he could see doubt behind her eyes.

"What if you want... company? If I remember correctly that apartment is pretty close quarters." He'd helped Aiden fix up the second bathroom, the one he knew the friends had shared when they'd all lived there together.

"It used to be. Now I've got the main room and Aubrey's got Elle's old room." She glanced around, avoiding his eyes as she spoke.

"What about you? What if you want... company? You still live with your grandmother," she pointed out.

"That's different."

"How?"

He thought about the last time he'd gone out on a date. The last time he'd been with a woman.

"It must be nice, seeing all your friends move on. Find love. Get engaged." He knew he was changing the subject, but had to know her thoughts on it. Several of his buddies had taken the leap in the past few years too. Two of them were even expecting or had kids already, something he was extremely jealous of.

"It is." Again, her eyes remained dull as she smiled across the table at him. "Why all the questions?" She leaned forward and lowered her voice. "Are you planning on getting hitched?"

He chuckled. "No, just curious as to what's going on in your life." He thought about it, then added, "So, your mother and Reed?"

When she rolled her eyes, he knew he'd pushed his luck talking about relationships.

"If you decide to get another job, just let one of us know. We'd hate to lose you but understand that not everyone can cut it at the camp."

He laughed. "Is that a challenge?"

"Just an observation." She nudged her plate aside after finishing only half of the food on it.

Since he'd cleaned his own, he pulled it towards himself and started finishing off the rest of her burger and fries.

"You won't be the first employee to leave," she added.

"No." He thought back to the scare they'd had with Ryan.

"How's that all going anyway?" he asked, knowing about the lawsuit the crazed woman had filed against the camp after she'd been fired shortly after pulling a gun on Dylan and Zoey.

"With Ryan?" she asked, shrugging. "Haven't heard hide nor hair from the woman since she stabbed Hannah. We heard that she spent a few months in prison after the multiple assaults against the camp. Thank goodness." She crossed her arms over her chest. "The last update from the Costa's lawyer was that she was broke and working in some dive bar in California, since no one else would hire her. After Leo Costa returned home and denied ever having met the woman, she's been... quiet."

"Do you think she's done or just hibernating until another reason to torment you five comes up?" he asked.

She sighed. "God, I hope she's done. I mean, there is no more fuel for her fire. Leo's back in town. From what Zoey and the others have said, Leo was her real target. Him and the Costa money that is tied up in Owen's new venture, Hammock Cove."

"That's right." He perked up slightly. "That new subdivision is set to open soon."

"They've already built the two model homes. You should drive by there and see it. They're absolutely gorgeous."

Owen had purchased the land near the outskirts of town and had created a huge subdivision, complete with golf course, multiple swimming pools, tennis courts, and more. He'd meant to swing by and check it out earlier but had been too busy fixing up his gran's place.

"I'll drive by tomorrow and check it out," he agreed, knowing he had the following day to himself. Due to his mood earlier, he'd finished almost every task on his to-do list.

Somehow, that thought got him thinking about the sisters'

SUMMER FLING

attitude towards him. The hurt from hearing their conversation last night surfaced again. Normally, he wouldn't have thought anything about it, but just knowing that Scarlett's first inclination was to turn away from a friend, which he had thought they were first and foremost, stung.

He'd promised himself last night that he was going to stop trying so hard with her, to distance himself. It was the reason he'd mentioned the possibility of the job change.

Looking at her now, remembering the way she'd responded to the kiss, he had to know the real reason she was trying to convince him to stay at the camp. Maybe he was torturing himself, but the thought that she might care had him asking.

"Why did you really stop by today?" he asked after Scarlett paid and they'd stepped outside. He'd tried to pay, but he knew better than to argue with Scarlett on some things. This was one of them.

She turned towards him; her brown eyebrows arched up in question. "I told you..." She started to make an excuse; he could almost see it on the tip of her tongue.

"I overheard your sister talking to you last night." Her face paled slightly.

"You... did?"

"I'm not a charity case," he added, his voice low.

"No." She shook her head quickly. "Of course not."

His eyes narrowed as he saw something close to pain and embarrassment cross her eyes. "Well, you can go back and tell your sister you did your duty." He turned away, totally prepared to walk back home, since it was only a few blocks away.

"You're bleeding again." She gasped and then rushed to his side, turning him away from her, lifting his shirt slightly. He could feel the material stick to his skin, thanks to the dried blood, which made him wince with pain. "Seriously, how can I be sure you won't bleed all over the place," she scolded him. She took his arm. "Come with me."

"I'm fine." He tried to jerk out of her hands, but she held on and pulled him across the street. "Scarlett," he warned, but she shushed him and continued to tug on his arm until he followed her.

He was so engulfed in his sour mood that he hadn't realized she'd taken him to the house she shared with her friends until they were on the front porch. The massive place was one of the oldest in town, a historic landmark, a beacon for all that was Pelican Bluff. He knew that the place sat empty often now, since the other Wildflowers had other living arrangements.

Stepping through the front door behind her, he got a moment to glance around the place. The setup was a lot like his grandmother's place, with the exception of the massive staircase that led up to the bedrooms. He could see a large formal dining room between the living area and the kitchen, which looked twice the size of his grandmother's.

The place could use a little work, but it was tidy and kept up. Even if the furniture was older and the style was late nineties, he was impressed.

"Nice place," he said when she shoved him on the sofa.

"Thanks," she said, moving out of the room into what he presumed was a bathroom. He heard her rummaging around. "Shirt off," she said when she came back into the room.

"I'm—" he started, but her eyes moved up to his and narrowed until they were just slits.

"Now," she said, and he knew she meant it.

He would have chuckled, but he was still reeling.

Pulling off his shirt, he hissed as the material once again stuck to his skin.

"Here," she said, rushing over to him. She nudged him until he was lying face down on the cushions. "Wow, I didn't think these would bleed this bad."

It was his fault. He had sat back several times in the booth, scraping the cuts on the seat.

He closed his eyes and waited as she cleaned his back.

As with earlier, it was complete torture having her fingers lightly play over his bare skin. It was extremely difficult to focus on anything other than how wonderful it was for her to touch him.

He must have made a sound, because she spoke softly to him, as one would with an injured child. Her soft voice soothed him, and he felt himself relaxing completely.

When he opened his eyes, the light had changed. He could see the soft hues of a sunset flooding the room with colors.

He shifted and glanced around and noticed that the room was empty. He sat up, thankful that he hadn't drooled on the sofa pillow. Finding his shirt tossed over the back of a chair, he pulled it on.

"Good." Scarlett came into the room, smiling. "You're awake."

"Sorry," he mumbled, still a little groggy. "I must have dozed off."

Her eyes moved over his face. "You had a rough morning." She set a tray of cookies and tea down on the coffee table. "Sit." She motioned towards the sofa.

"I'd better…" he started, but she stopped him.

"Levi, sit. I think it's past time we had a talk." She sat down in a large leather chair and started pouring the drink.

"I'm not a big tea drinker," he admitted.

"Neither am I; this is hot chocolate." She smiled at him.

"In August?" He shook his head but took the mug from her.

"It goes great with Betty's s'more cookies." She held the plate out for him.

"Seriously?" He looked down at the cookies and felt his stomach growl. "How did you get these?" He glanced up at her after taking a bite.

"Betty likes me." She shrugged. Scarlett leaned forward slightly. "She thinks I'm too skinny."

"She thinks everyone is too skinny," he agreed. "She gave me an entire pan of brownies when she first met me."

"Our second-best hire, after Isaac, of course," Scarlett joked as she finished off a cookie and handed him the plate to grab another one.

He waited for her to start talking as he enjoyed the treat. The room went darker, signally he'd slept the entire afternoon away. It wasn't any wonder; he'd barely had any sleep the night before, thinking about her, about his position in life. His options.

When the plate was empty and his hot chocolate was gone, she continued to look across at him as if she was waiting for him to speak.

He tried to lean back without causing his back too much discomfort. "This is your show."

CHAPTER SEVEN

He wasn't going to make this easy for her. She should have known. Nothing with him ever was.

She'd tortured herself by bringing him back to her place, but she felt so much responsibility for his injuries, she couldn't just let him walk away bleeding.

Then he'd gone and fallen asleep while she'd cleaned his cuts, giving her plenty of time to admire how sexy he was. Even more so when his blond lashes lay on his cheeks as his breath leveled while he slept.

Her first instinct had been to shake him awake, but then she remembered how tired he'd looked during lunch. She'd assumed it was pain, but looking back, she realized she'd seen him like that before, when the crew had pulled an all-night repair to fix a cabin's roof after a storm.

Was it a sign that she could read his moods more than she could her own?

Zoey had been correct—he'd been hurting and needed a friend. She'd seen the change in him over the past few months.

"I didn't stop by today because my sister forced me to," she started, watching him closely. When his eyebrows slowly moved up, she sighed. "I didn't."

"Okay, then why?" he asked.

Why had she? Because she'd tried to get him out of her head all day yesterday and had failed miserably.

"You're making this extremely hard," she said under her breath. The corners of his mouth twitched, showing off those sexy dimples of his. Her heart did a little flutter. Why was she denying it? She'd fallen hard long ago for him and had never really gotten over him. "Fine, I wanted to check in on you, because there is something between us." She motioned between them. "I'm not entirely happy about it, but… there it is."

His smile grew. "Why aren't you happy about it?"

This, this was why she'd denied it all this time. The smug look he was giving her made her back teeth grind together.

"Because you hurt me," she ground out.

His look changed. Everything about him changed. He softened and moved closer to her.

"I'm sorry for whatever it is I did," he said softly.

"You don't remember." It wasn't a question, but a statement.

"I don't," he admitted, "and for that, I'm even more sorry." He reached across the space and touched her hand, a move that caused her to soften and relax. "When you're ready, I'd love to hear what I did so I can properly apologize."

She narrowed her eyes at him, wondering if he was playing a game. Not trusting her voice, she nodded and took the last sip of her drink.

His eyes were moving over her, and she could tell that he was trying to assess her mood.

"Thanks for letting me crash at your place." He chuckled. "I hope I didn't put you out too much."

"No, not at all," she admitted, unwilling to tell him that she'd sat across from him the entire time, watching him sleep while pretending to read a book.

He glanced over at the grandfather clock that sat to the left of the fireplace, then whistled. "Wow." He stood up slowly. "I can't believe I slept so long. Gran will be worried about me." He pulled out his phone from his back pocket then waved it. "She has dinner ready and is wondering where I am," he said while typing a reply to her message.

"You love her." She didn't know what caused her to say it as she stood.

"Yeah, the only woman who has ever loved me right back." He winked and tucked his phone away. "Listen, I owe you, for… fixing me up." She watched as he moved a little closer. "What do you say to me treating you to some of the best home cooking in the Panhandle?"

She laughed. "I get that each day at work."

"Isaac can't hold a candle to my gran. She made chicken parm tonight." He leaned slightly towards her. "Isaac's been begging her for the recipe since he tried it out himself last year."

She thought about her dinner plans. As with before, they involved a bottle of wine, a book, maybe a frozen meal and… herself.

She liked Levi's grandmother, Mary Lynn. The woman was one of the nicest people in town and a huge supporter of the camp.

"Sure," she agreed. The thought of a quiet evening alone hadn't interested her. She'd been left alone all day yesterday with her thoughts about Levi, and after the lunch and seeing his sexy body half naked, she doubted she could ever get her mind off of him. The distraction of dinner with his grandmother might be helpful. "I can drive…" she started.

"How about we walk? After that nap, I need the air," he suggested. "Besides, it's only two blocks away."

She nodded. As they stepped out, she grabbed her light sweatshirt. Even though it was in the high eighties now, she figured it would be cooler when she walked home, and she might need it.

She was right. The breeze coming off the bay was cooler, signaling they would have rain either later that night or the following day.

"Nice night," Levi said once they were at the end of her sidewalk.

"Smells like rain soon."

"I love the rain." He reached over and took her hand, stopping her from walking. "It reminds me of our first kiss."

Her heart did a little flip as she lost herself in his blue eyes. "Levi." She sighed.

"I understand that you're still upset about something, but I think, that is, I was hoping you would give me a chance to make it up to you."

She watched him hold his breath and felt the hold on her heart loosen. She'd lived years with the sting of his betrayal. But since she'd returned to the camp, he'd done nothing but try to make her laugh and smile. She could try and give him a second chance, as long as she kept her heart secured behind the wall she'd built years ago. Maybe having a summer fling with Levi would be just what she needed to get him out of her system for good. After all, the guy couldn't really be as good as she'd built up in her mind. Could he?

"Of course," she nodded.

They walked hand in hand back to his place. The smells that hit her as they stepped inside the house caused her stomach to growl. It didn't seem like that long ago that they'd eaten lunch.

"Gran?" he called out. "I brought company."

"Back here." His grandmother appeared in the hallway, an apron wrapped around her waist that said 'Hot Shit' in fancy letters.

Scarlett smiled. "Hi, Mary Lynn."

SUMMER FLING

"Oh, Scarlett, what a wonderful surprise." She waved them back towards the kitchen area.

"Thank you for having me. I hope I'm not putting you out," Scarlett said, stepping into the kitchen.

"No, not at all, I always make plenty of food." His grandmother hugged her. "Levi, why don't you put an extra place setting out."

Scarlett stood back as the duo moved around the small kitchen as if they had spent hours practicing the moves. She couldn't count the times she and her mother and sister had worked around each other in their old kitchen in Jacksonville, before moving to the camp.

After her father had abandoned them, her mother had sunk into a slight depression, leaving Zoey and Scar to fend for themselves while trying to lift their mother out of the darkness.

Both sisters had gotten jobs to help pay for the monthly bills, since their father had left the family destitute after marrying a woman a few years older than Zoey.

Her father had not only taken his successful business and all the money when he'd left, but he'd cut all ties with his daughters until the day he'd died, when he'd called Zoey up and confessed from his deathbed how sorry he was.

Zoey, being Zoey, dropped everything and flew out to Vegas to deal with it all. Bridgette, their father's second wife, had divorced him a year earlier. And since their divorce settlement hadn't been to her liking, the woman had been there, waiting for another handout the moment she found out he'd died.

When Scar found out that he'd changed his will so that Zoey and she would inherit everything—millions of dollars—she at first didn't want to touch the money. But then her sister had talked her into putting it all into the camp. After all, the place could use it.

Zoey had stepped up and taken charge of the sale of their father's estate and business. When the first checks started flooding into Scarlett's bank account, she'd quickly moved them over to the camp's accounts. She was shocked by the amount of money that came after the liquidation of her father's business. Zoey again persuaded her to invest some of it instead of just letting it sit in her account, untouched.

Since her father hadn't left a dime to their mother, the woman who had given him everything, including her heart, before he'd left her behind, Scarlett and Zoey took care of her. Even though Kimberly continued to try and talk them out of it, neither of them planned on stopping anytime soon.

One of the best things they'd ever done was convince their mother to move into their old cabin on the campgrounds after it had been fully remodeled and turned into a home.

That was one thing she and Levi had in common—their family units were broken but still full of love. Everyone around town knew Levi's story. How his mother, who had been a young teenager when he'd been born, had OD'd on pain meds shortly after Levi's seventh birthday. Everyone knew that he didn't know who his father was, since his mother had taken that knowledge with her when she'd died.

Levi was extremely lucky that his grandmother had been there for him. He may not have grown up with a mother and father, but he was raised with love and had turned into one of the best people Scar had ever met, even if his past was shaded with betrayal and pain.

She couldn't deny that since she'd come back to town, he'd tried to make it up to her. Still, it would be nice for him to remember the major betrayal that had caused her so much pain for so long. She normally didn't play games, but after that summer together, he'd hurt her. His betrayal had come the same year, the same month that her father had left and married a woman half his age. Levi had hurt her as much as her father had, and she had never talked to her father again.

"Levi was telling me that you have a few more cabins almost

ready to open up?" His grandmother chatted as they all sat down around the table.

"Yes." She smiled. "Hillview Cabin and Beatle." She chuckled. "Which is nothing like it sounds. It has these amazing wood arches that Liam helped create over the front door, giving the entire cabin an almost bug-like shape. It's one of my favorites."

"Think the front doors like in the homes in The Hobbit," Levi said to his gran. "Big circle arches over the doors and windows."

"Right." She smiled. "Next time I'm out there, I'll have to take a walk and see some of the new cabins."

"You're welcome anytime," Scarlett said, taking the plate of chicken parmesan she offered her.

"I used to visit all the time, when Joe was running the place." She sighed and Scar figured she was thinking of fond memories of her friend.

"There have been quite a few rumors about your visits," Scarlett said.

Levi had been taking a drink of his water and started coughing and choking. Scar reached over without skipping a beat and pounded him on the back. Only when he winced did she remember the scratches on his back.

"Sorry." She shrugged.

His grandmother chuckled and waved her off. "Joe and I were close, but never lovers."

"Jesus, Gran," Levi said between coughs.

His gran chuckled. "Levi, you aren't the only one who can have fun."

Scar watched Levi's face turn red as he tried to suck in air. "You're killing me here," he said, taking another drink of water.

Again, his grandmother waved his words away. "Joe and I were best friends. More like brother and sister." She smiled and handed a basket of bread to Scarlett.

"Thanks," she said, taking a slice of garlic bread and handing the basket to Levi.

"I remember the day he got full custody of Elle." His grandmother sighed and leaned back, then her eyes moved over to Levi. "I'd gotten Levi when he was seven years old, but here Joe was, a single man, running a successful business and then"—she snapped her fingers—"overnight he was taking care of an adolescent girl." She smiled. "Needless to say, we had a lot of talks. He hadn't really helped raise his daughter, since his wife had been alive and taken the reins back then, but with Elle, it was all him. I had Levi, a boy." She chuckled. "And boy, he was all boy. I'd raised my Mary." Her smile faltered. "And I was so concerned that I would damage Levi like I'd damaged Mary." Levi reached over and took his grandmother's hand in his. The comparison of the lean, toned hand holding the older, frail one made Scarlett's eyes water. "I was so concerned back then that I'd do something wrong."

"You never could do anything wrong," Levi added softly. "You loved me. That's all I needed."

She smiled and then laughed. "That and food." She glanced over at Scarlett and rolled her eyes. "Lots of it."

"Still," Levi said, scooping another big spoonful of food onto his plate, causing both his grandmother and Scarlett to laugh.

CHAPTER EIGHT

*H*earing his gran and Scarlett laugh together was pure heaven. Sitting across from the woman he'd been infatuated with his entire life, listening to her joking and talking to his gran, was the best thing he'd experienced in years.

Even the pain of the scrapes down his back faded as he laughed and joked with them during dinner. He'd grown up trying to get his gran to smile. It had been his life's goal for as long as he could remember. She'd been through so much, losing her husband and her only daughter. And, to date, he'd done a smashing job. His gran had only recently shown signs of being lonely after her best friend, Robin, passed away last year.

Since her friend's death, she'd filled her time with book clubs, tea parties, and small-town events. She was even going to every town hall meeting.

He'd joked with her, after she'd complained about the mayor once, that she should run for office herself. He still believed she would be better than the good ol' boys that currently ran the town. Most everyone in Pelican Point wanted growth, but the group of old men who had been sitting on the board for more than a decade wanted to keep growth to a minimum.

He knew that Scarlett and her Wildflowers, as they called themselves, had had to jump through hoops to get the camp's restaurant and bars open. Thankfully, the men sitting on the city council had liked Elle's grandfather, Joe.

With Owen Costa's new home subdivision... well, money got you anything you wanted in these parts, something Levi knew a lot about.

His gran had raised his mother alone after her husband, Marco, had died overseas. The man, his grandfather, had been a top colonel at the time, leaving behind enough of his retirement and benefits that his gran could live comfortably for the rest of her life. Comfortably, not lavishly.

Which meant, early in his high school years, he'd gotten small odd jobs to help pay for repairs around the house that the income she'd been left hadn't accounted for.

Which is why he found himself still living with his grandmother at the age of twenty-four. It wasn't because he didn't think he could go out in the world and make a name for himself. But if he left her here alone, she would have no one to look out for her and care for her.

Everyone else in her life had abandoned her or died. There was no way he was going to do the same. Not after she'd sacrificed everything for him.

After dinner, his gran suggested he walk Scarlett home, something he'd had every intention of doing anyway. He and Scarlett stepped out on the front porch

"It's going to rain," Scarlett said, looking up to the darkened sky. Normally, they had beautiful sunsets all summer long, but tonight's sky was dark and grey.

"Yeah." He swung open the screen door and grabbed an umbrella and a jacket. "Thanks for coming to dinner," he said as they started walking slowly down the sidewalk.

"I like your grandmother." She looked at him sideways.

"She likes you." He smiled.

She chuckled. "Your grandmother likes everyone."

He frowned and shook his head. "No, not everyone."

"Oh?" she asked, her eyebrows slowly moving up. "Who in town does your gran have it out for?"

He shrugged. "She didn't particularly like Ryan."

Scarlett's steps faltered and he reached out to steady her. "Did your gran know her?" she asked.

"She stopped by the camp a few times and ran into her when she worked there. She and Isaac are friends. She still goes and hangs out in the kitchens at least once a week," he admitted, keeping his hand on hers as they walked.

"I can see that. You were right about your grandmother's cooking," she said smoothly.

He chuckled. "I'm right about a lot of things."

She smiled. "And your ego doesn't show it."

He moved closer to her, their shoulders bumping as they walked.

"How does your back feel?" she asked when they were halfway to her place.

He shrugged, the move no longer tearing open his skin. "Better. I guess I just needed a nap and a satisfying meal." He glanced over at her. "You never did really tell me why you stopped by today."

She sighed. "I told you…" she started, but he tugged on her arm, forcing her to stop and look at him.

"Scarlett, if we're going to start over, let's start by agreeing to not lie to one another."

She was silent for a while, then nodded. "Fine. I was worried. Even before Zoey said anything to me," she said quickly, holding her hands up. "You haven't been yourself for a while."

He thought about the sour mood he'd been in ever since her three friends had gotten engaged. For some reason, knowing that her friends were all moving forward in their lives while he was still stuck... where he was had a dark cloud over his normally happy mood.

"I'm okay," he lied and started walking. She tugged him to a stop. She placed her hands on her hips and glared up at him.

"We just agreed..." she started, but just then, the skies opened, and a torrential rain soaked them both. He tried to open the umbrella, but the wind almost jerked it out of his hands.

"Let's make a run for it," he said, grabbing her hand. They laughed as they rushed towards her front porch less than a block away.

When they stepped onto the porch, she pulled down the hood of her jacket. It had done no good. They were both complexly soaked.

Even his boxer shorts were soggy. The insides of his shoes squeaked as he took steps.

"I'm soaked." She laughed and removed her jacket and threw it over one of the benches on the patio. "I could have stood under a shower for an hour and not gotten this wet." She sat down and removed her shoes. "Go ahead." She motioned to the spot next to her. "I doubt this is going to let up anytime soon. I can throw some of your clothes into the dryer while we wait for it to stop raining."

He sat next to her and removed his shoes. There was at least half an inch of water in them. He laughed when he turned them over and a waterfall flowed from them.

"Thankfully I was wearing sandals," Scarlett joked. She'd set her shoes next to the door and had removed her outer shirt, leaving her in a tight, soaking-wet tank top. His mouth watered seeing it cling to her body.

"Well?" she asked, motioning to his shirt. "I've already seen you a couple times today without it. Don't get shy on me now." She stood up and wrung out her shirt. Water splashed everywhere.

His eyes ran over the way her jean shorts clung to her tan skin. She was perfection. He was so caught up in watching her that he hadn't yet removed his shirt when she turned back around.

He watched her face, lost in her hazel eyes. Then his gaze ran down over her lips, and he would have been mesmerized by them as well, but they were slanted down into a frown.

"Are you going to make me pull it off you?" she asked, moving closer to him.

Thoughts of her slowly undressing him, running those hot lips over his cool skin, played in his mind.

"Levi?" She snapped her fingers directly in front of his face, breaking the trance.

"Right." He stood up suddenly, causing their bodies to bump. He took her shoulders, holding her so that he wouldn't knock her over. When his hands registered that he was touching her bare skin, he felt himself grow painfully hard.

How long had it been? From the moment he'd spotted her walking across the campgrounds almost two years ago, he'd only had eyes for her.

"Sorry," he said softly, his body still brushing against hers. He felt his heart skip when her eyes ran over his face. When she sucked her bottom lip into her mouth, then slowly ran her teeth over it, he watched the motion like his life depended on it. "Sassy," he groaned.

He'd let her make the last move, had needed her to, but this time, it was his turn.

Dipping his head, he ran his mouth over those lips that he'd been dreaming about for years. He felt her sway and as he wrapped his arms around her. He enjoyed the way her body plastered against his, warming them both.

His fingers tangled in her long dark hair then ran over her jawline. Using a finger, he traced the curve of her shoulder and felt her suck in her breath.

"Levi." His name on her lips tasted so sweet.

"Sassy, I can't tell you how long I've dreamed of kissing you again." He traced his mouth down her neck, feeling the slight goose bumps rise over her skin.

"I…" Her fingers locked in his hair as she arched back, giving him more access. "Please," she sighed before reaching down and tugging on his shirt.

It landed on the porch with a wet plop. He ran his hands over her shorts and enjoyed the way they clung to her curves.

She'd changed so much since that first summer they'd been together. She'd filled out, everywhere. He'd never imagined that she would be everything he'd desire and more.

He took a couple steps backwards until his shoulders bumped into the screen door.

Reaching behind him, she yanked open the door. He moved to step up into the house but, since he was so occupied with kissing her, he didn't see her sandals lying in front of the door and tripped over them.

Feeling himself falling again, he held onto her and twisted slightly, making sure that once again he protected her with his body.

He landed hard on the floor just inside her doorway. Seconds later, she landed on top of him, causing the air in his lungs to whoosh out of his lungs. He groaned when he felt the skin on his back open once again.

"Sorry," she groaned. "Tripped over my sandals."

It wasn't really the fall or the weight of her covering him that had done most of the damage. But one of her knees had connected with his family jewels, causing pain to explode in his entire body. It was the only thing he could focus on.

"Are you okay?" she asked, starting to move aside.

He held onto her firmly, not wanting her to do any further damage.

"Levi, let me up so I can see if you're hurt."

"I'm fine," he grunted.

"It doesn't sound like you're fine," she said, her tone a little clipped.

He would have laughed, but his balls were still in his throat. "Don't move," he warned her. "Let me... catch my breath."

That seemed to do it. She relaxed over him, allowing him to focus on just how wonderful she felt, instead of his bruised balls.

"Feel better?" she asked after a moment.

"Yes." He sighed and started running his hands over her. He'd had a moment to think through several things.

He knew better than to jump back into a relationship with her. He wanted—needed—to show her how much this meant to him.

There was nothing that he wanted to do more than to carry her upstairs and make love to her all night long. But the fact was, if they had sex now, he was afraid it would be just that to her... sex.

He knew he had to gain her full trust back, because in his heart, he didn't want just sex. He wanted more. He had always wanted more with her.

"You're quiet," she said, still lying on top of him, unmoving.

"Yeah." He ran his hands up and down her arms. He pulled her up until they were standing in the entryway, she with the tight wet tank top and skin-hugging shorts, him in his soaked jeans.

"I'd better go," he said after a moment.

The pained look on her face almost broke him, but he knew he had to stick to his guns if he wanted a future with her.

Her entire body stiffened and, when he pulled her closer, she tensed in his arms.

"There's nothing that I'd rather do than carry you up those stairs and peel the rest of those wet, skintight clothes from you, but..."

"But?" she asked, looking up into his eyes.

"This has to be more than just sex."

Her eyes narrowed and she took a step away from him. "Why?"

"You know why." After a moment, she turned away from him. She started to pace the living room.

"I... don't want anything bigger," she said, glancing over at him.

"Yet," he added with a smile. She rolled her eyes.

"Levi, I'm not sure anything beyond really exists. Look what happened with my parents."

He sobered. "I'm nothing like your father. I would never hurt you."

"You already have," she admitted, causing a pain to spread in his chest.

"And I still don't know what I did..." he started, but she held up her hand and sighed.

"Jenny Carpenter," she said, narrowing her eyes and watching his face.

"Who?" He shook his head. The name sounded familiar, but he couldn't place it. At least now he knew it was because of someone. Someone he hoped he could convince her sister and the others to talk about so he could try and figure out what he'd done.

"That's all you get." She shook her head. "I'm sure you'll think of the rest." She walked over and picked up a sweater from the back of a chair and pulled it on.

He could feel it now, the chill in the air. He was standing in her living room, no shirt or shoes, with soaking-wet jeans as the wind blew through the front screen door.

"Sassy." He moved closer to her, but she held up her hands again.

"I can't." She shook her head. "I'll get you some dry clothes..." She started to walk away.

"No, don't bother, they'll just get wet on the walk home." He moved towards the door, picking up his wet shirt and shoes as he went.

"Levi," she called to him. "I'm really sorry I can't give you what you want."

"Can't?" He shook his head, then without thinking, stormed across the room and kissed her until he felt the water steam from his skin. Without another word, he turned and left. Her kiss, how she'd responded to him, was all the answer he needed. She may not be able to give him what he wanted now, but there was more than just a slight spark of hope. It was a full-blown raging forest fire.

CHAPTER NINE

Over the course of the next week, Scarlett was surprised that Levi avoided her. Well, maybe avoid wasn't the right word. He went about his business as usual instead of hunting her down or following her around.

She had to admit, as much as she'd found his attention annoying, the lack of it was even more so. Why had she lied to herself that she'd never enjoyed his attentiveness?

By the time she was getting ready for her next days off, she was seriously questioning if she should hunt him down herself. All she could think about that week was how he'd left her. The kiss had seared her body and had her lips vibrating for days.

At first, she'd been thankful he wasn't showering her with attention. Then she'd grown hurt, followed by angry. Now she was back to feeling hurt.

Hell, he'd muddled up her emotions so much that she no longer knew what she wanted. Which made her angry again.

What she needed was some time away from it all. Away from Levi, her feelings, and away from her thoughts. And she couldn't just spend that time muddling around in Pelican Point alone. What she really needed was a day of shopping and friends.

So, she set out to convince her friends to take the day off and spend it with her. After all, the last time they'd all had a day together was before the camp had opened.

After two days of nagging, they caved in. Of course, it took some doing to be able to move everyone's schedules around. But by her next day off, the five best friends were heading towards Destin in Scarlett's car.

"When was the last time we did this?" Hannah asked from her spot squished between Zoey and Aubrey in the back seat. The three of them were the smallest of the group and therefore destined to always share the back seat when they rode together.

"We've hung out a lot at the camp, but it's been almost a full year since we took a day off and had fun," Zoey responded.

"Days off are one thing. Fun days off are another," Elle responded.

Scarlett remembered several days in the past year that they'd spent together. Usually it was worrying over Elle when she was sick, or Hannah after she'd been kidnapped.

"So," Zoey broke into the silence that followed Elle's statement, "Scarlett and Levi…" Her sister left the question hanging.

"I know." Hannah giggled. "I can practically see the steam coming off them every time they're around one another."

"Shut up." Scarlett groaned.

"I don't know what happened during their last day off, but wowzah," Elle chuckled.

"Shut up. Shut up." Scarlett groaned again.

"So, are you going to spill?" Aubrey asked.

Scarlett wished she could close her eyes, but since she'd been picked as designated driver, she kept them glued to the road. "No," she answered after a few calming breaths.

"Come on." Her sister leaned slightly forward and tapped her on the shoulder. "Everyone can tell you two took it to the next base."

"Second base?" Aubrey gasped. "They passed second base finally?"

Everyone in the car laughed. "Oh, I think that base was passed a long time ago," Zoey added, leaning back again.

"Third base?" Elle asked. Scarlett could feel everyone's eyes on hers. She chose not to move, not even blink.

"Oh, I'm guessing they passed that one too," her traitor of a sister added.

"Seriously?" Hannah sighed. "Those are some fond memories, passing those bases for the first time with Owen."

"Seriously, stop," Scarlett said.

"Who started the whole base metaphor anyway?" Aubrey asked. "I mean, of course it had to be a man."

Everyone chuckled.

"Could you imagine if a woman had been the first to invent a metaphor for getting her hands around a guy's…?" Aubrey cleared her throat.

"Dick?" Zoey supplied.

"Seriously?" Elle shook her head. "You've been hanging out in the locker room too much."

"Womb broom? Trouser snake, Rumpleforeskin, knobgoblin, disco stick…" Zoey twisted up her lips and frowned as if she was thinking.

"Cave hunter?" Elle supplied, earning her a look and then more giggles.

"Silent flute," Hanna added, and everyone burst out laughing.

"Enough," Scarlett said getting everyone's attention. "No more penis names in my car."

"I told you I could do it." Aubrey smirked as she held out her hand towards Zoey. Zoey dug in her pocket and handed Aubrey a five-dollar bill.

"Did you seriously bet on getting me to say the word penis?" Scarlett gasped.

In response, Elle held out her hand with a giggle and took the five from Aubrey's hand. Then she held up two fingers and waved them in Aubrey's face.

"Enough." Scarlett rolled her eyes. "Seriously, how old are you?"

"Who cares. I now have five extra dollars to spend today." Elle snapped the bill between her fingers then tucked it away in her shorts.

"Maybe we haven't had enough time between these little... outings?" Scarlett hinted, but the fact was, she was smiling and enjoying herself. Even if she was the butt of their jokes.

The rest of the short drive into town was filled with the same, leading Scarlett to believe that her friends had needed the day off as much as she had.

Their first stop was at the outlet mall, where they spent more than three hours going from store to store, trying on items and buying things that they wanted or needed. It wasn't as if Scarlett didn't go into town often, she just didn't go with the people she deemed her sisters. Which, of course, made the trip far more fun. Not to mention that Hannah was like a walking clothes designer.

It was thanks to her that they had amazing outfits for their fancy dinners or costumes for the festive parties they hosted on an almost nightly basis.

Still, Scarlett was surprised at how well the five of them shopped together. It wasn't as if they'd practiced or had even done it often, but as they moved from store to store, they picked out things that they wanted for themselves or needed for the camp. Okay, most of the stuff they were lugging around in bags was things that they needed for the camp.

The items ranged from matching outfits for the friends for evening events to small items or furniture for a new cabin, which would be delivered next week. By the time they stopped for lunch, Scarlett had spent most of her extra spending money.

Since the sale of their father's business, she'd taken Zoey's advice on investing some of the money that had come in. Most of her stocks had paid off well enough that she had a bank account that she didn't have to worry about. Still, she had set a limit for herself each month to keep herself grounded.

Hannah and Aubrey had grown up with wealth, but they had never acted like the rest of the girls had in the camp. One of Scarlett's strongest memories was how Jenny and her cronies had flaunted their wealth, as if they'd done anything to deserve it.

The Wildflowers had never really focused on money. Their friendship was beyond any material things, which Jenny and the rest of the girls who attended the summer camp hadn't understood.

One summer, it had finally gotten out that Aubrey's father was Harold Smith, one of the wealthiest men alive. Jenny had desperately tried to befriend Aubrey after that. Of course, Aubrey had shut her down quickly.

It was strange. Even though all of them had come from money, they had all been cut off at one point. By the time they had decided to open the camp back up, they had all been pretty much broke.

Zoey and Scarlett's father had taken all of the money with him when he'd left their family for a younger woman.

The five friends had pooled together their savings and scraped pennies together to make it work for that first year, and it had given them the perspective they'd all needed.

They didn't need their families' money. They had each other.

"You're quiet." Elle nudged her. They were sitting in a restaurant in Destin, overlooking the calm emerald green waters on the gulf. Scarlett picked up her fancy blue drink, sans any alcohol, sipped it, then shrugged.

"I was just remembering our first summer at the camp." She smiled and glanced around the table. "How far we've come since then."

Hannah chuckled. "We were all skinny awkward girls. No wonder we became friends."

"You have never been awkward," Aubrey added as she dipped a coconut shrimp into the tangy sauce and bit into it.

Scarlett grabbed the last one before someone else could. "I was the only awkward one," she admitted, "being the youngest. I used to trip all over myself that first summer."

Elle laughed. "You fell off the pier so many times."

"Fell?" She arched her eyebrows. "You mean pushed by that one." She pointed to Hannah with her shrimp. Hannah reached over and snagged it from her fingers. "Hey, get off, that's mine."

Hannah laughed and shoved it in her mouth quickly.

"Easy, girls," Zoey added. "I ordered more." She motioned to the waitress who delivered another plate.

Scarlett took two and guarded them by wrapping her hand around her plate. Hannah laughed.

"Here's to Elle." Zoey held up her matching blue drink. "For bringing us all together that first summer."

"To Elle." Everyone held up their matching drinks. Scarlett glass connected with everyone else's. Her drink looked so bare next to the other's since she had disposed of her little umbrella and had eaten her fruit a few moments after it had been delivered.

She was thankful when the lunch talk turned towards her sister's wedding plans instead of what was between her and Levi. She didn't even really know at this point what was still between them. She'd been ready to take him up to her room and... well, take things to the next level or base... whatever.

It wasn't as if she could deny the attraction that she had towards him. Her body heated each time he was within a mile radius of her, against her will. It was as if her body had already made up its mind about sleeping with Levi.

"I know that look." Her sister nudged her. "What's wrong?"

"Nothing," she lied automatically, which caused Zoey to shake her head.

"Nope, can't do that. I know you too well. Is it the wedding plans? Did you not like the idea Aubrey had?"

"What?" She hadn't even been paying attention to what they'd been talking about. Looking at everyone, she realized she'd been so engrossed in her own thoughts that she hadn't been helping them plan her sister's bridal shower. Damn. "No," she answered again.

"She was too busy dreaming about Levi to hear my plans," Aubrey teased, nudging her under the table with her flip flop.

"Was not," she lied again.

"Wow, two lies in a row," her sister said, shaking her head. "Spill. What happened between you two that has Levi all..."

"Quiet," Elle supplied.

"Not happy," Hannah added. "He used to be the life of the party, but over the past week he's been moping around like a kicked puppy."

"Oh god." Aubrey faked a gasp. "Did you kick our poor Levi?"

"Shut up." She rolled her eyes. Then she leaned on the table, knowing she wouldn't be able to think straight until she confessed. Completely. "Fine." She threw her hands up. "I don't know what I did to piss him off."

"He's pissed at you?" Zoey asked, her eyes narrowing, indicating she was thinking. "What'd you do?" Someone nudged her under the table. "I mean, since we've been back here, you've been pissed at him. But not once have I seen him pissed at you."

"I'm not sure what I did. I mean, one minute we were kissing and pulling each other's clothes off, the next..."

"Wait." Aubrey held up her hand and then leaned closer. "You were what? Did I miss something here?" She glanced around.

"Tell us everything," Hannah said, resting her chin in her hands.

Glancing around the table at the faces looking at her, she knew there was no getting away from it now. She would have to tell her friends, her sisters, everything.

CHAPTER TEN

Why had he thought that staying away from Scarlett would be an acceptable plan? He was in complete hell. Here it was, just over a week after he'd kissed her, and he could still taste her lips on his.

By the end of the first week, he was in a foul mood. So much so that everyone around him noticed it. He was looking forward to his two days off. Time at home always seemed to center him.

He spent his first day off finishing all the work that needed to be done around the house. He even got the new hardwood flooring installed in the kitchen and painted the cabinets seashell cream, as his grandmother had wanted. Installing the little shell door handles had been a bitch, but since his gran was there helping, he'd had to refrain from cursing.

By the end of the night, he was back in the garage lifting weights to burn off the rest of his frustration.

He knew that Scarlett and her friends had spent the day together in Destin. Actually, everyone in the camp knew it since schedules had had to be moved around. No one had complained, since, as bosses, they allowed people to fill in for each other all the time if requested.

He'd had his pick of jobs in his life, but he'd never had another employer as relaxed as the camp. He knew that some employees were handled differently than the ones that were trusted. He liked the reward system the friends had set up the first year the camp had been opened. They'd tweaked it a few times, but now it just worked.

Security had gotten a little tighter around the grounds, especially after the whole Ryan issue. Not to mention Hannah's kidnapping from a dinner party. Now guests were given key cards and had to show them to security that moved around the grounds. Employees had colored badges they had to wear around their necks, which, in his opinion, helped guests out because it helped them stand out to guests who had questions.

He'd been concerned when Hannah had been hurt and kidnapped. After all, he considered all the Wildflowers close friends. But part of him kept playing over in his mind how he would have handled it if it had been Scarlett.

He knew his feelings cut deep. They always had. Even though for years he tried to hide and deny it, he was completely gone for her.

The fact that she didn't appear to feel the same way about him was a challenge. After all, at one point in her life she'd been crazy for him. They'd been crazy for one another. And there was no doubt in his mind that he was a better man than he'd been as a teenager. Still, what she'd said about him hurting her had him questioning things, especially after last weekend.

He racked his brain as he worked out, trying to play over the last summer they'd spent together. How things had progressed physically with them. They hadn't crossed the line of having actual sex, not for his lack of trying. But he wasn't a pushy person and she'd made it clear to him she wasn't ready… yet. Still, he'd gone as far as he could and had enjoyed every moment of his time with her.

Over the years, he'd built her up in his mind. She was every fantasy come true. Better. She was the woman who had gotten away. Dreams paled to kissing her again, to touching her. He knew he had to have more, he just needed time to come up with a plan. One where, if she kept her distance from him emotionally, he wouldn't end up getting hurt.

He'd just finished his last set and was finally feeling a little better when the bane of his thoughts strolled in the open garage door looking sexy as hell in tight shorts and a tank top.

"What are you doing here?" he asked softly, trying to block his sour mood from returning. He tried to avoid looking at her and focused on putting his weights away instead.

"Your grandmother told me I could find you out here." She looked around. "Your fortress of solitude?" she asked, moving around.

Years ago, when he'd been a teenager, he'd hung up posters around the old garage. He'd hauled an old fridge out there and kept it stocked with water and beer. At one point, he'd even dragged his grandmother's old TV and chair out there. They were still sitting in the corner where he watched sports when his gran wanted to watch her shows inside.

"I guess so." He shrugged and set his weight onto the racks. When he was done cleaning up, he turned to her and asked in a quiet voice, "What are you doing here, Sassy?"

She stopped walking around and shrugged her shoulders. "I... came by to see how you're doing."

He almost laughed, but instead answered, "I'm fine." He walked over to the fridge and started to pull out a water, then switched to a beer instead. "Want one?" he asked over his shoulder.

"Sure," she agreed and moved closer to him.

Using the countertop, he popped the tops on both bottles and handed one to her, then downed half of his before turning back towards her.

"What are you really doing here?" he asked, his eyes locked with hers.

She opened her mouth and he could tell whatever she was going to say was an excuse, so he raised his eyebrows and she shut her mouth into a cute little pout. He waited, watching her struggle with telling him the truth or coming up with something believable. He knew the moment the truth won out.

Her eyes changed slightly, and she sucked her bottom lip between her teeth, causing his dick to jump in response.

"I was worried about you. You've acted pretty... strange in the last week," she finally said.

He was silent as he thought. Sure, he'd been acting strange. Of course, he had. How was he supposed to act normal after what had happened last weekend? What he'd asked of her and she'd denied.

He knew all about her trust issues because of her father. He and Zoey had talked about how much Scar had been hurt when their father had left the family. Abandonment issues, hell, they both had them. Still, he focused on the good influences in his life, like his grandmother.

Scarlett had her mother and Zoey, not to mention the other Wildflowers, who stuck by her through everything.

Still, after last weekend, he'd hunted down her sister to find out just who Jenny Carpenter was and what he had done to cause Scarlett so much pain.

Zoey hadn't been much help. Not that she didn't want to be. He could tell that she'd wanted to give him more information, but she'd glanced around nervously, telling him that she was under direct orders not to say anything.

"I'll leave you with this one hint," she'd said, leaning closer to him and lowering her tone. "Jenny was Scar's arch nemesis and, after that summer... Jenny sent Scar a text message. An image." She narrowed her eyes at him. "Of you and her."

Since then, he'd racked his brain for what he'd done shortly after Scar had left to go back home that summer. He'd come up with a blank. He didn't remember Jenny Carpenter from camp, nor was she anyone he'd gone to school with.

Whatever he'd done to piss Scarlett off, he'd either blocked it from his mind or it had never happened, and Jenny had fabricated a story that had put a wedge between him and the woman of his dreams.

"I think I have a right to how I've behaved." He crossed his arms over his chest and leaned against the counter. The fact that her eyes watched his arms as he moved told him that the extra set that he'd done that evening had done its job.

Scarlett looked hungry. Which, of course, had him smiling.

When her eyes jumped back to his, he almost laughed.

"Problem?" he asked smoothly.

"No." Her eyes narrowed in annoyance. "If you're sure you're okay..." She turned to go, but then jerked around again. "You know what, no." She set her beer down and moved closer to him until she was a breath away. "You don't get to run hot one moment..."—she waved her hands in the air as if that was enough explanation, then poked him in the chest with her fingernail—"then go cold on me and ignore me all week as if nothing happened."

"Nothing did happen," he reminded her, enjoying watching her get agitated and riled up. Her cheeks were glowing pink as she marched back and forth in front of him, going over how hurt she was about something. It wasn't until she stopped directly in front of him again that he realized she was talking about the big event that must have happened with Jenny Carpenter.

"Sassy." He took her shoulders in his hands to stop her movement. "I really don't remember any Jenny Carpenter. Whatever she said or did, it was all a lie."

Instead of his statement having a calming effect, it seemed to piss her off even more. Her entire body vibrated as she jerked her shoulders free.

"I saw the pictures..." she said, her eyes narrowing.

He chuckled, which was apparently the wrong move. "Sorry," he said quickly. "Pictures can lie. There were lots of kids taking pictures at the parties I used to go to. I'm sure I'm in more than a few of those. The fall and winter after you left, I did everything I could to get the taste of you out of my head." His hands went to her arms as he pulled her closer, his body and mind already remembering the feel, the taste, the desire to be closer to her. "You left me." He sighed. "Then, when I tried to contact you less than a week later"—he sighed— "your dad and..." he started.

"You talked to my dad?" She jerked in his arms.

"He was the one who answered your phone."

"What did he say?" she asked, frowning slightly.

"It doesn't matter." He pulled her closer as his hands moved up and down her arms. "I didn't keep my promise to stay in touch with you."

Her eyes met his. "No, you didn't, and it hurt."

"I'm so sorry. I was young and stupid." He smiled down at her. "Trust me when I say that I won't be making that mistake again." He rested his forehead against hers. "I'm sorry I pulled away this week. I needed time to figure things out."

"Did you?" she asked.

He pulled back and looked down at her. "Yes, I still want more..." She opened her mouth, but he stopped her by covering it with his own in a soft kiss. "But I'm willing to start things off slowly and see where we go from there. If you're willing."

He held his breath as she thought things through. When she finally nodded, he released the breath.

"Good." He smiled. "How about I walk you home?" He reached down and took her hand.

"You really don't remember Jenny?" she asked once they were outside.

He glanced sideways at her. "No, should I?"

"She was the one who pushed me off the pier. Her and her friends."

He narrowed his eyes and thought. "The blond-haired one that always wore tight things two sizes too small for her?"

"Yes," Scarlett said, then stopped and looked up at him. "You and her never…"

He shook his head. "God no, she was a bitch."

Scarlett's eyes narrowed as she looked at him. Then she burst out laughing. "I've been so hurt and angry at you for years." Then she gasped. "Jenny did that on purpose."

"I wouldn't doubt it." He took her hand and pulled her close again. "She was out for your blood that entire summer." Then he stopped, pulling her to a stop. "You believed her." It wasn't a question as much as an accusation.

"I did." She sighed and shook her head. "My dad left us less than a month after we returned from camp. Things were… emotional for us that summer. I guess she caught me at a very vulnerable time." She tilted her head.

"And yet, for the past two years since you returned, you chose to believe a lie?" he asked, a little hurt that she'd held a grudge for so long. Then again, it had only been a few months after she'd left that he'd started dating someone else.

"How long?" she asked and moved closer. "How long was it before you found someone to replace me?"

He smiled and cupped her chin, then dipped down to run his lips over hers. "I never found someone to replace you. I've dreamed of these lips since the last time I kissed them." He sighed and then kissed her again.

"Kiss up," she said with a chuckle.

"Is it working?" he asked, pulling her closer, enjoying the way her body fit against his.

"I'll let you know, later," she teased, causing him to grow even harder next to her. "I have tomorrow off," she said, then smiled. "I traded my day off yesterday with Aubrey so she could go shopping with us today." She shrugged. "Maybe we can do something?"

Thoughts of spending the night with her wrapped around him flashed in his mind. God, how long had he wanted that? How long had he wanted her?

"How about I pick you up in the morning, and we can grab some breakfast and head to the beach?" he heard himself asking.

They were at the end of her walkway, and she turned towards him.

"The beach tomorrow sounds wonderful, but I was hoping you'd like to come inside… stay a while." She pushed her body against his and his dick took over his brain as he kissed her.

In the back of his mind, he kept telling himself that he'd just promised he'd take things slow with her. He still believed that if he slept with her now, at least in her mind, it would be just sex.

And he was even more determined now that this was going to go far beyond just sex. If his plan to get her to fall in love with him was going to work, he had to stick to his no sex rule.

But as her body rubbed against his and Scarlett took the kiss deeper, he decided that there was a difference between sex and having some fun sex time.

Pulling her up into his arms, he carried her up the front steps of the house and inside, determined to have as much fun sex time as he could, without crossing the line he'd drawn.

CHAPTER ELEVEN

Scarlett had gone her entire life waiting to be romantically carried up a set of stairs. Holding onto Levi, she nuzzled his neck as they stepped into the house. But when he stopped just inside the front door, she glanced up at him.

"My bedroom's upstairs," she hinted.

He frowned at the stairs. "I know. I'm thinking." He quickly turned away from the stairs and moved to the sofa instead.

When she opened her mouth to protest, he kissed her until she forgot all about not being carried upstairs. Her entire body melted as he ran his hands over her hips.

When he tugged her shirt over her head, she held her breath as he ran his eyes up and down her exposed skin. His fingers traced across her, sending bumps rising everywhere as he slowly explored her skin.

"Levi," she begged, reaching for his shirt, only to have him step away from her.

"No, I just worked out. I probably stink. For now, I'm going to enjoy myself with you." His eyes met hers. "This is what compromise means," he warned, then he dipped his head down and ran his mouth over the curve of her breast. She opened her mouth to argue, but he nudged her bra aside suddenly. Her knees went weak when his tongue dipped below to trace her nipple.

Crying his name, her fingers tangled in his hair, she remembered the first time she'd held onto him like this. How he had kissed her, pushed her shorts down, and slid a finger into her. She'd come instantly, not really knowing what was happening, but enjoying it so much she wanted more.

"Levi." She wrapped her arms around his shoulders and held on as he slowly undressed her.

"Yes, Sassy?" He chuckled against her belly button as his fingers worked the clasp of her shorts. When they dropped to the ground, she lost her ability to think. His mouth ran over her silk underwear, heating her, soaking her skin.

"Please," she begged. They had never crossed into full sex, back at camp all those years ago. Even though she'd enjoyed him touching her, getting her to orgasm, she had never once made him feel the way he had made her feel.

She'd promised herself not to be such a selfish lover this time. But when she reached for him, he gripped her wrists and nudged her down onto the sofa.

"Hold still," he warned her as he knelt between her legs.

"Levi, I want..." she started, but then she gasped as his mouth covered her silk panties. Her legs wrapped around his shoulders, and she held on when he nudged them aside to slide his mouth over her.

"Oh god," she moaned, her fingers getting lost in his hair as she arched into his kisses.

"My god," he agreed. "You taste like spring. I've dreamed..." He moaned and ran his mouth over her again. When he dipped a finger into her this time, she tried to convince herself to hold out, to wait until she could please him, but it was too much. It felt too wonderful. He felt too wonderful. She felt too much for him, even though she wanted to deny it. She couldn't stop her body from building up.

"Sassy, let go," he said against her thigh. "I need this."

"No, Levi, I want..." Then he did something with his thumb, brushing it against her clit as his fingers worked inside her and stars exploded behind her eye lids as she cried out his name.

"Yes, that's it," he encouraged her. "Please," he said, kissing her again.

She was in a daze. She was pretty sure that he wrapped a blanket around her and then held onto her until she fell asleep. The long day of shopping caught up with her, causing her to drift off in his arms.

When she woke several hours later, Levi was gone. She found a note on the coffee table, scribbled on one of the bookmarks she'd picked up from the library.

"I'll be here to pick you up at eight. Goodnight, Levi."

"Damn him." She tossed the bookmark down and sat up. She didn't realize that she was still completely naked under the blanket until she stood up.

Grabbing up her clothes, she marched up the stairs, mumbling the entire way about stupid unrealistic romantic notions in books and movies as she went.

When she glanced at the clock, she realized it was only half past midnight. What the hell was she supposed to do with herself now?

Then an idea came to her. Starting a bath, she tossed in one of her pink bubble packets and lit the candles surrounding the tub.

When she snapped a picture of herself, she made sure that only the non-essential skin was showing. There was no way she was going to send him a picture of anything that could accidently get shared around.

Just her belly button and a little leg showed above of the pink bubbles. She was happy that part of their excursion that day had been an hour filled with pedicures and that she'd picked a hot pink for her toes.

It took a couple tries before she finally got the picture she wanted. When she sent it off to him, she added a short message.

-Looks like you missed a spot.

She chuckled and enjoyed the warm water as she waited for a reply. She didn't think it would take long and had to only wait about two minutes.

-You'll pay for that.

She laughed and hugged the phone to her.

-Promise?

-Go to sleep. I'm going to keep you busy all day tomorrow.

-Can't, I'm too… worked up.

His next response took a little longer.

-Then touch yourself and think of me.

-Is that what you're doing?

-Now I am.

She smiled and ran her hands over herself, almost dropping her phone in the water as she went.

-I need a picture… to help.

-LOL, nope.

-Come on, something like I sent.

A moment later, a picture of his ear came through, causing her to laugh.

-So sexy.

Then another picture came, this one of his feet, outside of his bedsheets.

-That's about it.

-That'll do.

She smiled. Already, she could feel herself growing tired again.

-I think I'm going to crawl out of this bath and into bed now.

-God, now you have me fully awake.

-Good.

She smiled and then added,

-Now you know how I felt a few minutes ago when I realized you'd left me.

-Until tomorrow.

His last words played over in her mind as she crawled in between the cool sheets and closed her eyes. What exactly was he promising her would happen tomorrow?

The memory of what he'd done to her earlier that evening played over in her mind as she drifted off to sleep.

When her alarm woke her, she stretched her arms over her head and then remembered what her plans were for the day. She jumped out of bed and rushed around preparing, very eager to start the day.

By the time Levi knocked on her door, she had a bag packed with everything she would need for a day at the beach and with him.

When she opened the door, she was surprised by a large bouquet of wildflowers.

"I don't know your favorite, but I assumed..." He handed them to her. "You know, because of what you and your friends call yourselves."

She laughed and hugged the flowers to her face to breath in their mixed scent.

"I love all flowers equally," she answered. "Come on in, I'll put these in a vase."

He followed her into the kitchen where she busied herself finding a vase and filling it with water.

When she turned back around, he was there, pulling her into his arms. Even though the kiss was light, her body reacted instantly when it bumped into his.

"What are the chances I could talk you into a late brunch?" she asked, nodding towards the stairs.

Instead of answering, he chuckled. "Can't, I've made plans." He took her hand. "Are you ready?"

She sighed and then followed him out of the house. He stopped to pick up her beach bag for her and tossed it over his shoulder.

"Okay, so what's the plan?" she asked as he helped her into his Jeep.

"A short drive first." He set her bag in the back seat and then moved around to get in. "Brunch"—he wiggled his eyebrows—"water, beach, swimming, more beach, more water, more swimming, then sometime later we'll eat the lunch I packed, then eventually, around sunset, dinner." He picked up her hand and kissed it.

She couldn't help but smile at his attempt to rile her up. "I'm all yours for the day." She sat back as he drove out of town. She didn't care where they were headed. He'd removed the soft top and the doors from his Jeep, and she was thankful she'd braided her hair and added a cap to her attire.

The wind in her face was almost magical as it wiped away all her stress. She should really spend more of her days off like this instead of cooped up in the house reading.

It wasn't as if she didn't get enough time outdoors, since most of her days were spent rushing around the camp helping with outdoor activities.

But being outside for work and being outside for fun were two different animals.

Now, since she was on her own time, she didn't have to abide by anyone else's timelines. Thankfully, she didn't have to rush around to be somewhere for another group activity or to help new guests to their cabins. She really enjoyed her work, but lately her time off was just not what she'd hoped. Yesterday being the exception.

"I'm not taking you away from your grandmother today, am I?" she asked as they turned onto the beach road.

"No, Gran has her book club meeting today, then her knitting class, followed by a baking class she signed up for last week."

"She's taking a baking class?" Scarlett asked, remembering how well his grandmother baked.

Levi chuckled. "No, she's teaching a group of people who signed up at the library how to bake." He glanced over at her. "You'd be surprised at how many adults don't know how to bake."

She bit her bottom lip and silently wished she had more time to learn herself. It wasn't that she was a terrible baker, she could just use some extra skills.

"You know," she thought out loud, "that's not a terrible idea." She shifted towards him. "Would your gran be interested in holding those classes at the camp? I mean, I'd have to figure out the logistics of it, but I don't see why we couldn't offer cooking or baking sessions."

"She'd love it," he answered quickly. "She's been trying to fill her time lately." He sighed. "Since her best friend died last year"—he shook his head— "I think she's struggling, and staying busy seems to be helping her."

"Then it's settled. I'll see what we can come up with and talk things over with your grandmother."

When they pulled into a small parking lot, Scarlett looked around. Since she'd returned to the area, she'd been too busy with the camp to have time to explore all the different beaches and towns. She'd walked this beach before, but hadn't spent a lot of time here.

"This looks... amazing," she said getting out of the Jeep and reaching for her bag, but he was there, pulling it and a few more things out of the back of the Jeep. "You're going to need some help carrying all that," she joked when he picked up two beach chairs.

He frowned. "Okay, you can carry the bags." He handed her his bag and hers. They started walking down the white sand towards a small cluster of white buildings. "We should be all set up for brunch." He motioned towards a small deck area.

A few yards down the beach sat a small gazebo with a table, chairs, and food.

"How did you set this all up?" she asked, following him into the area.

"We can set our stuff here until we're done eating." He set down the chairs and the cooler he had in his hands. Then he reached for her bags and set them beside the rest of the stuff. When he took her hand, a waiter appeared.

"Mr. Grant?"

"Yes." He smiled. "This is Scarlett."

"Perfect, we have everything ready for you." The waiter nodded. "Would you like something to drink?"

Levi looked over at her. Scarlett shrugged. "Mimosas?"

"Perfect." Levi smiled and held out a chair for her.

"Okay, how did you set this up?" she asked when the waiter disappeared to get their drinks.

"This is part of BB." He shrugged. "I have an old friend who works here. He arranged it all."

"BB?" she asked, glancing around. She'd seen the small circular gazebo on her walks along the beach but hadn't realized what it was. The table with its white tablecloth and matching covered chairs looked like something straight out of a beach catalog.

"The Beach Bar." He chuckled. "It's kind of underground." He frowned. "No, not underground, just... for a select crowd. Locals and some very high-paying customers know about it."

"I guess I wasn't in that category." She shrugged, then sat back when the waiter came back with a pitcher of mimosas. He poured them each a flute and then ran through the brunch menu.

She ordered Fosters French Toast with fresh berries, then she took a sip of her drink and took in the view.

"We couldn't have asked for a better day," she said, motioning to the clear water in front of them.

"We're supposed to get more rain later this week," he agreed. "I'm thankful you changed your days off." He held up his drink towards her.

"Me too." She tipped her glass to his. "Thank you for setting all of this up." She leaned back in her chair, trying to remember the last time she'd gone out on a date this fun. Never.

The last dozen or so failed dates ran through her mind quickly. How had things gotten this bad with her?

It wasn't as if she'd dated a lot. Actually, her last date had been before she'd left Jacksonville. She knew she had issues with trusting men, especially after what her father had done to her and her family.

Then she remembered all her pent-up anger towards Levi and how she'd found out they were all unjustified. Levi hadn't betrayed her. Whatever he was, he wasn't someone like her father.

Her mind screamed and an instant of panic filled her, so she busied herself with slowly taking a sip of her drink until the moment was over.

"What was that?" he asked, and she realized he'd been watching her.

She shrugged and tried to think of something else to talk about but couldn't come up with anything.

"Sassy?" He leaned closer to her and took her hand. "It's just us. Talk to me. What is causing that lost look in your eyes?"

CHAPTER TWELVE

He watched Scarlett's mood darken slightly as she fought with telling him her thoughts, then she sighed and rolled her shoulders.

"Fine, it's just... I was remembering the last time I went out on a date." She cringed.

"That bad?" he asked. He could tell there was something deeper bothering her but didn't want to push her.

"The guy actually showed up two days late and tried to convince me I had misunderstood his text. When I showed it to him, he laughed and said his phone had autocorrected and that I should give him another chance."

"Did you?"

"I was bored." She shrugged. "I shouldn't have. He ended up taking me to a pool house where I stood around watching him and his buddies play pool all night while sipping a drink. When I made it home, I had to order a pizza, since I somehow had assumed dinner would be in the four-hour span somewhere."

"Wow." He shook his head. "The guy knew how to show a woman a good time," he joked.

"Tell me about it." She rolled her eyes. "He tried to invite himself in when he dropped me off." Levi tensed at that thought, and his hand jerked in hers slightly. "As if." She laughed and he relaxed a little. No, whatever Scarlett was, she wasn't a pushover. "Two days later he called me up and asked to take me out again."

"I take it you let him down gently?" he asked, his eyes searching hers.

"I wouldn't use the word gentle." She smirked.

"Have you had many bad dates?" he asked, curious.

She ran her eyes over him and took another sip of her drink. "A few. You?"

"No," he answered. "But then again, I've been the one driving."

"You've never had a woman set the date? Why is it still a thing in society that men dictate evenings out?" She glanced around quickly. "I mean, don't get me wrong, this is amazing and there is no way I could have pulled something like this off without at least a weeks' notice. And you did it all after leaving my place late last night."

"I've had a few times when a woman set the mood of the evening. But we were already dating at the time."

She leaned her elbow on the table and rested her chin in her palm. "Oh?"

He smiled. "Okay, let's get this out of the way. I've had two semi-serious relationships. One in high school, the year after you left camp. The other was two years back." His smile slipped a little.

"What happened?" she asked.

"The first time"—he leaned back and looked out towards the beach— "Robin's family moved away," he answered easily.

"And the second?"

"Carrie was... after something I couldn't give her," he admitted, still feeling the sting of rejection.

"Which was?" she asked, smoothly.

"Wealth," he admitted, feeling foolish. The memory of Zoey's large engagement ring surfaced, and he kept his eyes away from hers.

"Stupid." Scarlett sighed. "My father's second wife was like that."

Suddenly, he remembered hearing how the woman had attacked Zoey shortly after their father's death. After she'd found out she hadn't been left a dime in her ex-husband's will.

"Still, it's pretty nice." He glanced sideways at her. "You know, to have that cushion." He took a deep breath and poured her some more drink. "I mean, your sister..."

"What?" She stilled, her hand halfway to her glass.

His eyebrows shot up. "Nothing, I mean." He cleared his throat. "She really likes that rock Dylan gave her."

She softened and smiled. "Yes, that's different."

"Oh?" He poured himself some more drink and sipped. "How so?"

Scarlett tilted her head and watched him. "That was his grandmother's ring. He was going to buy her one, then his father returned and... well, since he was the first Costa to get engaged"—she took a drink and watched him—"he got dibs on the ring."

Levi thought of his own grandmother's wedding ring. The one his grandfather had given her all those years ago. He'd never met the man but knew about him from his gran and all the pictures around the house.

Marco Grant had been military through and through. He'd been born into a family who had all served and even died so that others could have their freedom. Levi had believed at one point that he'd join up himself, but his gran had talked him out of it. Besides, if he'd left, she would have been left alone again, and he doubted she could have handled it.

There was no way he would ever want her to remove the

rock on her finger for him. Not when he knew how much she'd loved Marco.

"Did you think my sister… that money was the reason she and Dylan…"

"No," he broke in. The conversation stopped as their food was delivered.

"Wow, this looks amazing," she said after the waiter left.

"Dig in."

"You were saying?" she asked after the first bite.

He sighed. "No, I know Zoey and Dylan got together before everyone knew the brothers were… well, who they were."

"Then why mention her?" she asked and suddenly he felt stupid for thinking that money would have even been an issue with her. She wasn't like Carrie. Scarlett had grown up with wealth and if the rumors were true about the money her and Zoey were getting from their father's estate, still had enough to be comfortable.

"Levi?" she said when he didn't answer her.

"I guess I'm still harboring thoughts from when Carrie was around," he admitted.

Scarlett reached over and took his hand. "Money isn't important to me. This is nice and all," she said, motioning around them, "but I'm just as happy sitting on a beach, reading my book from the library, and having a homemade turkey sandwich." She leaned closer. "Which I suspect your grandmother helped make for our lunch."

He laughed. "That's good to know."

After brunch, they made their way down to the water's edge and set up their chairs and towels. He enjoyed watching her peel off her shorts and top to expose a sexy red bikini. Hell, he'd seen her naked last night, but somehow in the small red suit he found her even more appealing.

Taking a cool dip in the water, he enjoyed when her soft body pushed against his as the waves crashed around them.

They laughed and flirted in the water until she mentioned being thirsty, then they sat under the small umbrella he'd brought along and talked.

He couldn't remember ever having more fun at the beach or on one of his days off.

She told him that she'd played the flute in grade school and had sucked at it since she was musically challenged.

He told her how his gran had forced him to take piano lessons as a child and that he still played during some of her gatherings for her church.

"You should play during our next talent show," she suggested. "We have a school reunion this weekend, but after that..." She nudged him. "I'd love to hear you play."

He smiled. "You have already. Three weeks ago, when the Palmers had that little gathering?"

She frowned. "No, that was Carol."

"Nope, Carol was out sick that night. I filled in for her." He shrugged.

"That was you?" She shook her head. "I guess I was too busy to glance over at the piano."

"You were too busy ignoring me, you mean," he joked. Her smile slipped slightly, but then she nodded.

"Okay, yes, I have been avoiding you. Avoiding this." She looked down at their joined hands. "I was wrong." She sighed. "Wrong about you and Jenny." She glanced up at him and he watched her eyes heat. "Makes me wonder what else I was wrong about."

His body reacted instantly to her. Would she always have this power over him? Just looking into those smoky hazel eyes, he knew the answer. He was completely gone for her.

"We could spend a lifetime finding out," he teased, knowing she needed to keep things light with him. After all, it was only day one of his plan to win her back.

They swam a little more, ate lunch when they got hungry,

took a long walk down the beach, swam more, and then dried off in the sun until it started to sink below the horizon.

"I have dinner planned." He thought about the reservation he'd made online.

"How about we head back to my place?" she suggested. "We can grab a pizza on the way and watch a scary movie?" She moved closer to him. "Then, I can pay you back for last night."

"Okay," he answered so quickly that Scarlett laughed. "It's just..." He ran his hands through his hair and then stopped thinking when she wrapped her arms around him.

"I understand." She smiled up at him. "We've been dancing around one another for the past two years." She lowered her voice. "I'm done running from this. I still don't know where it will lead, but I'm willing to give it a shot if you are." He nodded, not trusting his voice. "Good, then let's clean up and get out of here."

Without saying anything, they packed up all their gear and hauled it back to his Jeep.

He hadn't realized the drive to the beach took so long until there was sex on the line. He almost forgot to stop by the local pizza place and pick up a pie for later. Thankfully, he remembered at the last moment and pulled into the parking lot.

"What kind of pie do you like?" he asked after shutting down the Jeep.

"Okay, don't kill me, but I like Hawaiian. It's the best." She answered.

He chuckled. "Pineapple on pizza." He shook his head. "I guess for you, I'll try anything." He got out, then held up his hand. "You wait here, I'll get it."

He stepped into the pizzeria. He was next in line to order when he spotted a familiar face.

"Hey, Corey." He shook his friend's hand. "What are you doing back in town?" He'd gone to school with Corey Leggatt. One of the reasons he and Corey had gotten along was that both of them were high school mistakes, as they called themselves.

Corey's parents had been in the same grade as Levi's mother and both women had gotten pregnant around the same time. Corey was less than a month older than Levi, instantly making them friends in school.

"Hey, man." Corey laughed. "My folks' reunion is coming up. We're back here spending some time with my grandparents. Trying to enjoy some fun and sun." He waved to his grandparents and his parents, who were sitting across the room enjoying their drinks while they waited for their food.

Corey had lucked out with parents who not only stuck together through the teenage pregnancy but were still together more than twenty years later. That thought had a slight ache spread near Levi's heart.

"Cool," he sighed, then remembered Scarlett mentioning the reunion at the camp. "Oh, hey, I'll see you around then. I'm working out at the camp where the reunion is happening."

"I heard." Corey slapped his back, then moved up to take his order when he was called. "Congrats. It seems like a pretty cool deal out there. Makes me wish I wasn't stuck behind a desk all the time," Corey said.

"City life will make you soft," Levi joked as his friend walked across the room.

"Hey, it pays the bills and gets me loads of women," Corey joked back quickly.

After ordering their pizza, he tried to avoid watching the family across the room from him.

As a kid, he'd never really thought about how much it hurt to not have a mom and dad. His gran had been everything she could to him. Everything he'd dreamed of having. Until he'd spent the night over at Corey's house when he was ten. After one night of seeing what a real family could be like, Levi had dreamed of something different. Something more. He'd tried to keep those hopes locked away from his grandmother, since he didn't want to hurt her feelings, but he'd been so young, and his grandmother was a wise woman. She'd tried to cheer him up the best she could and eventually, he'd put it in the back of his mind.

"You okay?" Scarlett asked as he got back in the Jeep.

"Yeah." He smiled, but she shook her head.

"Levi." She took his hand, stopping him from putting the Jeep into gear. "It's just us. Talk to me. What's causing that lost look in your eyes?"

The fact that she was repeating his own words back to him had him sighing and pushing his hands through his hair in frustration. It was silly, as an adult, to let this kind of thing still affect him. But here he was, almost twenty-five and wishing once again he could have what other people had. A slice of normalcy. A family.

The look in her eyes told him that she wasn't going to let him off without an explanation, just like he'd demanded one of her earlier. If he wanted things to move forward with her, he was going to have to tell her about his own past desires.

Glancing around, he sighed. "Not here. Let's talk back at your place."

CHAPTER THIRTEEN

Stepping into the house with Levi felt different than it had the night before. He'd walked into the pizzeria happy and almost walking on air. When he'd returned, it was as if the weight of the world was on his shoulders.

Something had caused him to come crashing down to earth, and she was determined to find out what had caused his mood change.

Tossing her beach bag down, she took the pizza from his hands and walked back to the kitchen. Flipping the oven on warm, she set the box in it and then turned to see him watching her from across the kitchen.

She pulled out a bottle of wine and poured them each a glass.

"Sorry, we don't have beer," she started to say only to stop when he downed the glass and set it aside.

"I didn't have a family growing up." He started moving around the kitchen, his long legs eating up the small space so that he had to turn several times and make a large circle around the bar area. "My friend Corey was like me. His mother and mine were in the same class." He turned to her, his eyes almost unseeing. "They were friends. I don't know how close, but from my mother's yearbook, close enough to be seen in several pictures together. Anyway, Corey was born a month before me. His folks, shortly after graduation, got married and..." He sighed and rolled his shoulders. "They were in the pizza joint tonight with Corey."

She moved over to him and touched his arm. "I'm sorry."

"Growing up, I tried to let my grandmother be enough for me. I really did. She gave up so much for me. The first time I saw Corey's family together was the first time I realized I was missing something in life."

"Levi, not everyone gets the family they deserve," she said softly as she thought of her own messed-up childhood. How her father had, even before the divorce, been absent most of her life.

"No," he agreed as he wrapped his arms around her. "Since that day, my biggest wish in life has been to have a family of my own. To make something great, something I never had growing up."

Scarlett tensed. She'd been trying to avoid thinking about her own future. One thing she'd promised herself after her parents very messy divorce was that she was never going to fall into the marriage trap. No man was ever going to hurt her the way her father hurt her mother.

"I know the thought of something more in a relationship scares you." He pulled back slightly and looked down at her. "That's why I'm trying to take things slow with you." He sighed. "Which is why we should eat that pizza and then I should kiss you before I head home."

She opened her mouth to argue, but he stopped her by placing his lips over hers.

"Don't argue with me, Sassy. I'm not in the mood." He rested his head against hers.

"Don't I get a say in any of this?" she asked, feeling frustrated.

"Sure." He smiled and dropped his arms to his sides. She

swayed slightly, missing the feeling of his strength against her. "Go ahead." He motioned towards her.

She had so much she wanted to say, but at the moment all she could think about was having his arms wrapped around her again. She wanted to enjoy the feeling of him touching her. To know what it would be like to be with him. Even if the possibility of getting hurt outweighed her desire for him.

"I don't want you to go," she admitted.

His eyes darkened and for a moment she thought he was going to reach for her. Then he tucked his hands in the pockets of his shorts.

"Trust me when I say I don't want to leave either."

"Then stay." She moved closer to him, but he stopped her by holding onto her shoulders and keeping her at arm's length. "Screw the future," she blurted out. "None of us know what's going to happen tomorrow. I may not be able to promise you forever, but I'm here right now." She shifted slightly until her body finally came up against his. "Let that be enough for tonight."

He bent down and kissed her and, for a moment, her entire body shook with the desire radiating from him.

"I have commitment issues," she said between kisses as she tugged him towards the stairs. "I may always have them, but I trust you." She pulled back and looked into his eyes. "You may be the only man I can say that to." He smiled suddenly.

She gasped as he hoisted her up into his arms. "If you're sure," he asked, waiting, and she felt her heart kick in her chest at being held in his arms.

"I am." She smiled and then laughed when he started taking the stairs two at a time. "My bedroom's at the end." She motioned to her door when they reached the landing.

"You make me feel stupid." He chuckled when they stepped into her darkened room. "Drunk and stupid." He bent down and kissed her.

"Good, because that's how you make me feel," she said as he lowered her slowly to the floor. Her body brushed against his until her feet touched the ground.

Wrapping her arms around his neck, she kissed him until she was breathless. His hands nudged her shorts down her hips slowly, sliding the jean material until it pooled at her feet.

She stepped out of them and reached for his shirt. She ran her palms up his six-pack, over his chest, as she removed his shirt. Tossing it on the ground with her shorts, she reached for his swim trunks, but he took her wrists and pulled them over her head so he could slowly pull her tank top off.

She stood in front of him in her swimsuit as his eyes ran over her hungrily.

"You are so beautiful," he whispered as his fingers traced her collarbone.

"You saw me in this all day." She chuckled and reached to release the clasp.

He stopped her. "I know, but that doesn't mean I don't want to enjoy removing it from you." He traced the material over her skin. The feeling of his fingertip running over her had her eyes closing as she sucked in a breath.

She felt herself sway slightly until his arm wrapped around her waist as he continued his soft exploration of her.

His finger dipped below the material, tracing around her breast, causing a low moan to escape her lips.

"You're torturing me," she complained.

In response, the straps of her top floated away, leaving her exposed. She watched his eyes heat, then she smiled as he bent his head down and traced the same motion with his tongue.

"Perfection," he said before taking her nipple into his mouth and sucking lightly. She gripped his hair, holding him as she felt her entire body pulse with each suckle.

"Levi," she groaned, trying to hold herself in check. There

was no way she was going to be a selfish lover for a third time with him.

Reaching for him, she unsnapped his shorts and pulled them down his narrow hips quickly before he could complain.

He jerked slightly as she wrapped her fingers around his length, enjoying for the first time the feel of him in her hands.

"My god," she moaned with pleasure. "You've been keeping something from me." She smiled as he glanced up at her.

"Not by choice." He chuckled.

"If every woman knew what kind of package you had, you'd be in big trouble at the camp," she teased as she continued to stroke his length. He was larger than any other man she'd experienced before. For a moment, she wondered if she really knew what she was doing. What had she gotten herself into?

Then his fingers trailed down her stomach and nudged her swimsuit bottoms down over her hips. When he dipped a finger into her, she gasped and held onto him as he once again took over.

"I can't think when you do that," she complained, reaching for him again.

"Good." He shifted, and she realized he'd walked her backwards. Her knees hit the side of her bed. Instead of letting him pull her down, she reversed their positions and placed her hand in the center of his chest and nudged him until he fell backwards on her mattress.

He chuckled. "Okay."

"My turn," she said as she slowly moved over him. "I did warn you," she reminded him as she ran her eyes over him. "I'm going to eat you up," she said as she ran her mouth over the line of each of the muscles in his six-pack. "I've never seen someone as defined as you." She enjoyed the way he sucked in his breath as her mouth moved over him.

His fingers were tangled in her hair and when she trailed her tongue over the length of him, his grip tightened.

"Sassy." It came out as a warning.

"Don't fight it," she said before taking him fully into her mouth. She couldn't help the groan that escaped at the feeling of him hardening even further in her mouth.

She liked to think she was a skilled lover, but with Levi, everything seemed new. She wanted to spend the rest of the night exploring him, enjoying him but, suddenly, he hoisted her up until she straddled his shoulders. When his mouth found her pussy, she cried out and arched back as her eyes closed.

"I owe you," he growled out against her skin.

She shook her head, but she was enjoying the feeling of his wet tongue inside her so much that she couldn't function. Her mouth and body weren't connected any longer.

His hands gripped her hips, forcing her to move over him until she slowly rode his mouth, taking what she wanted.

"I'm not stopping until you come," he warned. "Let go," he said against her heated skin.

When a finger dipped into her heat, she cried out and did as he demanded.

As with before, she floated and only vaguely registering him sliding a condom on. He laid her down and covered her, and she felt him slowly slide into her, stretching her, filling her.

She arched, her nails digging into his shoulders as she wrapped her legs around him.

"Levi?" Her eyes met his.

"I've got you," he said smoothly, leaning down to kiss her as he continued to move until he was fully embedded in her.

She'd never felt so alive as she did that very moment. Her ankles locked behind his hips as she silently prayed that he would take her any way he wanted.

When he started to move finally, she watched his eyes darken until she could no longer hold onto her control. His kisses matched his movement and soon she lost herself in the best sex she'd ever had. She felt herself building up again and knew that this time, she was going to hold out for him.

"Sassy, come with me," he said against her ear. "I need to feel you tighten around me." He pulled her earlobe into his mouth and sucked gently as she convulsed around him, vaguely registering his release at the same time.

They must have slept for a while. When she woke, it was to the sound of Levi's stomach growling against her ear.

Laughing, she sat up and looked down at him. His blond hair was sticking up in places. When he cracked his eyes open, she could see that he was happy and horny again.

"Food first," she warned, trying to move out of his arms.

"Oh, I intend to eat." His grin spread as he lifted her and once again had her straddling his face.

She could get used to this, she thought as she held onto the headboard as he pleased her for the second time.

When they finally made it back downstairs, the pizza was devoured quickly. Levi pulled each piece of pineapple from his slices and piled them on her plate. She gladly ate them up and laughed as he made funny faces at her.

"Pineapples don't belong on pizza," he said.

"Neither does honey, yet..." She poured another dollop on her crust and bit into it with a moan. "Here we are." He chuckled and shook his head in response. "Come on, tell me you don't have some food fetish yourself?" She narrowed her eyes at him.

He tilted his head and thought about it. "Chocolate and peanut butter."

She made a noise and rolled her eyes. "Only a trillion people love that combination."

"Okay." He held up a finger. "I've got one. Pickles and red pepper."

She thought about it. "I could try that. What about French fries and milkshakes?"

"Chocolate milkshakes," he corrected.

"Of course." She laughed.

His eyes darkened and she could tell suddenly he was thinking about sex again. Dipping her finger into the honey, she slowly brought her finger up to her mouth and sucked the sweetness from her fingertip. His eyes grew darker as he set the rest of his slice down.

"Sassy," he sighed.

"I bet we could get really sticky…" She repeated the move, only this time, bringing her finger up to his mouth.

When he took it into his mouth and sucked, she closed her eyes and enjoyed the feeling of his tongue wrapped around her finger. His hands wrapped around her wrist and tugged until she moved across the space to sit on his lap. Feeling his hardness against her, she smiled.

"I think you could grow to like honey on anything," she teased.

His fingers bunched against her hips. "Now you've done it." He shoved the pizza box aside and hoisted her onto the table.

She giggled until he finished pulling all her clothes from her. When he turned the honey bottle upside down over her body, slowly letting the sticky fluid trail over her breasts, belly, and the V between her legs, she stilled.

"Levi," she warned.

"Shush." He dipped his mouth over her. "I'm busy. I have a sticky mess to clean up."

CHAPTER FOURTEEN

Half an hour later, he carried Scarlett into the shower. Both of them were so covered in sticky residue, he doubted one single shower would remove all the mess.

"I'm never going to get all of this off." She laughed as she used a washcloth against her skin.

"Let me." He took the cloth from her and instantly felt himself growing hard again as he slowly ran it over her.

There was no way he was going to be sated in just one night.

He watched her lean back and enjoy the feel of him running the cloth over her skin. Taking some more soap from the container she showed him, he let it bubble up and then covered her skin with it, gently removing the rest of the honey residue from her body.

"Next time we'll try chocolate sauce," he said, watching for her expression.

"Next time, we lay plastic down." She smiled.

He laughed, remembering the mess they'd left downstairs on the table. "Right," he agreed. He dipped down to kiss her.

"Would it be bad if I kept you up all night?" He sighed against her lips.

"I don't have a class until ten," she answered.

He quickly thought about what his day was supposed to be filled with. "I've got a group to take kayaking at nine." He groaned.

His hands continued to run over her soft skin and hair. He'd helped her scrub the honey from her long locks when they'd first stepped under the water.

"Shower sex can be just as... slippery." He smiled and was thankful he'd brought another condom into the shower with him.

"Are you ready for more?" she asked, her eyes going to his cock, which instantly jumped in response. "Wow." She smiled.

"Sorry, I've been wanting you for a while," he said between kisses.

"Don't be sorry." She wrapped her arms around his shoulders.

"I could spend a lifetime lost in your arms," he said against her skin. He felt her stiffen slightly and kissed her until he felt her relax again.

Making slow love to her in the shower was even better than their sticky-quickie in the kitchen.

When they finally made it back to her bed, he was exhausted and knew that if he didn't have to set an alarm for the morning, he could easily spend the following day with her wrapped around him.

Dressing the next morning was one of the hardest things he'd had to do. She busied herself getting ready and, after a few minutes, he could tell she was avoiding him.

To stop all the weirdness, he pulled her into his arms and kissed her until he felt her melt.

"This doesn't have to be weird," he told her. "I want to see you again tonight."

"Okay," she said with a smile. "Dinner..."

"I'm scheduled to help out all week. There's the big party tonight then the reunion." He knew he was already on the schedule for that. No matter what, he planned on spending as many of his nights with Scarlett as he could.

"Okay." She wrapped her arms round his shoulders. "After dinner then."

He nodded. "Think your sisters will make a big deal about us?"

She laughed. "For sure."

He shrugged. "It doesn't have to be weird."

"No," she agreed. "It doesn't." She kissed him. "Now, you'd better go before your late. You don't want to piss off your boss so soon after sleeping with her."

He chuckled but kissed her again until he felt her body heat. "I'll see you later."

For the first time in two years, he didn't really want to go into work.

As he took the small group out on the calm bay in the kayaks, he couldn't keep his mind from last night.

Even when the pretty blond guest went out of her way to flirt with him, his thoughts remained on his Sassy.

Flirting came with the job description, if you wanted to make tips, so he knew how to do it well. His heart had never really been in it, except with Scarlett.

He found Scarlett and her friends at lunchtime and sat next to her, rubbing knees with her under the table while everyone talked about the coming dinner party.

He didn't know if everyone had caught on about them yet, but it was only a matter of time before they did. The fact that Scarlett hadn't berated him for anything during lunch should have been the biggest clue of them all.

When he'd joked with the rest of the group about something,

she'd been right there laughing with all of them instead of scowling at him like she had in the past.

No matter what her friends thought, he knew they respected him and Scarlett. After all, Zoey had been the one to encourage her sister to go see him. She had to know there was something between them.

Since his schedule was full that day, he only had a few minutes to hunt her down and kiss her behind the swimming pool pump house.

"I'm running late," he told her before taking her in his arms and pulling her behind the small building.

"Your boss will understand." She sighed and tried to hold onto him.

"Can't." He chuckled. "My boss's sister will ream me when I don't show up to help her set up for the volleyball game." He glanced over his shoulder to see if Zoey was at the sand court yet.

"Tell her you got in a fight with me. She'll believe it." Scarlett smiled up at him.

"Do you think she knows yet?" he asked, resting his forehead against hers.

"She does now," a voice said from directly behind him, causing him to cringe.

"I can explain." He glanced over his shoulder and winced at the look Zoey was giving him.

"On your own time, buddy." She gripped his arms and tugged him away from her sister.

Levi glanced back at Scarlett and mouthed, "I'm sorry," to her as Zoey pulled him towards the courts.

"Think she bought it?" Zoey asked as soon as they were out of earshot.

His steps faltered. "You… you're not mad?"

As an answer, Zoey doubled over with laughter.

"Oh, that was rich." She pretended to wipe a tear from her eyes.

"Okay," he said slowly.

"Please." She waved him off and then handed him the volleyball flags and motioned for him to set them up around the sandy court. "Everyone knew the moment Scarlett walked into our breakfast meeting with a huge I-just-had-the-best-sex-of-my- life look on her face."

He stilled, unsure what to say, which had Zoey laughing again. Then she shoved him on the shoulder.

"Set up the flags. People are starting to gather for the game."

Glancing around, he realized there was a small crowd gathering. Rushing around the makeshift sand court, he set up the boundary flags and then took his place as referee as Zoey explained the rules of the game.

He was halfway through the game when he realized Scarlett was sitting at the pool bar, watching him.

The distraction caused him to miss a call, and one of the guests yelled at him. For the rest of the game, he tried to focus, even though he was highly aware she was watching him as she sipped an iced tea.

When the game was over, Zoey shoved him towards the bar area. "Go. I'll take the next game since you can't seem to focus." She winked at him.

"Thanks. I owe you one," he called over his shoulder. He jogged across the pool deck and stopped in front of Scarlett. He ran his eyes over her camp shirt and khaki shorts.

"Hey." He smiled at her and took a sip of her tea.

"Hey." She smiled.

"Got a break?"

"I do." She tilted her head and glanced over towards the game. "Do you?"

"Your sister thinks I'm too distracted to referee." He ran a finger up her arm. He felt her vibrate under his touch and smiled.

"You are. The last call was clearly out, yet you gave them the point," she teased.

"Oh?" He moved closer and wrapped an arm around her narrow waist. "We could stand here and debate my skills at referring a volleyball game, or…"

She gripped his shirt and pulled him towards the pathway as he chuckled. "Where are you taking me?" he asked when she turned off the pathway into thicker trees and brush.

"Somewhere we can be alone."

He hadn't expected her to drag him into a small storage shed where they stored some of the used sports equipment.

"Sorry," she said when she bumped up against him as she shut the door behind her. "I thought this was bigger than it is." She looked around. "And cleaner." She frowned.

He chuckled as he pulled her closer to him. "You won't hear me complaining." Kissing her in the cool, dark storage shed was just as thrilling as kissing her last night. He felt his entire body heat at her slightest touch.

The shed was beyond dirty, so he tried to keep the mood light, but the longer they spent in the small space, the more he wanted her.

"How soon can we cut out of the dinner party tonight?" he asked against her ear. Their breathing was labored, and he would have to take a very long walk or an extremely cold shower in order to be seen anywhere in public.

"Not soon enough," she answered as she glanced down at her watch. "I have to go get ready soon." She rested her forehead against his chest. "Tell me you're going to be wearing your tux tonight?"

"It's required. Why?"

She sighed before she answered. "I've dreamed of pulling it off you." She glanced up at him shyly.

"Really?"

"It's a fetish. My James Bond fantasy." She smiled.

He chuckled. "Okay, two can play at this. I've always liked you in that little red dress. The one with the straps in the back." He ran his hands over her shoulders.

"Noted. I guess I'll see you tonight." Then she lifted on her toes and kissed him once more before leaving him in the dark shed.

What was he supposed to do now? Stand in here until his dick went back down. Hell, he could still taste her on his lips, which meant that unless he did something drastic, there was zero possibility of him being on time for dinner.

Stepping out into the daylight, he glanced around. Finding himself alone, he figured his best bet was to head towards the small private beach area and take a short swim in the cool water. That way he could kill two birds with one stone—get clean and allow his desire to dissipate.

He was so focused on getting to the edge of the water that he didn't spot the blond woman stepping out of the water.

"Oh," she gasped, her hand sliding over his chest, telling him instantly that she'd maneuvered it so they would bump into one another.

"Sorry." He started to skirt around her, but her nails dug into his arms, holding him in place.

"Levi?" The woman's tone turned excited. "Is that you?" She did a little gasp and he could tell instantly it was fake.

"Sorry," he said again, focused on the goal of getting in the water before he embarrassed himself.

"It's me." She giggled. "Jenny Carpenter, well, Baker now." She held up her hand showcasing a massive diamond.

Shit, Levi thought. Two weeks ago, he wouldn't have known who the woman was. And if Scarlett hadn't reminded him of all the hell that she'd put Scarlett and her Wildflowers through all those summers ago, he would have tried to be friendly with her, since she was a guest. Now here she was, practically plastered to his body, and with his raging boner still going strong thanks to his time with Scarlett.

He took hold of the woman's shoulders and forced her back a step. "I'm sorry." He shook his head, deciding it was best to play dumb.

She slapped him playfully on his shoulder. "Of course you remember me. All that crazy fun we used to get into here on the campgrounds." She didn't give him a chance to respond and just kept talking. "When I heard this place had opened back up, well, I just knew Robert and I had to come take a look at it." She glanced around as if realizing she'd forgotten her husband. "He's around here somewhere. Anyway, I heard from Stephany that you were working here and was wondering when I'd bump into you." Her eyes ran up and down him. By this point, he'd lost the last proof of his desire for Scarlett, thankfully.

"I'm sorry, Jenny, I have work…" He started to turn back towards the main buildings of the camp, since he no longer needed the dunk in the cool water. But she was still gripping his shoulders, holding him still.

"Someone told me that you are still single." She smiled and moved closer to him. "I just can't imagine why some woman hasn't gobbled you up yet." She purred the last.

"You heard wrong," he said, setting her aside before she could rope him into anything else. "Now, I have to get back to work." He turned and left the beach. He didn't have to look back to know that she was pouting at his back and watching him closely.

Steering towards the dining hall before he went to shower and change for the dinner hour, he found Aubrey putting the finishing touches on the dinner decorations.

"Red alert," he said, stopping next to her. "Jenny Carpenter, now Baker, is on the premises."

"What?" The glass candleholder she was setting on the table

slipped from her hands and crashed to the table. Thankfully, it didn't break. "Seriously?" Aubrey recovered and glanced around. "How did you..." Her eyes narrowed. "I'll warn the others." She turned to go, then stopped and glanced back at him. "You'd better be on your best behavior tonight."

He would have chuckled, just knowing that Scarlett had been pissed at him all these years because Jenny had been conniving, but instead he nodded. Still, he had hoped that the rest of the Wildflowers would have some trust in him after all these years. He couldn't explain it, but knowing they didn't stung.

"Trust me, it's not me you have to worry about." He almost growled it as he stormed out of the room.

CHAPTER FIFTEEN

"I don't know what I did to piss him off," Aubrey was telling Scarlett as they got ready for dinner, "but I've never seen him so mad before."

"I don't think he was mad at you." She bit her bottom lip, remembering how he'd found out that Jenny had tricked Scarlett into thinking there had been something between the two of them.

She'd confided in her friends what Levi had told her, and they had all agreed that they believed his version of the story.

"No?" Aubrey turned so that Scarlett could zip up her dress.

"No." She sighed. Since tonight was another ball, they each would be wearing the long evening dresses Elle had picked out for them last year.

She had really wanted to wear the short sexy red dress with the thin straps in the back for Levi that night, but she pulled on a long flowing red dress with the thin straps instead.

He had his tux he had to wear, and she had her own uniform. If she'd shown up in the shorter dress, Elle would have never let her live it down.

Aubrey's pale pink dress was almost identical to Scarlett's

red one along and the rest of the Wildflower's dresses. Elle wore her signature silver, and Hannah wore blue while Zoey often wore black.

She liked that the five of them always coordinated their outfits for big events. It kept her from destroying her closet to find something each time they had to dress up. The other day, she'd gone through five different outfits just to spend the day at the beach with Levi.

"So, you and Levi, you're getting serious?" Aubrey asked, zipping Scarlett's dress up.

"We just spent the weekend together," she admitted, happy that her face was turned away from her friend so she couldn't see the fear in her eyes.

"You know we all love him," Aubrey finished up. "He's the right man for you. The two of you have been dancing around this for... well, forever." She chuckled.

Scarlett's eyes narrowed. "What about you and Aiden?" she asked, and Aubrey's face flushed before she turned around.

"The man doesn't know I exist." She shrugged and finished putting on her lipstick.

"Bull." Scarlett took the lipstick from her and applied some on her own lips. "He practically falls over his feet each time you walk by."

"No, he doesn't." Aubrey looked shocked.

"You should make a move." Scarlett smiled. "If he's too shy..."

"He is not shy," Aubrey started. "Busy, I believe is the word you are looking for. He not only oversees the cabins on the camp, but now he's heading up Owen's housing project. Not to mention trying to finish up Dylan and your sister's house before their wedding this fall."

"Right." Scarlett smiled. "Less than two months away." She tried to hide her sadness. But Aubrey, being the good friend she was, heard it and took Scarlett's shoulders until they were eye to eye.

"Dylan won't hurt her. Something tells me that all the Costa brothers are life-longers. God knows they aren't cheaters." She chuckled. "No one would dare cross a Wildflower." Aubrey smiled. "Now, we're going to be late for dinner, and we want to show Jenny Carpenter up."

"Right." Scarlett's smile grew as she looked at the pair of them in the mirror. "We are definitely hotter."

"Damn right we are." Aubrey laughed and slapped Scarlett on the butt. "Now, let's go."

Stepping into the dining hall, it was hard not to scan the crowded place for her arch nemesis. So, she focused on greeting guests and being helpful, showing everyone to their assigned tables and telling them where the bathrooms were.

When they had opened the camp back up, one thing they had all agreed on was that each evening needed to be unique for their guests. They had set up a schedule so that, each night of the month, dinner was centered around a different theme.

Tonight's theme was "A Night of Fancy," which meant most guests were dressed in their finest. Of course, there were those stragglers that wandered in still in their normal attire. All were welcomed as long as they had changed out of their beachwear.

If guests didn't want a fancier dinner, they were welcomed to eat from the same menu outside at the pool dining area.

In the last two years, the guests had confirmed their love for the dinner themes.

During the holidays, they had everything from costume parties to masked balls. The dinners during the holidays were some of the busiest, with almost all of the guests getting into the spirit.

Less than fifteen minutes later, Jenny Carpenter strolled through the front door on the arm of a silver haired heavy-set man. The fact that the man could have easily been Jenny's grandfather caused Scarlett to do a double take.

Was this really her husband? Scarlett ran her eyes over

Jenny. The woman looked the same. Exactly the same. It was as if she hadn't aged a day in eight years. Then Scarlett realized that Jenny still looked like a teenager—unsophisticated, unrefined.

One thing Scarlett had prided herself on since she and her friends had opened the camp was that they had learned how to showcase class in everything they wore. Even their camp uniforms.

Jenny was wearing a white dress that was two sizes too small for her body. Her blond hair was curled and flowing over her shoulders, showcasing what was obviously a new pair of breasts.

Scarlett knew plenty of women who had gotten breast augmentation, and most of the time she admired the jobs. But Jenny's were straight up stripper tits. Large fake double D's that didn't fit her tiny body frame, just like everything else she wore.

Scarlett's eyes moved back over to the older man and wondered if Jenny even liked her husband. They weren't holding hands or even touching. Aubrey had told her that she'd asked around and found out that Jenny had spent the day at the pool, alone, flirting with any man that walked by.

"Good evening," Scarlett greeted them with a smile to hide the fact that she knew who Jenny was.

Scarlett watched as Jenny's eyes ran over her, and she could see the instant dislike that flashed behind them.

"Good evening," the man said with a smile. "We're the Bakers."

"Welcome." Scarlett's eyes moved over to Jenny. "You're in from…?"

"New York," Jenny answered, her chin going up slightly as if she was proud that they came from the city.

"I hear they're having some rain up there right now," Scarlett said with a smile and turned her eyes towards her clipboard, even though she already knew which table they would be seated at for the duration of their stay. "I'll show you to your table. This will be your assigned table for your entire stay with us. You know, so you don't get lost." She motioned for the couple to follow her.

Walking around the dance floor, she showed them the table on the side of the room, near the bar.

"I hope this will suit you," she said, motioning to two spots with their nametags on the plates. "Chef Isaac has prepared a wonderful menu tonight for you to choose from." She smiled and removed the place cards. "Linda is going to be your waitress tonight." She waved Linda over. "If you need anything..." She started to walk away.

"You don't remember me?" Jenny said, stopping her.

Scarlett's eyes rose slightly. "Of course, I do," she said with a smile. "Welcome back to River Camps, Jenny."

"It's Jen now." She said looking down her nose at Scarlett. "I never would have thought that the five of you would be working here," She added with a smirk.

"Working?" Scarlett chuckled. "Yes, I suppose you could say we all work here." She sighed and, suddenly, her desire to rub her success and her wonderful life in this woman's face dissipated. "Please, enjoy your stay."

She turned and walked away, making her way towards the bar, where Levi was mixing a drink, watching her.

"So?" he asked, and she realized he must have watched the entire exchange.

She shrugged. "I decided I didn't have to prove anything to anyone. Least of all her."

He handed the drink over to its owner and then took her hand up to his lips. "Wise." He smiled. "You're much more magnanimous than I am."

She laughed. "Tell me that when you saw her you spit in her face."

He sighed. "No, I'm afraid I was so concerned that she was

going to spread a rumor about our little bump-in at the beach that I…"

"Oh?" Scarlett leaned across the bar and smiled when she saw Levi's eyes travel to her low cleavage. "What happened at the beach?" she whispered.

His eyes jerked back up to hers. "Nothing." His voice cracked, causing her to laugh. He cleared his throat and repeated himself. "Nothing."

She stood back up, smiling at him. "Later, Levi Grant, you're going to owe me."

"Yes, ma'am." His smile turned wicked. "I am."

She felt her knees go weak and, without saying anything, retreated back to her spot across the room.

"Wow," Zoey said a few minutes later when she approached her. "She looks the same."

"Who?" Scarlett asked, since her heart had yet to settle down from flirting with Levi.

"Jenny." Zoey rolled her eyes. "Who else?"

"Oh." Scarlett's eyes moved across the room to where Jenny was cutting her husband's steak dinner for him and looking annoyed while doing so. Scarlett held in a chuckle. Scarlett turned back to her sister. "Apparently it's Jen now." She mimicked the woman's tone then giggled. "Seriously, why do women that young marry someone three times their age?"

"Money," Elle said, stopping beside them. "Robert Baker is the head and heir to Stuffit's."

"The frozen meals?" Scarlett asked with a frown.

"No." Elle laughed. "That's Stouffer's." She chuckled again. "Stuffit's Bakery's in New York. It's a chain that goes back more than a hundred years."

"Oh." Scarlett shrugged. "Never heard of it."

"You've never been to New York." Zoey pinched her arm.

"Ouch." Scarlett swiped at her sister's hand. "So?"

"So." Elle lowered her voice. "The man is richer than... well, not quite richer than Aubrey's old man. But close."

"That rich?" Scarlett looked at the older man again. "I don't care if he has more money than god. I wouldn't marry him or anyone else for money."

"That's good to know," Levi's voice sounded from directly behind her.

It was amazing how quickly her sister and Elle disappeared once Levi appeared.

"What are you doing here?" she asked, turning towards him.

"It's my break time and I thought..." He broke off when she took his hand.

"Yes, and yes," she said as she pulled him towards the front door.

"Let's actually walk this time," he said, glancing around. "I'm not letting you stuff me in some closet dressed like this." He motioned to his tux.

She chuckled. "A walk sounds wonderful. I could use some fresh air."

They strolled hand in hand, winding around the lit pathways.

"So?" he said after a moment of silence. "Want to talk about it?"

"There's nothing to tell." She shrugged and turned to him when he came to a stop under one of the lights.

"The woman was the cause of hurt and pain you carried around for years," he reminded her and pulled her into his arms. "Surely you want to tell me how it makes you feel seeing her again."

"I feel..." She thought about it. "Sorry for her." She tilted her head and looked past his shoulder to the dark starlit sky beyond. "I mean, she married a man who could easily be her grandfather, all for money." She shivered slightly.

Suddenly, Levi pulled his jacket off and wrapped it around

her shoulders. She didn't want to tell him that she wasn't cold. She enjoyed the smell and his warmth coming from the jacket too much. She hugged it to her body.

"Money is important to a lot of women," he said. She could hear the sadness in his voice.

"Like Carrie?" she asked as her eyes ran over him. He was even more handsome in the shadows dressed in the tux. Like her fantasy of running into a sexy James Bond and having him sweep her off her feet.

"Yes." His eyes met hers.

"Did she break your heart?" she asked, curious to know if he'd ever crossed into the big L. She didn't know why it mattered to her, but she held her breath until he answered.

"No." He shook his head. "I thought she had."

"Then?" she asked, unsure why she was pushing him so much.

His eyes returned to hers. "You came back to Pelican Point." His eyes locked with hers.

Once again, she felt her knees go weak, but he was there, wrapping his arms around her tightly as he pulled her close against his body.

"I'd forgotten that I'd already lost my heart years ago," he continued. "Seeing you again reminded me that I'd given it away that last night we were together." He bent his head and brushed his lips across hers slowly. "It's no longer my heart to break since it's in your hands." He sighed and rested his forehead against hers. "I know you don't want to hear it, but…"

"No." She closed her eyes and shook her head slowly. "I can't."

"I know." His thumb nudged her chin up until their eyes locked again. "But there it is. I've been in love with you since I saw you standing on that dock, wearing your cream-colored shorts and that pink top, waiting for me all those years ago."

Her breath hitched and she felt her chest tighten. She didn't deserve him. He was more than she could have ever hoped for. More than she could handle.

She didn't trust forever-afters. Even with Levi.

Taking a step back, she dropped her arms, letting his jacket fall to her feet.

"Levi, I..." Her eyes scanned around, looking for an escape route.

"No." He reached for her, but she was already in motion, rushing back to the crowded dining hall where she could melt into the crowd and hide all the hurt that welled up inside her. All the pain that her father had caused her, all the pain that Jenny had caused with her lies.

Even if she could trust Levi with her heart, there was no way he should trust her with his.

CHAPTER SIXTEEN

"I screwed up," Levi said to Zoey after he'd found her in the kitchen, trying to mooch a cookie from Betty. The woman was glaring at Zoey, and he thought it a wise idea to pull Zoey out of the line of fire.

"It's just one," Zoey said to Betty, waving him away.

"One that our guests won't get to enjoy," Betty replied easily with a smile.

As he pulled Zoey aside, she grabbed up a cookie and stuck her tongue out towards Betty, who laughed as a reply.

"She has plenty. I skipped dinner." She stuffed the entire cookie in her mouth.

He would have laughed at her, but he was too worried he'd screwed things up with her sister.

"What did you do now?" she asked after taking a drink from her water bottle.

"I told your sister..." He shut his mouth. "Well, I didn't really say the three words, but... came damn close to it. Close enough that she dropped my jacket in a mud puddle"—he held up his ruined jacket and frowned down at it—"and ran back to the dining hall in those high heels of hers. I think she could have won a few awards with that sprint."

Zoey smiled. "She'll come around." She slapped him on the shoulder. "Go see Brent about getting another jacket for tonight." She started walking back to the baked goods, and he took her arm as Betty motioned towards Isaac, who started walking towards them.

"Are you sure?" he asked. "You didn't see the fear in her eyes."

Zoey sighed and took his shoulders. "My sister took everything that happened between my parents harder than even my mother did." She snapped her fingers suddenly. "My mother. You should go talk to her. She's back from her trip to Montana with Mr. Spy Pants."

He chuckled. "Reed Cooper."

"Yes." Zoey smiled. "If they get married, I refuse to call him Daddy. It's going to be Mr. Spy Pants." Zoey held up her hand. "I've already settled on it. Anyway, she's back home now. She would know the best approach to my sister's heart. Moms know everything." She tapped him on the shoulder. "Now, if you don't mind, I have to try and swindle dinner from my employees." She rubbed her hands together and turned to face the head chef.

Levi left Zoey begging for a plate in the kitchen and made his way back up to the bar.

When he arrived, he was thankful to see Liam Costa standing behind the bar, helping Britt out.

"You got this?" he asked the man.

"Sure." Liam winked at him. "Heard you and Scar were…"

Levi growled and the man shut his mouth.

"Sure, I've got this." Liam chuckled. "She just headed out the front."

He thought about going after Scarlett for a second, then made his way towards the back door. The back path would take him towards her mother's cabin.

River Cabin sat away from all the other guest cabins, which

was why the Wildflowers had given it to Zoey and Scarlett's mother within days of opening the camp up. It had also been their cabin each summer, making it special to the group.

Levi had hung out with Kimberly Rowlett more times than he could count. The woman lived on the grounds and enjoyed taking part in many of the fun activities. Reed Cooper, her new boyfriend, lived in a massive mansion across a small inlet of water that sat across from the campgrounds.

The rumor was that Reed was an ex-military spy. Only a handful of them knew it was true, since he'd helped rescue Hannah last year.

Still, the man was retired, and seeing Scarlett's mother with him, happy, went a long way with her daughters and the rest of the Wildflowers, who had adopted her as their den mother.

He knocked on the door after making sure her light was on and he wouldn't be waking her.

She opened the door with a smile. "Zoey called." She motioned him inside. "She says you have something you want to talk to me about?" The woman motioned for him to sit in the small living room area.

River Cabin was one of his favorite cabins on the property. Half of it hung over the small stream that trickled under the massive porch.

Its tall two-story windows looked out over the water and, during the day, you could see the nature and beauty that surrounded the house.

Now, however, the large windows sat dark, reflecting their images back at them, thanks to the lights.

"Yeah." He sighed as he sat down.

"Would you like something to drink?" she asked.

Kimberly Rowlett was a perfect cross between the two sisters, with the exception that she'd let her dark hair turn its natural silver years ago. The woman could easily pass for Scar and Zoey's sister instead of their mother if she dyed her hair dark again. But the silver locks suited her much better and they set off her eyes nicely.

Thanks to all the activities on the grounds, she stayed in great shape. He'd seen her on more than one occasion enjoying the zip lines with Reed, taking yoga classes, and even playing water volleyball.

"No, thank you." He rested his elbows on his knees and leaned forward slightly. "I think I screwed up with Scarlett."

"Okay?" She sat across from him. "Why do you think that?"

"I…" His eyes met hers and he swallowed. "I told her how I feel about her."

Kimberly's smile was instant. "Good for you."

"No." He shook his head and frowned down at his hands. "She ran." His eyes moved back up. "Literally ran away from me."

Kimberly chuckled. "Scar is… has always run away from things she fears."

"No, she's courageous. I've seen her face—"

"Emotionally," Kimberly finished. "She may come off as strong—and don't get me wrong, she is—but when it comes to matters of the heart…" She shook her head and her eyes turned sad. "I'm afraid that's all her father's doing."

"I'm not her father."

"No, you're not." She nodded. "Any fool can see that. Trust me when I say this, Scarlett is no fool. She may let fear hide her heart, but if you're persistent, and patient, you are the man who can crack that tough outer shell she's protected her heart in."

He thought about Kimberly's words the entire walk back to the main building. Seeing that the party was still going on, he decided to try and find Scarlett one last time.

Kimberly was right. He'd promised Scar that he'd be patient and then, the first chance he'd had, he'd spewed his feelings all over her. Smooth.

Most of the guests had left for the night, returning to their own cabins. Still, there were half a dozen couples left dancing to the music or still eating and drinking.

Scarlett and her friends were parked at the bar, chatting. When he approached them, they all scattered like flies.

"Was it something I said?" he joked, but Scarlett's lips didn't even twitch.

"Hey." He touched her shoulder. "I owe you an apology." He ran his hand over her bare shoulder.

"No." She shook her head as she closed her eyes. "I knew this wouldn't work."

"Stop right there," he interrupted her. "I overstepped when I promised I wouldn't. I'm sorry."

She sighed and nodded quickly.

"How about I buy you a drink?" he asked, trying to change the mood.

"I could use a glass of wine."

Instead of asking Britt, he stepped behind the bar to pour her a glass himself. He leaned across the bar top. "Would you like that shaken or stirred?"

Her smile flashed quickly. "I can't stay mad at you."

"Good, because I was looking forward to us playing spy." He wiggled his eyebrows. "I've got a surprise for you...somewhere on my person." He leaned back and ran his hands over his body. "You'll have to find it."

He watched her eyes heat and enjoyed the way she slowly sipped her wine. When her tongue dipped out and licked her lower lip, he realized he'd lost his control of the situation. She'd taken the reins and was in charge now. He swallowed hard and leaned closer again.

"Do I get a clue?" she purred, and he knew instantly he'd successfully changed the mood.

"Real spies don't need clues."

Her eyes narrowed as she scanned him from head to toe.

"What do you say you show me your rooms?" he whispered.

She set her glass down and held out her hand for his.

As they walked out, they had to skirt around Jenny, who was very drunk, while her husband tried to help her out. Jenny was falling all over the place, her tall heels flopping around in her hands as she tried to flirt with anyone who would give her attention. Anyone except her husband.

"Brent, would you mind helping Mr. and Mrs. Baker get back to their cabin?" Scarlett said as they passed by the waiter. "And make sure they are left alone for the rest of the night."

"Sure thing, boss lady." Brent saluted them. "Night."

"Do you know," Scarlett said as they stepped outside, "that Brent has flirted with every single one of my friends but not me."

"Jealous?" he asked, feeling a twinge of his own jealousy surface at the thought of Scarlett wishing Brent would flirt with her.

"No." She chuckled. "I'm glad. I'm terrible at turning men away."

He laughed and pulled her into his arms. "Everyone except me," he reminded her.

"Right," she said with a smile. "You're the exception."

His heart jumped in his chest. As far as deep heartfelt confessions went, he figured he'd take Scarlett's little admission as another positive step.

"So," she said as they headed up the stairs to her apartment, "is this surprise above or below your clothes?"

He chuckled. "You're a cheater." He took her hand and pulled it to his lips. "No hints." He stilled when she started running her hands over him.

"I don't like surprises." She smiled up at him.

"Trust me, you're going to like this one." He pulled away and rushed up the stairs with her on his heels.

The moment they stepped into her private bedroom, he

sidestepped her and walked around, taking in the differences between this room and the one at the house in town.

"You live here," he said, glancing over his shoulder.

"Yup, that's what a bedroom is." She smiled and leaned against the closed bedroom door, watching him.

"No, I mean, the bedroom in town was nice, but there wasn't anything of yours there." He picked up a stuffed animal and smiled. "This room is full of your things. Your personality really comes through in here." He laughed at the posters on her walls.

"I hung those before I knew I was going to be bringing a man in here." She groaned.

"Fun." He moved over to her desk, and she rushed over and shut a book that had been laying open. He smiled as she stuffed it in one of the drawers. "Your diary?"

"No, just a book I was reading." She blushed, and he moved closer to her.

"Did it have sex in it?" he asked, watching her face closely.

"Maybe." She shrugged.

He took her wrist in his hands and pulled her closer.

"I like you in heels." His eyes met hers. Their lips were almost level with one another's. "I like this dress." His eyes moved to her cleavage spilling out of the top of the red silk. "Not as much as the shorter one, because, hey, technically, I'm a leg guy, but..." He sighed, trying to show her that it would do.

She smiled up at him. "All men love boobs."

He chuckled. "When they're spilling out like this." He ran a finger over her and she sucked in her breath as she leaned her head back. "Something tells me you did this for me."

She chuckled. "I might have."

He nudged the material down her shoulder and marveled at the skin he'd exposed. "Beautiful."

Her hands moved up his shirt, over his chest, pulling the borrowed jacket off his shoulders. It hit the floor with a plop, and she started working on the buttons of his shirt while he reached around for the zipper of her dress.

As he slowly slid her dress down her body, her hands fisted in his shirt while she swayed.

"Levi," she moaned when he brushed the back of his hand against her.

"You're not wearing anything under this," he said softly against her skin.

"No, there's no... need." She pulled his shirt all the way off his shoulders. "Where's my present?"

"Surprise," he corrected.

"Where?" She reached for his pants.

"My pocket," he said with a smile. Her hands greedily searched his pockets. When she pulled out the little vibrator, she giggled.

"Try it. It's pretty powerful."

"Where did you get this?" she asked, flipping the switch and then gasping as it jumped to life.

"You sell them downstairs." He laughed. "Remember?"

She rolled her eyes. "You did not go into the camp store and buy this. Now everyone will know that we... that you..."

"That I used it on you?" he said smoothly, taking the thing from her. Her dress was hooked on her hips but, with one tiny tug, the material fell to the floor.

Scarlett stood in front of him in nothing but a sexy pair of silver heels that clasped around her ankles.

"Beautiful," he said again as he took her hand and helped her step out of the dress.

She bent down and picked it up, tossing it over a chair that sat in the corner of her room. "Hannah will kill me if I wrinkle it."

"Come here." He nudged her towards the bed, then kissed her until she melted against his bare chest.

"I really like the tux," she said, trailing her lips down his collarbone. "But I really like you in half a tux even more." She was running her hands over his chest and arms. "You're like a male stripper."

He chuckled. "Have a lot of experience with male strippers, do you?"

She blushed slightly. "No, but we all went to Vegas a few years... No." She shook her head.

He kissed her. "Here I was thinking you weren't the shy type."

"I have another confession." She sighed and rested her forehead against his chest. "I've never... used a vibrator before. I mean, a dildo, but... nothing that... moves."

He nudged her chin up with his fingers and smiled at her. "Perfect. I'll be the first to show you how it works then. Sit." He moved between her legs. "On the edge of the bed." He helped her scoot forward, then knelt between her legs.

"My shoes." She started to reach down to remove them.

"No, leave them." He smiled. "Leg man"—he pointed his thumb at his chest—"has a heel fetish as well."

She smiled, then he held up the vibrator. "Levi?"

"Do you trust me?" he asked, using his hands on her inner thighs and spreading her legs wider. Their eyes locked and she nodded as she licked her lower lip.

"Lay back. Tell me if I do something you don't like." He smiled as he turned the vibrator on. When he touched it to her inner thigh, she arched and giggled.

He moved it slowly up from her knee until he reached her pussy. When he touched it to her skin, she gasped and flew up, her eyes glued to his.

"I..." She shook her head. "I don't think..."

He chuckled and laid a hand on her flat stomach and gently nudged her until she lay down again. "Sassy, relax and enjoy."

He started again, this time trailing kisses over the inner part of her thighs. When she started moving her hips against his mouth and the vibrator, he knew his surprise had hit the mark.

"Sassy?" He pulled it away from her, only to have her hand come up and hold it to her.

"No, don't stop. Please," she begged as she wrapped her legs around his shoulders. "I know I'm being selfish, but…"

He smiled. "Please, I get off more when you are."

"Really?" She groaned and moved even faster. "Levi, I'm going to come."

"Let go," he begged her, knowing he meant more than just physically but understanding she would need more time.

He lost himself watching her face as the guard that she'd wrapped around her heart unraveled another notch.

CHAPTER SEVENTEEN

Scarlett lay in Levi's arms the following morning, listening to the soothing sound of his heartbeats.

In that very moment, she realized she was in trouble. She'd never felt this way about someone before. The only thing running through her mind was the desire to stay right where she was for as long as she could.

The things he'd done to her last night were nothing short of magical. She'd finally gotten her chance to show him how wonderful of a lover she could be about halfway through the night.

She'd done things to him that had equaled what he'd done to her. Well, except with the little vibrator that he'd purchased downstairs in their shop.

When the Wildflowers had joked about carrying a line of sex toys and lubricants in the lobby store, they'd had no idea how much extra money that decision would bring in. Less than a month after opening the shop's doors, they were having to restock and grow their inventory.

She'd been curious about the items, but not enough to purchase something of her own. She would die of embarrassment if her sister or any of her friends found out what was currently tucked away in her nightstand drawer.

Hearing Levi's breathing change, she moved slightly against him. She had a mid-morning riding group she had to take out, but she still had plenty of time before she needed to get ready.

"Good morning," she purred as she ran her hands over his chest and arms. God, she loved the way he felt against her.

He stretched slightly, then his arms wrapped around her and hoisted her up over him.

She giggled and held on as he pulled her down into a kiss.

"Yes, it is a good morning." He sighed against her lips. She felt herself grow wet as he began moving his hips against hers. Just feeling him grow hard against her had her body reacting instantly.

When he gripped her hips and guided her to slide down on him, she held onto the headboard and took what she wanted from him, leaving them both sated.

"I take it back," he said against her ear when she fell onto his chest panting. "It's not a good morning, it's a great one."

She couldn't stop the smile from coming, nor could she keep it from her lips for the rest of the morning. She didn't think there was anything on earth that could dampen her mood.

After her normal breakfast meeting with the rest of the Wildflowers and her morning ride, her body was still flying high on the pulsating wave caused by Levi's hands.

That was until she bumped into Jenny shortly before lunch. The woman was sitting by the pool in a stark white Brazilian bikini that was slightly see-through and way too small for her body type.

Flashbacks of all the terrible things that Jenny had done to her surfaced the closer she got to the pool area. If Scarlett hadn't been asked to fill in for Britt behind the pool bar, because the woman was home sick with the flu, she wouldn't have been near the pool at all. But as it was, the moment she stepped out of the clearing so the pool area was in view, she saw Jenny reach up and grab Levi's head and pull it towards her own. Jenny ran her mouth over his jaw, or at least she tried to.

Levi had been trying to set a full drink down on the table beside Jenny when the attack happened. As he jerked away from the unapproved attention, Scarlett could tell immediately what was going to happen.

Levi pushed away from Jenny quickly, causing the drink, one of their signature Sunset Bursts, which consisted of bright blue and red mixes, to teeter on the tray he'd been holding. The tall glass, with its paper straws, umbrellas, and several fruit wedges on the rim, started to fall. It landed directly on Jenny's chest, spilling the bright liquid all over her white swimsuit.

What happened next had Scarlett holding in her laughter. The one thing she could say about Jenny was that she was an excellent actress.

Jenny jumped up from her chair squealing as she tried to brush the mixing colors from her suit. Her arms thrashed around her as she threw insults at Levi.

Levi dropped his hands to his side, took a giant step backwards, and looked around uncomfortably. When his eyes landed on hers, she could see the plea for help in them from across the pool. Scarlett knew that Levi had done nothing to instigate the kiss, but a flash of concern flooded his blue eyes.

Scarlett rushed over, grabbing up a few clean towels from the bar area along the way.

"Here, let me help..." She started to use a towel to sop up most of the bright drink, only to have Jenny shove her hands away.

"Get away from me," she screamed as she grabbed the towel from Scar's hands.

"We're just trying to help," Scarlett said calmly. "Levi, why don't you..."

"Bullshit." Jenny jerked her head up towards Scarlett, her

eyes burning with anger. "This suit was very expensive. Don't think I won't demand that you repay me for it along with damages." She continued to dab at the suit but then gave up when all she was doing was spreading the red and blue over the now-colored material. Jenny tossed the towel down at her feet. "You and your friends have always had it out for me." Her eyes moved to Levi, then back to Scarlett's. When she moved forward, Levi took her arms to pull her back, as if protecting her, but Scarlett wedged herself between the two of them. If Jenny was going to attack anyone, Scarlett was stepping directly in line of fire. "I didn't believe you would stoop to their level," Jenny tossed over to Levi.

Levi moved to open his mouth, but Scarlett jumped in quickly.

"As we've said, we were just trying to help you clean up. If you hadn't tried to force yourself on—"

"Force myself?" Jenny squealed. Her voice drew the attention of everyone in the area that hadn't already been watching the exchange. "Force myself?" She laughed. "That's rich. The man was practically drooling on me. When I rejected his advances, he did this." She motioned to her ruined suit. Jenny's eyes narrowed and she moved closer to Scarlett, shoving a finger into her chest. Levi tried to move around and block her, but Jenny wasn't having it and turned her body and all of her attention towards Scarlett instead.

Scarlett knew that there was nothing either of them could say at this point that would matter. So, they stood there, side by side, listening to Jenny spew her hate towards them.

When Scarlett believed she was almost done with her tirade, she calmly apologized and offered, again, to make things right.

Instead of accepting the offer, Jenny jerked a fingernail into Scarlett's chest again and glared up at her.

"You think I don't know exactly what you and your friends are doing?" She smirked. "Oh, have fun around here while it lasts. After the way you've treated me, I'll make it my life's mission to ruin you." She growled out the last in a low tone.

Scarlett was about to step out of the woman's way but only had time to gasp as Jenny brought her hands up and shoved Scarlett's shoulders hard enough that Scarlett lost her footing, tripped on the towel Jenny had tossed down, and started to fall backwards.

Everything seemed to happen in slow motion.

She reached out for Levi, who was less than a foot from her, but Jenny pushed between their bodies, leaving Scarlett's arms to flail in the air as she fell. Scarlett only had time to scream out as she fell into the shallow end of the pool.

She hit the water hard and gasped with pain, water flooding her nose and mouth.

Her ass hit the bottom of the pool first, followed by the back of her head, at which point, everything went dark.

When her eyes opened again, she was lying in a pool chair soaking wet as Levi hovered over her, dripping water from his hair onto her face. Scarlett coughed up the water she'd swallowed while Levi grabbed her into his arms and held onto her.

"Get Lea up here quickly," Levi yelled to someone.

"I'm okay," Scarlett said between coughing and spitting up pool water. When she tried to get up, he held her still. "No, don't move," he said gently. "You got knocked out."

"I hit my head." She reached up and touched where she had hit the bottom of the pool. Feeling an egg sized bump on the back of her head, she hissed.

"Easy." He used one of the towels she'd brought over for Jenny to wipe her face. "Where does it hurt?"

"I have a bump." She motioned to her head, then moved slightly and realized she'd hit her hip on the bottom of the pool as well. "And my hip."

"I couldn't get to you." He groaned and wrapped his arms around her again. "You went down so fast."

"It's okay." She closed her eyes for a moment. "I'm okay."

"What happened?" Zoey cried out as she rushed towards them.

"Jenny. She pushed Scarlett into the shallow end..." Levi said quickly.

"I bumped my head."

"She was unconscious when I pulled her out of the pool," Levi supplied.

"What?" Zoey sat next to her and scanned her eyes. "Her eyes are unfocused. She might have a..."

Just then Lea approached, pushing the growing crowd of people aside.

"Doctor coming through," she said loudly.

For the next few minutes, she was looked over by their resident doctor, Lea Val. The woman knew her shit, which is why they'd hired her to work at the camp part time. It was a smart move, seeing as most of their guests were over the age of fifty and spent their vacation doing sports and activities they normally wouldn't.

Since they'd brought her on board, Lea had been kept busy with twisted ankles, the occasional sunburn, and earlier that year, a mild heart attack. If they hadn't had her there, the woman would have died. Even though they had med kits and defibrillators spread around the grounds, Lea was the reason the woman had been able to go home to her family.

"I don't like the look of your pupils," Lea said to her. "I'm going to call..."

"No," Scarlett groaned. "I don't want to go in."

"Too bad." Lea shook her head. "I'm the doctor, not you." She glanced up and nodded to Levi. "I'll call it in, but we could probably get her there faster ourselves."

"I'll drive." He hoisted her up in his arms and following Lea towards the parking lot.

"I'll drive," Dylan corrected, coming out of nowhere and catching up with them.

"Fine," Levi said and followed the man towards his car while Lea talked on her phone, following them.

They all crammed into Dylan's Tesla. Levi held onto Scarlett in the back seat while Lea sat next to them. Zoey was sitting in the front seat, talking to the rest of the Wildflowers on speaker phone, filling them in on what had happened.

"Do you think we should call the police?" Zoey asked to the car.

"No," Scarlett groaned. She'd been keeping her eyes closed, since the brightness of the day was causing her head to spin.

"I think you should at least file a report," Dylan said. "Remember when we didn't file one at first for Ryan and how that came back to haunt us?"

"Agreed," Zoey answered. "Elle, go ahead and call Brett to file a report. Hannah, see if you can round up some witnesses willing to talk."

"Consider it done. Scar, get better. Zoey keep us posted," Elle said before they hung up.

"How are you holding up?" Levi asked.

She would have opened her eyes, but at this point, her entire body was aching. "Fine," she lied between clenched teeth.

"Liar," he said softly. "We're pulling into the hospital now."

"I don't like hospitals."

"You won't be staying long. I just want a scan," Lea answered. Scarlett had almost forgotten the woman was in the car, even though she kept checking her pulse every few minutes.

"How am I doing, doc?" she asked, her eyes still closed.

"Your BP is one-twenty over eighty." The car was silent. "That's normal."

Scarlett heard a couple sighs. "Good," Zoey said. "Do you think she has a concussion?"

"We'll know more after we get a CT scan," Lea answered.

"You work at the hospital too, right?" Dylan asked.

"Yes," Lea answered. "Which is why I won't be handing Scar over to someone else." Lea's hand rested on Scarlett's. "You're all mine."

Scarlett smiled slightly. When she chuckled, her head felt like it was going to explode. Reaching up, she tested the knot on the back of her head and winced. It was easily double the size it had been earlier.

"It's getting bigger," she groaned.

"You know what they say," Dylan said. "To make an omelet…"

"Yeah, well, it's my egg on the line not yours. Besides, I'm not very hungry…" At the thought of food, her stomach revolted.

"Here," Lea said, shoving a small bag into Scarlett's hands. "I came prepared."

Scarlett emptied her stomach into the barf bag. "Sorry," she said, wiping her mouth as the car stopped.

"I'll park and meet you inside," Dylan said as Levi lifted Scarlett into his arms again.

Scarlett held on as Levi and Lea rushed her into the emergency room. The moment Levi laid her on the gurney, she started shaking uncontrollably. It was probably because her clothes were still wet from the dip in the pool and the hospital's air-conditioning was running at full throttle.

"I'm cold," she said as lights and sounds bombarded her, forcing her to once again close her eyes tight.

"I know, we'll get you a blanket," Lea said. Moments later one was set over her carefully.

Scarlett tried to listen as Lea talked to the medical staff, filling them in on her condition, but her head was started to grow dull and she couldn't stop shaking.

"We're going to take you back for a CT scan now," Lea said softly. "Levi's going to go with you."

Her hand was squeezed, and she realized Levi had been holding it all along.

"I'm right here," Levi said to her.

"I'm cold," she complained again.

"It's shock," Lea said softly. "We'll take care of you."

"Shock?" She tried to shake her head. Why would she be in shock? It wasn't as if she was really hurt. Was she?

Tears dripped from her eyes as she was rolled through the hallways. It was far too bright for her to open her eyes since her head was killing her at this point.

When they stopped, she cracked open an eye and saw Levi watching her.

"Doing okay?" he asked, his voice and eyes filled with concern.

"Yeah," she said between her chattering teeth.

He was rubbing his hands up and down her arms, which helped. They were in a dark room, waiting, while Lea and a nurse worked on the large scanner across the room from them.

"I know you don't want to hear this right now," he said in a deep voice as he leaned a little closer to her. She could see tears pooling in his eyes, which broke her heart to see. "But I love you."

CHAPTER EIGHTEEN

Levi sat next to Scarlett in the small dark room she'd been given after the CT and MRI scans had both come back confirming a concussion. Lea had assured them that there was no bleeding on Scarlett's brain, but there was possibly some bruising. They would know more after the swelling subsided.

They were going to keep Scarlett overnight and possibly a second night if she didn't show signs of improvement.

She'd stopped shaking, but still complained of being cold and dizzy. She'd thrown up two more times and for most of the time kept her eyes closed tight.

He knew she wasn't sleeping, since her breathing wasn't shallow enough. That and she kept squeezing his hand as if reassuring herself that he was still there.

He continued talking to her in a low voice, assuring her that things would be okay.

When the door opened, he glanced over to see all of her friends shuffle in, each one of them holding a bundle of flowers. Kimberly and Reed stepped in seconds later.

"Your Wildflowers and mother are here," he said softly.

Scarlett's eyes opened slightly, and a smile formed on her lips.

"Flowers," she sighed and closed her eyes again.

He held a hand over his lips to signal that they needed to be as quiet as possible. "She's fighting a headache."

"We'll set these here for when you feel better." Hannah set her vase on the table next to the bed. Elle and Aubrey followed along until the small table was full of different colored flowers.

"Zoey filled us in," Elle said to him. "We just wanted to stop in and see how she's doing."

"She," Scarlett said, "is fighting off the mother of all headaches."

Levi stood back as her friends crowded around her bed.

"I'm going to run... get a coffee. I'll be back in a few minutes." He quickly left the room.

Stepping outside, he saw Zoey and Dylan sitting across the hallway in a small waiting area. The pair had their heads bent together, talking quietly.

"Hey, know where there's a coffee machine around here?" he asked them, looking around.

"Sure." Dylan jumped up. "I'll take you to it. I could use a cup."

"Me too," Zoey said, but Dylan turned towards her. "Tea, I'll get you some tea." He started walking away.

Suddenly, everything was so clear to Levi. The last few times he'd run into Zoey, she'd been mooching food from the kitchen staff. Smiling, he slapped Dylan on the back. "So, is there something everyone should know?"

"What?" Dylan's steps faltered and he glanced back at Zoey with a slight frown. "No," he denied quickly. So quickly, Levi laughed.

"Jesus, it's written all over your face."

"What is?" Dylan frowned.

"Easy, buddy. I'm not going to spill the news."

"There is no news," Dylan replied as he started walking again.

"Sure, there isn't," Levi said easily as he fell into step. "Your secret's safe with me."

Dylan stopped in front of a large coffee machine, and Levi slid in his credit card to order. "There's no secret," Dylan said a little sterner.

"I get it. The wedding is almost a month away." Levi shrugged and waited as the coffee poured into the cup. "But it isn't as crazy as it used to be, you know…" He glanced around and lowered his voice. "Babies before marriage is not that big of a deal nowadays. Hell, I'm one of 'em."

"Jesus." Dylan swayed on his feet and Levi reached to catch him.

"You really think she's…" His eyes moved back down the hall where Zoey had been. She'd obviously disappeared into the room with the rest of her friends to visit her sister.

Levi frowned. "Isn't that what you meant when you said you were going to get her tea?"

Dylan shook his head and took a deep breath. "No, she had an upset stomach earlier. She thinks it was because of Scarlett's injury. I just thought tea would be better…" He dropped off when Levi laughed.

"Sorry, bro. It's just the way she's been wolfing down the sweets lately. I guess I jumped the…" He stopped talking when Dylan's face paled.

"That's what…" He shook his head. "Gotta go." He rushed from Levi's side, and Levi saw him disappear into Scarlett's room. Less than a minute later, he came out with Zoey and disappeared down the hallway.

"Shit." Levi sighed as he took his cup of coffee. "Guess I stepped into that one." Since Scarlett's friends were still in the room with her, he decided it was a good time for a short walk.

Besides, he could use some fresh air. He didn't like hospitals either.

When he stepped outside, he pulled out his phone and called to fill his grandmother in on everything that had happened, letting her know that he might not make it home that night, since he wanted to stay with Scarlett.

When he stepped back into Scarlett's room half an hour later, Zoey was sitting by her sister's bed, holding her hand.

"Lea just left the room," she said softly and smiled at him.

"And?" he asked, moving over and taking Scarlett's free hand. He knew instantly that she'd fallen asleep.

"Lea thinks we can take her home tomorrow. They want to keep checking on her tonight and suggest we go home and leave her to get some rest ourselves."

"I'm staying," he replied.

Zoey smiled. "I told Lea you would. She said she'd clear it with the staff here so you can stay."

"Thanks." He brought Scarlett's hand up to his lips. "How long has she been asleep?"

"I'm not," Scarlett replied softly. "Yet."

He winced. "Sorry." He kissed her knuckles again.

"It's okay." She sighed and opened her eyes slightly. "Where did everyone go?"

Zoey chuckled. "You must have slept through them all leaving." Zoey stood up and stretched. "I'm going to head out myself. Dylan stepped out for a phone call. I'll see you in the morning. Want me to bring you a change of clothes?" she asked Scarlett.

"Please. Some yoga pants and a T-shirt will work."

"Will do." Zoey moved to leave, but he jumped up.

"I'll be right back," he said to Scarlett and followed Zoey out the door.

"Hey." He took her arm. "I, um, didn't meant to get you in trouble."

"Trouble?" Her eyebrows shot up in question.

"Yeah, I, um. Guessed." He nodded towards her.

Her eyes narrowed, then widened. "Oh." Her hand went to her stomach. "It's not... I mean..." She shook her head. "How did you know?" She lowered her voice as she looked around.

He smiled. "I didn't, not really. I mean, you were ready to MMA for that cookie the other night. Then Dylan mentioned he'd get you tea instead of coffee and... well..." He ran his hands through his hair. "Like I said, it was a guess. I thought Dylan knew."

Zoey sighed and closed her eyes. "I only found out this morning."

"Really?" He smiled. "Congratulations."

Her face lit up. "Don't tell my sister yet. I... we..." She shook her head. "We wanted to tell everyone all at once. But not here, not like this."

He hugged her. "My lips are sealed." He kissed her cheek.

"That better be a brotherly kiss," Dylan joked as he approached them.

"It's a 'congratulations and your secret is safe with me' kiss." He held out his hand for Dylan's.

"Thanks." Dylan's face lit up. "We're going to tell everyone..."

"Tomorrow," Zoey supplied. "When my sister returns home." She smiled at Dylan, then turned back towards him. "Take care of her tonight. Call me if anything changes."

"Will do." He nodded. "Don't worry, she's in great hands here. Lea's sticking around, right?"

"Yes." Zoey laughed. "Scarlett is her favorite of us Wildflowers." She sighed and leaned closer. "It's because she keeps sneaking her cake."

Levi laughed. "I'll see you in the morning," he said before returning to Scarlett's side.

When he stepped in, she was asleep again, so he settled himself next to her and watched her while she slept.

The night stretched out longer than normal, since nurses or Lea appeared almost every hour to check on Scarlett. Just when he'd close his eyes, someone would walk in to take her vitals.

For most of the night, Scarlett slept through the interruptions.

When he woke in the morning, Scarlett was sitting up in the bed, watching him.

"Your neck is going to hurt," she said, smiling at him.

It was true. He'd slept in the recliner with his head tilted at an odd angle. Standing up, he stretched before walking over to sit next to her on the bed.

"How are you feeling?" he asked.

"Rested." She smiled. "I still have a knot on my head." She reached up and tentatively touched the back of her head. "But I'm no longer seeing double." She sighed. "Which is a shame, since two of you were far better than one."

He smiled and pulled her into a light hug. "Joking is a great sign."

"I want to go home," she said, holding onto him.

"Lea says that after she checks you this morning, she'll probably send you home. Hungry?"

She placed a hand over her stomach and frowned. "I'm starving, but I'm afraid I'll upchuck whatever I eat again."

"You can start slow."

"I'll try."

As he got up to hunt down something for her, she grabbed his arm, holding him still. "I know you meant what you said, yesterday."

"You don't have to say anything in return." He sat back down next to her. "I know you're not ready to hear it. Hell, it snuck up on me, but I meant it." He took her face in his hands. "I now you need time, and I'm willing to give you as much as you need. I just wanted you to know how I felt, in case…" He closed his eyes at the thoughts he'd had yesterday after seeing her at the bottom of the pool, unconscious.

She sighed and he opened his eyes again. He could see the uncertainty in the amber pools, along with fear.

"I'll go hunt something down for you to eat." He leaned in and kissed her. "Don't go anywhere."

She nodded and he felt better that at least she hadn't kicked him out or tried to talk him out of loving her. At this point, he was pretty sure nothing could talk him out of it. His entire heart had jumped into her hands.

Three hours later, he stepped out of the shower in her room and pulled on his backup work uniform. He knew Scarlett was propped up on the sofa in the living room, surrounded by her friends and family.

Someone had suggested he needed a shower and a shave, so he'd disappeared into her room with the duffle bag that his grandmother had dropped off for him earlier that morning when she'd visited Scarlett in the hospital.

Scarlett had been right about his neck. The hot water worked out most of the aches, but what he really needed was a night holding Scarlett, knowing she was going to be okay. Really okay.

She'd gotten a clean bill of health from Lea, with a promise that she would stop by later that evening to check on her progress.

Lea had gone over what to expect next, the dizziness, the lack of appetite, and other side effects. Scarlett was told to take the rest of the week off from work, which meant the first thing the five friends had talked about was how to fill in her schedule.

He knew they'd make it work, even if it meant most of them would be working double shifts to help out. He'd seen the friends pull together before when one of them had been out of commission, either because of a sickness or after Hannah had been injured by Ryan.

When he stepped into the living room, he was surprised to see Officer Brett Jewell sitting next to Scarlett. His partner stood across the room and took notes.

"Here." Scarlett motioned towards him. "He can fill in the blanks."

"Afternoon," Levi said, shaking the man's hand. He'd known Brett most of his life. The man had been in the class above his in school and had gone on to help them on the campground several times when they'd been hunting for Ryan or when the Costas had been in trouble with their cousin Joel.

"Afternoon." Brett shook his hand. "We're just trying to fill in a few blanks for our report."

"Right." He nodded and sat next to Scarlett, wrapping his arm around her shoulder. She snuggled into his chest and he relaxed slightly. "Doing okay?" he asked her softly.

"Yes, just tired." She yawned. "Answer Brett's questions so we can nap." He smiled at that thought. He knew he was probably needed around the camp, but Dylan had assured him they would fill in for him again today.

"We'll make this quick. What time did Mrs. Baker arrive at the pool?" Brett asked.

Levi thought about it. "Just before ten."

"How many drinks did she have before the one that spilled on her?" Brett asked.

"That would have been her third, but something told me she was already a few drinks in before she arrived."

"Was her husband with her at any time?" Brett asked.

"No." Levi frowned. "I didn't see him. Just her."

"From what a few guests have said, she tried to pull you down on top of her?" Brett asked.

"No, she pulled me down to her and tried to kiss me," he corrected, not looking around the room at the rest of the people still there. "I moved away quickly, spilling the drink on her. I suppose I should have guessed her move, after..." He shook his head.

"What?" Brett asked.

"She'd asked me when I delivered her second drink if we could go someplace... private. I gracefully declined and then delivered the rest of the drinks that had been ordered."

"Did she do anything that time to you?" Brett asked.

Levi shook his head. "No, and like I said, I hadn't expected her to pull me down the next time. I tried to step between her and Scarlett, but..." He glanced over at Scarlett and frowned. "I wasn't fast enough."

Scarlett took his hand. "You couldn't have known. I wasn't ready for the push either." She smiled at him.

"I think that'll cover it." Brett stood up and motioned to his partner. "We'll update the report."

When the two officers left, Zoey pulled out her phone and sent a text. "I'm getting everyone up here for a meeting," she said to the room. "We need a plan. The Bakers have decided to leave the camp early and will be out of their cabin by tonight."

"Thank god," Aubrey said to the room.

"We're all here," Elle said, looking around.

"Not all of us." Zoey looked around. "Dylan, Liam, and Owen are on their way up."

"Oh." Aubrey rolled her eyes. "We need the men now?"

"We can call Aiden up if it will make you feel better?" Elle said to Aubrey, who replied by sticking out her tongue.

"What I have to say involves them," Zoey clarified. She stood up and started to pace in front of the windows. The fact that he knew what she had to say had him smiling.

"What are you so happy about?" Aubrey asked him, pointing in his direction.

His smile fell away quickly. "Nothing." He shook his head and avoided everyone's eyes.

"Liar," Aubrey accused him.

"Leave him alone, he's had only a few hours of sleep." Zoey jumped to his defense.

"They have a secret," Aubrey accused.

"Aub." Scarlett sighed, and had Aubrey shrugging.

"Sorry, I missed breakfast and lunch," she replied.

"Good news then." Dylan walked in. Each of the brother's held large brown boxes from the kitchen. "We brought food."

"Yeah." Aubrey jumped up and grabbed a box.

"Isaac wanted to make sure Scarlett got better. Oh, and Betty sent up some baked goods just for you." Dylan handed Scarlett a box. "Only for you." His eyes moved around the room.

"The lengths a girl will go to to earn a few brownies around here is criminal," Aubrey joked as Scarlett pulled out a brownie and bit into it.

"You should have some of the lunch first," Levi suggested. "To take it slow."

Scarlett shook her head slightly. "Everyone knows when you're concussed, you eat dessert first." She rolled her eyes then groaned and held her head. "Okay, no eye rolling for me for the next few days."

"That will be a miracle," someone said quietly.

As everyone settled around eating their food, Levi's eyes moved over to Zoey and Dylan as he waited for them to share their news.

They ended up waiting until everyone was almost done eating. Dylan stood up and disappeared into the kitchen, returning with a bottle of champagne and glasses for everyone.

"That's what we were missing," Elle chuckled. "Day drinking."

Dylan filled all of the glasses and passed them around. "To family." He held up his glass and pulled Zoey to his side. Levi was the only one who noticed that Zoey hadn't been handed a glass. Dylan looked down at Zoey and smiled. "To our family, which in about nine months will be adding a new addition."

The entire room was silent for about ten seconds, then a burst of happy cheers exploded as Elle, Hannah, and Aubrey jumped up and surrounded Zoey.

Scarlett sat next to him, completely still and quiet as her friends surrounded and congratulated her sister.

"You okay?" he asked quietly.

"A baby?" She shook her head. "They're having a baby?"

He realized that everyone had stopped talking and turned their eyes towards Scarlett.

"Scar?" Zoey moved over to her and sat next to her sister. "I wanted to tell everyone together. I only found out yesterday morning. Before..."

Scarlett grabbed her sister into a hug. "I'm going to be an aunt," she said with a smile. "That's the best news I've heard all year."

CHAPTER NINETEEN

That night, Scarlett laid in Levi's arms, trying to calm her mind down. She'd had no problem sleeping earlier in the day, but now, in the middle of the night, she was wide awake.

Her mind refused to shut down and kept playing the fact that she was going to be an aunt over and over. Her sister was going to have a baby. A baby!

At one point in her life, Scarlett had dreamed of having a family. Then her father had left, and Jenny had texted her that picture of Levi and her at the bonfire.

Her mother had claimed that she'd put a shield around her heart that first year and had grown cold and distant from everyone. Since they could no longer afford to go to the camp the following summer, she hadn't had her Wildflowers to talk her out of protecting herself against another possible broken heart.

The only thing she'd known how to do was turn everything off.

But now, thinking about her sister having a baby, she felt something shift inside her. The desires she used to have were trying to break through her carefully shielded heart.

Looking over at Levi as he slept next to her, she remembered hearing him say he loved her.

In her dazed state, her first thought was to repeat those words back to him. But, after she'd surfaced from the fog and cleared her mind, she'd realized she'd been lucky she hadn't.

She couldn't afford to love him or any man, for that matter.

The pain she'd gone through as a teenager had damaged her to the point that her trust in anyone outside of her tight circle was completely shot. But Levi was slowly sneaking into that circle. So had Dylan, Liam, and Owen, among a few others on the campgrounds.

They were family now, even though they technically weren't yet. Zoey and Dylan's wedding was set for a month from now. Scarlett and the others were still working to finish up the final details. Zoey had even purchased her wedding dress and picked out the four bridesmaid dresses the Wildflowers would wear.

She rolled slightly to relieve some of the pain on her hips and cringed slightly.

"You okay?" Levi jerked awake.

"Yes, just sore." She finished shifting until she felt comfortable.

"Better?" he asked, wrapping his arms around her.

"Yes." She sighed.

"Can't sleep?" he asked her, his voice gruff.

She sighed and shook her head. "No, I can't shut down."

"We could... watch a movie?" he said slowly. His slurred speech told her that he was still half asleep.

"No, go back to sleep. I'll fall asleep eventually."

He rolled until he was looking directly at her. "Sassy, what's wrong?"

She bit her lip and debated telling him her thoughts.

"Is it about your sister and the baby?" he asked.

"Partly."

His hand came up and brushed gently down her arm. "You're happy for them though, right?"

"Very," she answered truthfully.

"Then what is it?" he asked, his hand stilling on her hip.

"Fear," she admitted. "At one point, I'd hoped to have that."

"A family of your own?" he asked, interrupting.

She nodded.

"What changed?"

"My father left us. And then I got that text from Jenny the following day."

He stiffened. "She texted you the day after your dad left?"

"Yes. It was as if she knew. Just like yesterday. She knew that I was coming around the corner and wanted me to see you and her kissing. That's why she pulled you down like she did."

He was silent for a moment. "I think you're right. Before she did, she kept glancing over towards the pathway. I thought she was waiting for her husband."

"Why does she hate me so much?" Scarlett shifted until she was sitting up. "What did I ever do to her?"

He sat up next to her and wrapped an arm around her shoulders. "Well, you did win me over that summer when she wanted all my attention. Especially when she tried so hard to flirt with me. It was obvious she wanted me."

She chuckled. "Egotistical much?"

"No, hear me out." He shifted until he was looking at her. "When did it all start?"

Scarlett thought back. "The first summer I showed up at camp and ran into her at the pool with the rest of my friends." She smiled when he frowned.

"Okay, that tosses my egotistical theory out the window." He shrugged with a low rumble in his chest. "So, it's not about me."

She laughed, already feeling much better, her mind moving from her sister and the baby to something different. "You're doing this on purpose," she accused him.

"What?" he asked, innocently.

"Making me laugh and relax." She sighed and leaned against his chest, feeling tired.

"Maybe." He held onto her. "Laughter always helps get your mind off problems."

"Does it always work for you?" she asked, holding back a yawn.

He was silent for a moment, then answered. "Yeah, it has. My entire life. Gran taught me laughter really was the best medicine after my mother died."

Scarlett was quiet for a moment. "She died of an overdose?" She'd heard tons of rumors. Everyone had, but she figured it was time to talk with him about it herself.

"That's what Gran told me. I had just turned seven." He was quiet again and she thought for a moment that he was done talking about it. "It's strange, I remember things differently than Gran does."

"Like what?" She sat up a little to look at him.

"Well, for starters, I remember my mom and my gran fighting that morning about…"—he sighed—"my father."

She sat up. "Do you think your grandmother knows who he is?"

"No." He shook his head. "Gran was trying to find out that morning. My mother was crying as she told her that she had someone try and contact him, but they had told her that he'd been mad when he found out that my mother hadn't aborted me like she'd told him she would."

"You…" She swallowed hard, her heart beating faster. "Your mother was going to abort you?"

"No." He shook his head. "My grandmother insisted that thought had never crossed my mother's mind."

"But your dad thought it had?"

"Apparently."

"Sounds like your life is better off without him in it then."

"Yeah." His arm tightened around her. "Then the day that she died, my mother left me with my gran so she could go to work."

"What happened?" she asked.

"Instead of going to work, she apparently went back to her apartment and OD'd."

"I'm sorry," she said softly. "How does your gran remember it?"

"She says they weren't fighting about my dad, but about something else."

"What?" she asked, looking up at him.

"About a trip my mother wanted to take me on. She wanted to take me out of the country for a while. Gran wasn't too keen on my mother taking me so far away from her," he said with a frown.

"Sounds like she had good reason to keep you close."

"Yeah." He scooted them back down until she was almost lying across his chest. His hand was rubbing her back slowly, causing her to feel more relaxed.

"I'm sorry you lost your mother so young." She held in a yawn.

"Me too. Part of me has always wanted to know who my father was, while the other part knows that any man who would have wished my mother would get an abortion isn't the father that I dreamed of having anyway."

She hugged him. "Thank you for getting my mind off my own problems."

He chuckled. "Sure, now you can think about mine."

She smiled as she ran her hands over his chest. "No, but it does help getting to know you more. I've gone all these years thinking I understand you completely. I was wrong. You are not the man I've been thinking you are."

"Oh?" His hand stilled on the lower part of her back.

"No." She glanced over at him and smiled. "You're much

more." She kissed him and then laid her head back down. "I think I could sleep for days now." She yawned again.

"I'll be right here when you wake," he promised as she fell asleep.

When she woke the following morning, she felt almost back to normal, except for the massive bump on the back of her head. She could hear Levi in the shower and made a quick decision to join him.

"Good morning," he said with a smile. "I thought we determined this shower was too small for the both of us," he joked as he wrapped his arms around her naked body.

"We've got to do our part to conserve water." She smiled. "For future generations."

He laughed and ran his soapy hands all over her. "Think you feel good enough to head down for breakfast?"

"Yes," she groaned. "Get me out of this apartment. I'm going stir crazy."

"It's only been a day," he reminded her.

"A day and like fifty hours of sleep." She rolled her shoulders.

"You have a large bruise here." He ran a finger gently over her hip and back.

"That part of me hit the bottom of the pool first."

"Does it hurt?" He scanned the rest of her body for bruises.

"Only when I sit," she joked, pouring shampoo into her hand. The moment she started scrubbing her head, she winced.

"You okay?" he asked.

"I forgot about this." She rubbed the large bump. "It's gone down some."

"Let me see." He touched her head gently, running his fingers over the area. "I guess it's a good thing you have a hard head," he said when he was done.

"It's a good thing you were there to fish me off the bottom of the pool." She wrapped her arms around him.

"That too." He sighed. "I should have never let her get that close to you." He rested his chin on the top of her head gently.

After showering and dressing, they made their way down to the employee's dining room.

Her friends were slightly upset to see her dressed and sitting in their normal booth when they walked in fifteen minutes later.

"You are supposed to be in bed," Zoey said, sitting next to her. Her sister's eyes scanned hers as if looking to see how she felt.

"I'm fine," she told her and laid a hand on her sister's. "Did you tell Mom yet?" she asked, knowing she had to change the subject.

"Yes, we went over to her place last night after our meeting and told her." Zoey smiled. "She's so excited, I think she spent the rest of the night buying things for the baby online."

"We weren't supposed to do that?" Elle asked with a slight frown. "I've already got stuff on the way."

Zoey laughed. "Jesus, we haven't even had our first doctor's appointment yet. Let's just... slow down." Her sister's eyes scanned everyone, and Scarlett could see a slight hint of fear in them.

Picking up her sister's hand, she smiled. "You're going to be an amazing mother."

"Oh god." Tears started flowing from her sister's eyes. "I'm so...."

"Scared?" Aubrey supplied.

Zoey shook her head. "Happy," Zoey finished with a chuckle. "I mean, we weren't planning this to happen this early, but..." Her sister's hand went over her flat belly. "It's just... right. You know? We'll be in our new house by the time we get back from our honeymoon, or so Aiden says. Things were a little slower because of his other projects, but the timing is just... right."

"To a new Wildflower." Hannah held up her glass of orange

juice. "We should have mimosas, but…" She smiled. "This will do."

"To another Wildflower," Elle repeated, holding up her own glass.

The five friends tapped their glasses together and drank.

"You guys are weird," Levi said, shaking his head, but he was smiling. "If someone can watch Sassy here for me, I'm going to head out to check and make sure someone is covering my first shift at the slides."

"Dylan has you covered," Zoey said, but Levi stood up. "I have to run an errand." He leaned down and kissed Scarlett on the cheek.

"Tired of me already?" she joked.

His eyes turned soft. "You can't get rid of me this easily." He smiled. "I'll meet you back up in the apartment in an hour."

"Take your time." She sighed. "I'll be around."

She could already feel her energy draining, but she wanted to do a few things before she locked herself back up in her room again.

"He has it bad for you," Zoey said after Levi left.

"Yeah." She sighed.

"Hey, that's a good thing," Elle said with a smile.

"I'm not sure I'm capable of returning the same feelings." She knew she could say anything to her best friends. They knew her too well to try to hide anything.

"Why? Because your dad decided to screw your mom and leave her for Bridgette?" Elle said, shaking her head. "Your mom isn't even that messed up over it. I mean, have you seen how cute Kimberly is with Reed?" Elle sighed and rested her head in her hands. "They are like the perfect couple from a travel magazine." She suddenly sat up and snapped her fingers and turned to Zoey. "Do you think your mom and Reed would pose for some promotional pictures for the camp?"

Zoey laughed. "Mom would, but Reed might have to kill the photographer if the pictures ever got out."

"Oh." Elle sank back and frowned. "Right, Mr. Spy and all."

"Ex-spy," Hannah reminded them, then turned back to Scarlett. "Why are you so apprehensive? I mean... it's Levi. He's one of the nicest guys I know. He'd never hurt a fly. I don't think he's the cheating type."

"No," she agreed, "he's not."

"Then what's the problem?" Aubrey asked.

Me, Scarlett thought. I'm the problem. But she just shrugged her shoulders and bit into her bagel.

CHAPTER TWENTY

When Levi walked back into the apartment, Scarlett was propped up on the sofa, watching an old black-and-white movie. She looked absolutely bored, and he laughed.

"Here." He set the bag of items he'd gone to town for on the coffee table in front of her.

"For me?" She sat up slowly and reached for the bag.

"I know you can't stand sitting still for too long, so I got a little something to help us through the boredom."

"A puzzle?" she asked, smiling down at the first box she pulled out of the bag.

"Among other things." He sat across from her.

"What's this?" She held up a deck of cards.

He smiled. "Read it." He leaned closer and watched her eyes as she read. When they grew large, he smiled.

"These are…" She tucked the cards close to her and glanced around. "Sex cards," she whispered.

He chuckled. "We'll play with those later." He took the cards from her and she dug into the bag again.

"I also got a handful of other games." He motioned to her

bookcase. "Since I know you can't really read with a splitting headache…"

"I don't…" She started to deny it, but since she'd been just rubbing her forehead, she shut her mouth. "Fine, I do. That's why I was watching a movie."

"Which you were completely bored with."

"It was growing on me." She shrugged.

"This will be much more fun." He pulled out a board game. "What do you want to play first?"

She was still frowning at him, so he leaned forward and took her hand. "When I was eleven, I broke my leg at the beginning of summer. When most of my friends spent the hot summer days playing at the beach or at the local pool, I was stuck on the sofa. My grandmother bought me a bunch of games like this and turned my summer into one of the best that I can remember." He shrugged. "You only have a week. I had five weeks of this. Give it a try."

She smiled and nodded. "Okay, but I get to be the car." She took the box from him and smiled.

For the next few hours, they played games. He found out quickly that Scarlett was extremely competitive and often reverted to cheating tactics to win. Of course, since she was using flirting as a diversion to distract him, he didn't complain too much.

They were laughing about a word she'd just placed on the Scrabble board when Zoey walked in with their lunches.

"Your sister is a cheater," he joked easily.

Zoey laughed. "Tell me about it." She rolled her eyes. "She's also a sore loser."

He laughed. "I found that out with Monopoly."

"Oh god, you didn't play that with her, did you?" Zoey shook her head. "She buys everything."

Levi laughed. "And she hordes the get-out-of-jail cards."

"Yes." Zoey smiled and set the bags down. "How are you feeling?" she asked Scarlett.

"Much better. I think I'll be ready to—"

"Nope," Zoey said quickly.

"But—"

"Nope. End of the week. That's the doctor's orders." Zoey leaned closer. "And you do not want to piss off Lea. She may like you the best, but trust me when I say, she can be vicious if you don't obey her directions."

"How's it going out there in the real world?" Scarlett asked, grabbing her sandwich from her sister.

"Busy, but nothing we can't handle." She sat next to Scarlett and took out her own sandwich. "We've filled in for each other before." Zoey shrugged. "Jenny and her husband left last night." Her eyes moved up to her sister's.

"Did she say anything?" Scarlett asked.

"No, other than she tried to blame you and Levi for attacking her first. But since we had everything on video…" She shrugged. "They left town after paying a fine. I told them they wouldn't be getting their deposit back."

He'd forgotten that there were cameras installed in most of the campground's major areas. Ever since the first big party, security had been key to the survival of the camp.

"I bet she didn't care about that," Scarlett said.

"Actually, she threw a fit about it." Zoey rolled her eyes. "From what I hear, her husband handed Stuffit's over to his oldest son a few years ago. Rumor is it that Jenny has flown through the old man's fortune and the son won't be giving them any more money any time soon."

"Then why plan a vacation down here?" Levi asked.

"I bet she was just trying to rub our noses in her wealth while she still had some," Scarlett said, setting down the rest of her sandwich. Levi could tell instantly that she was tired again.

"If you don't have it, you shouldn't spend it," he commented. "Tired?" he asked Scarlett.

"Some." She sighed and rested her head back against the sofa. "Beating you at games all morning has worn me out," she said with a smile. Levi chuckled.

"I let you win." He winked.

"I've got to get back to work." Zoey stood up and cleaned up the mess. "Oh, there are two slices of pie in there for you. The kitchen staff sends their best," Zoey added. "And now that the news is out that I'm eating for two"—she rubbed her flat belly —"I no longer have to beg for extra dessert." She pulled out a large slice of pie and hugged it to her chest. "This one is for junior," she said as she walked out.

"She is so going to milk this," Scarlett said, putting her feet up on the sofa.

He walked over and placed a blanket over her.

"Lie down with me?" she asked, shifting the pillow under her head.

"I've got a few things to do." He nodded to this computer. "I'll be here, but I've got some research I want to do while you rest."

"Okay." She closed her eyes. "Save my slice of pie for later."

"No promises," he teased, but she was already asleep.

While Scarlett slept, Levi got on online and did a quick search. He started out by researching everything he could about Jenny and her husband.

Zoey's information seemed spot on. There were articles about the family problems, including a wedding photo of Jenny and the old man standing in a Vegas church, all alone. Jenny even looked drunk then.

When a camp reminder popped up about the school reunion for that weekend, he changed his search parameters.

It wasn't the first time he'd looked through the old yearbooks online, searching for a face that matched his own. Or one that resembled it at least.

He'd seen plenty of pictures of his mother and her best friends. From what he could tell, her best friend had been a girl named Leslie Cummings. There were more than a dozen pictures of the two girls together over the years.

Which made sense, since they were in charge of the yearbook committee for their entire junior high years.

He'd searched for Leslie Cummings over the years but had come up blank. Whatever had happened to her, she'd left Pelican Point and never returned.

It didn't stop him from looking. If he could find his mother's best friend, maybe she could shed some light on who his father was and what had really happened that last day of his mother's life.

The more he looked, the more frustrated and discouraged he grew. Would he ever know anything about either his father or his mother's best friend?

He spent over an hour searching the pages of old yearbooks and school photos. When his eyes started hurting, he shut down his laptop and crawled under the blanket with Scarlett to shut down for a while.

They woke when someone came into the apartment.

"Sorry," Aubrey said softly as he sat up quickly. "I was told to bring you this." She set a large brown bag on the coffee table and he instantly smelled food.

"I'm going to gain so much weight this week," Scarlett groaned, sitting up next to him.

"How are you feeling?" Aubrey asked as she sat down.

"Rested," she answered and yawned. "And hungry again."

"She didn't finish her sandwich earlier," Levi supplied. "Or touch her pie," he reminded Scarlett.

"Right." She pulled the bag towards her. "What's on the menu tonight?"

"Steak," Aubrey told them. "It was heavenly. "I've got to change and get ready for the dinner rush."

"Oh." Scarlett pouted. "It's fifties night. I like fifties night."

"You can go next month," Aubrey reminded her.

"Yeah, I suppose." Scarlett pulled out a container and opened it. "I'm seriously going to gain weight if Betty keeps sending me up these desserts."

Aubrey laughed. "I'm sure Zoey can take them off your hands if you want. She's totally milking this pregnancy thing. She had double dessert for lunch." Aubrey got up and headed towards her room.

"Did you get enough sleep?" he asked Scarlett when they were alone.

"Yes." She set the container down. "I'm not even hungry." She looked up at him. "You know what? I could use a walk." She stood up and he followed her, realizing his legs were a little stiff as well.

"Let's do it." He held out his hand for hers.

"We'd better put the food away so we can enjoy it later." She took the bag and walked into the kitchen. He helped her put everything away before grabbing a light jacket for her.

"It's probably eighty degrees out." She laughed.

"Humor me." He shrugged. "I didn't like seeing you shiver when you were in shock."

She took the jacket and wrapped it around her waist. They walked two full circles around the campground's pathways, talking about the camp and how likely it was that Jenny would return for more revenge.

"I mean, look at what happened with Ryan. The woman was nuts," Scarlett said as they headed back towards the main building.

"I'm not denying that, but security is a lot tighter around here now. Jenny is now on the no-go list."

Scarlett chuckled. "I just love knowing that she can no

longer step foot in the place she used to spend all her summers at."

He stopped and pulled her into his arms. "Revenge is sometimes sweetest when it's a backlash to someone trying to dish it out."

"True. If she hadn't been drunk at the pool and pushed me, she and her husband would still be here for another three days, showing off all their wealth. We would be ignorant to the fact that she married a man three times her age just to spend all of his money." She sighed. "I guess a concussion was worth it."

"No." He shook his head as his entire body tensed at the thought. "I never want to see you like that again."

She leaned her head against his chest. "Okay, maybe not. But still, I'm glad she won't be coming back here."

"I moved my days off to match yours," he told her out of the blue. "I'm hoping to spend them with you."

"I'd like that." She smiled up at him. "Since I'm not supposed to do anything too strenuous, I think we can spend the entire time inside..."—she leaned up and kissed him—"playing other games that I'm really good at."

He chuckled. "That sounds like a plan." He kissed her.

They walked back towards the main building, hand in hand.

When they passed the boat house, they heard arguing and turned to see Aubrey storm towards them.

"Is everything okay?" Scarlett asked, concerned.

"Yes." Aubrey looked jittery. "I just..." She glanced around. "Yes, everything is fine." She marched away, heading towards the main building.

"What was that all about?" Levi asked Scarlett.

"I'm not..." She stopped and glanced over when she heard hammering. They both moved over to see Aiden hammering a new piece of two-by-four into the dock. The way he was swinging the hammer told them both that he was pissed. "Interesting," Scarlett said as she tugged him back onto the path and towards the building.

"Are they..." he started to ask, looking over his shoulder.

"No, not officially."

He thought about it for a moment. "Are we official?"

She chuckled and pulled him to a stop. "I think any couple would be official after what you did."

He held onto her and took a deep breath, enjoying her soft scent, the way she felt in his arms, and the feel of her next to him. "I did what any man would have."

"Not that. Although, you did win major brownie points for jumping in and saving me. Zoey showed me the video." She shivered. "It's strange to see yourself being pulled out of the water unconscious."

He'd seen the video too. Brett had wanted him to confirm what was being said during the silent footage.

"What then?" he asked, pulling her a little closer.

"What you said to me," she hinted.

He smiled instantly. "I love you."

She slowly swallowed and then nodded. "Yeah, that."

"I'll get you to say it back to me someday," he promised. As a response, she rested her head on his shoulder. "But only when you're ready," he promised. "Come on, we'd better go enjoy our dinner and desserts before your sister finds them and gobbles them up."

CHAPTER TWENTY-ONE

*I*t was strange. Over the next two days Scarlett didn't even really miss work. If Levi wasn't keeping her busy by playing games with her, then one of her friends was entertaining her in one way or the other. She took more leisurely walks than she normally would have and ate more desserts as well.

She was expecting that by the time she was back at full capacity, she was going to be five pounds heavier than before she'd been pushed into the pool.

On the night of the big reunion party, everyone, including Lea, agreed that she was able to help with decorations. The campground guests' dinner hour had been moved up and, after the last couple left the dining hall, work on decorating for the bigger party began.

Of course, she'd been given the job of filling all the balloons using the large helium canister Elle had purchased after their first party balloon fiasco.

How were they supposed to know that blowing up two hundred balloons would take so long and almost cause the five friends to pass out? Besides, helium balloons were so much better than ones that laid on the ground. So Scarlett sat in a chair and filled balloons and tied different colored strings to each one.

They even had a net of sorts that she could let the balloons drift up into afterwards. The job was mindless and boring.

Still, she was out of the apartment, and she was able to watch the other elaborate decorations going up around the main dining hall and talk to the other employees.

An extra benefit was being able to watch Levi lift and hang the heavier decorations. It was so fun to watch the man move. Clothes or no clothes, the guy set off her sex meter. Let's face facts, Levi broke her sex meter.

"Pay attention." Zoey moved over and poked her in the arm. "You're going to—"

Too late. The balloon she'd been filling popped, causing both of them to jump and squeal at the same time.

"That's the third one in the last five minutes," Zoey complained.

"Sorry." Scarlett tossed it in the trash and started on a new one.

"Enough torture." Zoey grabbed the deflated balloon from her hands. "I'm sure we can have you working on something else." She glanced around and smiled. "Aubrey could use some help folding napkins." She motioned towards the bar area.

Scarlett groaned.

"Hey, don't blame me. Everyone's tired of jumping each time you get busy watching your man work and end up literally popping something." She laughed and nudged Scarlett towards the bar. "Go." Her sister sat down and took her place.

Scarlett made her way across the dining hall, enjoying the streamers and decorations that were already in place.

"Hey," Levi said as she passed him. "Did your sister kick you off balloon duty?"

"Yes." She frowned.

"Good. I'm up on a ladder here. Every time you popped one, I almost lost my footing."

"Sorry." She frowned, suddenly concerned about him being up so high.

He chuckled, then rolled his eyes as another balloon popped.

"How are you feeling?" he asked, moving down the ladder towards her.

"I'm one hundred percent," she said, knowing it was the truth. Even the bump on the back of her head was completely gone. She still had a slight bruise on her hip, but it was a nasty shade of green and yellow, which meant, in a day or two, it would be gone completely.

"Good." He turned his attention towards Liam, who was holding the other end of the string of lights they were placing. "Gotta concentrate," he told her and moved back up the ladder. "My boss is a real…"

At that moment, Hannah moved over and yelled at the pair of them for putting the lights in the wrong place.

Scarlett chuckled.

"What are you doing?" Hannah turned to her. "Why aren't you…" She glanced around and, after seeing Zoey filling balloons, she motioned towards the bar. "Help Aubrey."

"Yes, sir." Scarlett gave Hannah a quick salute, and then shuffled off before she was yelled at again.

"Every party we have, she turns into a drill Sargent," Aubrey whispered as Scarlett sat next to her.

"True." Scarlett chuckled as Hannah continued to boss everyone around. "But you've gotta admit, she throws some of the best damn parties around."

"Agreed." Aubrey smiled.

"So," Scarlett started after a few minutes of silence, "want to tell me what that was all about the other night? With Aiden?"

Aubrey stiffened, then glanced around the dining hall quickly.

"He's not here. He's working out at Owen's neighborhood job site," Scarlett supplied.

"Nothing," Aubrey said as she kept her eyes turned downwards.

"Nothing?" Scarlett lowered her voice. "All that yelling wasn't about nothing."

Aubrey sighed. "Have you ever liked someone… that doesn't like you the same way?"

She was about to say no, but then shut her mouth and nodded instead. After all, for those first few days with Levi, back when she'd been a teenager, she'd believed he hadn't even known she was alive.

Not to mention the past two years of skirting around him. She hadn't even admitted to herself that she liked Levi during that time, until recently.

"You like Aiden?" she asked.

"I can't." Aubrey sighed. "I mean, I thought I did, but…" She shook her head. "It's just… I can't," she repeated.

"Can't? Or won't?" she asked.

Aubrey shifted and then shrugged. "Both."

"Why not?" Scarlett asked. "He's single, so are you."

"It's not that…" She glanced around again. "It's complicated." She stopped folding the napkins, resting her hands on the bar top.

"How so?" Scarlett asked.

Suddenly, Aubrey turned towards her. "You and Levi. Is it serious?"

Scarlett was about to tell her not to change the subject, but then realized Aubrey was trying to make a point.

"Levi's told me that he loves me," she admitted. She hadn't even told her sister that part yet.

"He has?" Aubrey smiled and leaned closer. "And?"

"And?" Scarlett frowned. "I can't love him back."

Aubrey bit her bottom lip and then asked. "Can't? Or won't?"

Scarlett thought about it. "I don't think I'm capable." She stopped folding the napkins as well and looked down at her hands. "I mean, with everything that my dad put us through... To protect myself, I locked up my heart and threw away the key." She sighed. "I really do like Levi and even trust him more than I have any other man, but…"

Aubrey sighed and nodded. "Yeah, I know what you mean." She picked up another napkin. "Can't and won't." She sighed.

"Hey." Scarlett laid a hand over Aubrey's. "I'm trying, though, and Levi is really patient with me. I'm sure Aiden is…" She didn't know. After all, Aiden and she had mostly worked together before the camp had opened. It wasn't as if she hung out with the man a lot. He was really a mystery to her. Sure, she liked him and thought he was smoking hot, as did every single woman that had a heartbeat, but she didn't know him well.

"He's complicated and so am I," Aubrey finished.

"Talking?" Hannah stopped beside them and leaned in. "Is it important? Are you willing to share with the group?" She motioned around to the room. Both Aubrey and Scarlett looked horrified. "No?" Hannah said sweetly. "Then fold. We have less than an hour to finish this before party guests start arriving."

"Tyrant," Aubrey said to Hannah's back.

Hannah glanced over her shoulder and stuck out her tongue towards Aubrey.

"But you have a cute butt," Aubrey said loudly, causing Hannah to laugh. "See." Aubrey nudged Scarlett. "I told you she could laugh." To which Hannah raised her finger and flipped them both off.

Aubrey and Scarlett laughed and then finished folding the napkins in record time.

Two hours later, Scarlett stepped into the dining hall and was amazing at how different everything looked. Somehow, with the millions of string lights hovering above everyone's head, everything looked fancier.

Scarlett was put on working the front desk. She was tasked with handing out everyone's name tags and making sure all the guests signed in.

She didn't mind the job, since it allowed her to sit in the front and out of the loud music the band was playing inside. She knew that by the end of the night, anyone working inside would be almost deaf. It wasn't that the cover band was bad, just one of the loudest they hired.

But all of the guests seemed to like it, since it sounded like they were all having a ton of fun. As people trickled in, two women from the celebrating class helped her greet their fellow classmates. On several occasions, Scarlett was asked whose daughter she was. Someone had even mistaken her for a woman named Gabby. Or course, the guy had been really drunk when he'd stumbled in.

She and the rest of her friends had worn their standard black dress suits, the same one that most of the waitresses and waiters wore on a nightly basis. During parties like this, they found it easier than trying to slip into a dress and heels and be mistaken for guests. After all, most of the attention should be on the reunion classmates and not the staff of the camp.

"How's it going out here?" Hannah asked almost an hour into the party.

"Fine." She smiled. "I think most of the guests have arrived. How's it going in there?"

"Good. We may need you on the bar with Levi." She sighed and looked back into the room. "I'm seriously questioning if we purchased enough booze for tonight."

Scarlett laughed as she moved to stand next to Hannah. "Do you think our twentieth reunion will be anything like this?" she asked, looking through the doors. People were crowded onto the dance floor, bumping and grinding against one another.

"God, I hope so." Hannah smiled. "I mean, it's funny." She leaned closer. "Some of these people look young enough to be

SUMMER FLING

our age. While others..." She motioned to an overweight, bald man trying to flirt with one of their waitresses. "I'd better go help Kathy," she said, rolling her eyes. "When you want, head over to the bar and lend a hand. I'm sure they can finish handing out name tags." She motioned to the two women who were still sitting at the sign-up table.

Scarlett had briefly talked with both women and found out that they had organized the entire party but didn't plan on going inside to enjoy themselves at all.

"We are what you would call the class nerds," one of them had told her initially.

"Everyone always made fun of us in school," the other woman had said.

"Then why throw the reunion party?" Scarlett had asked. "You two must have put a lot of effort into all this."

Both women were pretty, and everyone who came along seemed shocked that they had changed so much and said they would have never guessed who they were.

The blond one whose name was Sue had been talking about her husband and kids not being able to make it down here for the party. Vickie, the brunette, was a little heavier set, but still very attractive and soft spoken.

They both shrugged at her question. "If we didn't do it, no one else would have," Sue had answered.

Scarlett had wondered who in her graduating class would organize her reunion. It wasn't as if she'd known a bunch of kids she'd gone to school with. Scarlett and Zoey had been moved out of their private school the summer their dad had taken off on them. Zoey had graduated a year after that, leaving Scarlett to finish school without any close friends.

"Will you two be okay out here? They need my help inside," she asked after Hannah left.

"Yes," both answered at the same time. "We've got this. There's only a few more on the list that haven't arrived yet."

"When you're done, come in and have some fun. I'll be at the bar. First drink's on the house."

"Thanks." They both chuckled.

Scarlett made her way across the crowded room, trying not to bump into people as she went. When she stepped behind the bar, she was thankful for the extra space.

She hadn't thought that the local school would have such a large class, even with all the spouses attending.

"Hey." She touched Levi's back so he wouldn't bump into her.

He glanced over at her and smiled. "Thank god, the cavalry is here," he said to Britt.

Britt smiled and nodded. "Help yourself to a customer," she joked and went back to work.

For the next hour, Scarlett worked behind the bar, filling drink orders as quickly as she could. She didn't know how to mix a lot of drinks, but most of the orders were for light beer or shots. The fancier drink orders she left for Levi, Liam, or Britt.

"We need glasses," Britt said to her when there was a slight lull in the lines. "Could you go help collect them and clean them?"

"Sure thing, boss." She saluted and grabbed a tray. Any excuse to move around instead of just standing in one place. She was tired of being stuck behind the bar and wanted to get out into the crowd for a few minutes.

She was on her third run of picking up empty glasses when she bumped into the back of a tall man. After making sure the glasses on her tray didn't tip over and hit the floor, she glanced up to apologize to the guy and froze.

She was so shocked by the man's appearance that she actually stuttered and dropped her entire tray, sending the three empty glasses on it hurtling towards the ground to shatter.

CHAPTER TWENTY-TWO

"You have to come here," Scarlett tugged on Levi's arm.

He glanced over at her. "I can't take a break—"

"No." She shook her head, sending her hair, which had been neatly tied back in a low bun, flying around her face. "Levi, now." She glanced around. Her eyes were huge and instantly he worried something was wrong. She called out towards the end of the bar. "Liam, take over for Levi."

"I don't think you two have time for a quickie," Liam teased.

Scarlett narrowed her eyes at him. "It's important and, no, it's not a quickie." She almost growled it at the man.

"Fine." Liam chuckled and shrugged.

"What's going on, Sassy?" Levi asked as she tugged him towards the dance floor, his concern building the more she pulled on him. "Is something wrong?"

"No." She shook her head, then said with a sigh, "Nothing's wrong, it's just… that." She motioned her hands towards the crowd dancing on the floor.

"Hey, I'm game if you are. I mean, you know I love showing off my moves." He brought her in close.

"No." She shoved on his chest. "Look closer." She leaned in and took his face in her hands and pointed his eyes at a couple who were dancing slowly in the crowd.

"So?" He shrugged and turned back to her. "I don't get—"

"Levi, looook." She repeated the motion with his face. This time, instead of skimming over the couple, he actually looked at them.

Two heart beats in, he was pretty sure his heart stopped all together. He felt his palms go clammy, and his breathing even stopped.

"Levi?" Scarlett said, wrapping her arms around him. "That's your dad," she whispered.

He swallowed and felt his heart kick in his chest as if it had just started up again.

Everything that he'd planned on saying to the man when he'd finally found him fled his mind.

"Levi?" She tugged on his arm. "Go talk to him."

"No." He shook his head and took a step backwards, just as the song ended.

"We're going to take a fifteen-minute break," the singer of the band said into the microphone. "Now's a great time to take that smoke break," he joked, and soft prerecorded music started playing over the speakers.

Most of the people exited the dance floor, making their way towards the bar area to refresh their drinks, including the couple that he'd been watching.

"They're heading this way," Scarlett said into his ear as her hand took his and forced him not to move. Not that he could have. He was pretty sure his shoes were nailed to the spot on the floor, since his legs and the rest of him were suddenly disconnected from his brain.

Levi knew the moment the man noticed him. He was sure that the look that crossed his face was the same one that had been on Levi's moments ago. At first, the guy's eyes, which matched Levi's perfectly, scanned over him. Then they bounced back to Levi's face and held there. The man stopped walking and his chin dropped slightly. Then he moved towards them quickly.

"Who are you?" the man said, anger filling his voice. Levi noticed a slight accent but couldn't quite place it.

"Michael?" The woman he'd been dancing with tugged on the man's arm.

"Michael?" Levi had regained his wits in that brief moment. "Do I get a last name for the man who abandoned me?" Levi asked, his tone filled with sarcasm.

The man's eyes narrowed even further as something close to pain filled them.

"Not here." The woman grabbed Michael's hand and started tugging him towards the front door.

"Levi?" Scarlett said softly, getting his attention. "I'll come with..." She glanced around. "Elle, we need a few minutes," she called out to her friend.

Levi was too busy watching his father's back to pay attention to anything else going on around him.

"Come on." Scarlett took his hand and pulled him towards the front door, following the couple. "Let's hear what he has to say." She squeezed his hand lightly.

He didn't speak. Even when the four of them stepped out into the darkened patio area, he remained quiet, unsure now of what he could say. It was as if, after spotting the man, his brain had seized up.

"This way." Scarlett motioned towards the pathway. "We can have a more private chat here." They all followed her down the pathway to a small clearing where several benches were set up. There was a fire pit in the middle that, during colder nights, usually had a fire in it. Benches circled around the pit for guests to enjoy. Currently, they were the only ones in the area.

"Who are you?" Scarlett asked, turning on the man.

"We can ask the same," the woman hissed back in a low tone. "Just who do you think you are, approaching us at this very public party? How did you even get in here anyway?" she asked Levi, her eyes burning into him as if he was putting them out in some way.

Levi's eyes moved back to his father's. "Michael what?" he said, ignoring the woman.

The man sighed. "Michael Stiles," he answered after a moment. "This is my wife, Leslie."

"Did you go to school with my mother? Mary Grant?" Levi asked, trying to block out any emotion from his tone.

"Mary?" Michael asked, looking as if he'd been punched in the gut, which confused the hell out of Levi.

"I did." The woman stepped forward and for the first time, Levi looked in her direction. Instantly, he recognized the woman.

"You were my mother's best friend. Leslie Cummings." He felt his heart skip again, then his eyes nodded towards his father. "You knew… who my father was?"

"Stop calling me that," the man said, running his hands through his blond hair, a move so familiar and close to his own move that Levi's stomach rolled.

Really assessing him, Levi realized the man could have been his brother instead of his father. His hair was a little longer with the same curls that Levi often had when he grew his own hair out. Both men were clean shaven and were wearing dark suits for the party. If he hadn't known better, Levi would have assumed he was looking into a mirror instead of at the man who had abandoned his mother and him.

"Isn't it very obvious that's what you are?" Levi spat out. "All you have to do is look at us." He motioned between them. "We're almost fucking identical." Levi's voice raised slightly. He tried to take a few calming breaths when Scarlett's hand gripped his arm. He turned back to Leslie. The woman looked the same as she had in all the photos she'd posed in with his mother. Her short dark hair was cut in a new style, and she was wearing a green dress that hugged her thin body. She was short, even with the black heels she was wearing. "Did you know?" he asked her.

"I..." She turned her eyes towards Michael. "I left town."

"That's not an answer," he pointed out. "My mother had me when she was a sophomore in high school. You had to know about me."

They were both quiet as the man turned towards the woman and looked down at her.

"We don't have to explain anything to you," Leslie said. "Mary's gone. She killed herself."

"What?" Levi gasped and swore his head spun. "What?" he said again as his entire body jerked.

He felt Scarlett's hand jerk in his and then she was pulling him towards one of the benches and shoving him down in it.

"What the hell?" Scarlett confronted the woman. "Why would you say something like that? Levi's mother died of an—"

"Overdose." The woman smirked. "Seriously? Didn't Mary Lynn ever tell you the real story?"

"Did you know?" Levi said softly through the ringing in his head, his eyes returning to his father's.

"That Mary died?" He nodded slowly. "Leslie told me when she came to visit me that first time."

"You're Norwegian?" Scarlett asked and suddenly Levi recognized the accent.

"I'm from Copenhagen," he answered.

"That's why I couldn't find you." Levi laid his head in his hands and closed his eyes. "All these years." He sighed.

"We live in Miami now," Michael added.

"Michael," Leslie hissed, "we don't owe him anything."

"No." Michael sighed.

"I don't know how you got in here, since this is a private party. I'm going to make sure that both of you are thrown out of here." Leslie grabbed Michael's hand and jerked on it until he followed her back down the pathway.

Scarlett sat next to him and took his hand in hers.

"I'm sorry," she said softly.

"Why? You had no idea that the man was going to brush me off for a second time." He sighed and leaned back in the chair, only realizing they'd sat in one of the big rocking benches that Liam had made when the thing started to sway.

Scarlett wrapped her arms around him and held on. "I can't believe..." He heard her sniffle. "Someone would do..." She sniffled again.

"Hey." He tugged on her chin until she looked up at him. The big tears sliding down her cheeks almost broke his heart. Here it was, his darkest hour. He'd finally confronted the man he'd dreamed of berating his entire life and instead of feeling sorry for himself, Scarlett was doing all the crying. "I've had twenty-four years to be pissed or cry over the loss of that man. I've wasted enough tears and anger already." He smiled down at her as he wiped a tear from her cheek with his thumb. "You shouldn't waste any of yours. He's not worth it. Besides, I had the best childhood I could have ever asked for." He sighed. "My gran loved me enough for a dozen fathers and mothers."

She smiled as he wiped more tears from her cheeks.

"I'm sorry," She reached up and touched his face. "About your mother."

He sighed and rested his head back against the bench. "I can't deny that part of me had wondered."

"You don't have to go back in there," she said after a moment.

"No." He shook his head. "We are needed behind the bar. We still have a few hours before the party ends. I can't leave Liam and Britt to this crowd. Besides, I won't let him bully me into submission."

She nodded. "I'm here." She reached up and took his face and laid her lips over his.

"We all are," came a soft voice across from the fire pit. "Sorry." Zoey stepped out of the darkness. "Elle said you were having an emergency. I, um, spotted the couple marching back into the party and well, guessed what's going on." Levi held in a groan. "Am I right?"

"Yes." He stood up, pulling Scarlett up with him, and wrapped his arms around her. "That man, Michael Stiles, is my father."

Just saying those words out loud made his stomach roll. He promised himself that later he'd research the hell out of the guy. But for now, he was going to push it to the back of his mind.

Zoey walked over to them both and silently wrapped her arms around them. "I'm sorry," she said softly. When he heard her sniffle, he chuckled.

"Okay, enough tears. The man doesn't deserve them."

"No." Scarlett looked up at him. "But you do," she said with a slight smile.

When the three of them stepped back inside, the band was already playing again. The line at the bar was back under control for the moment and he thought about him and Scarlett skipping out on the rest of the night.

Then he spotted Elle standing by the edge of the bar talking to Liam. When Scarlett and Levi stepped up to the bar, she moved over towards them.

"I'm so sorry," she said softly. "Just so you know, the Stileses approached me. They were very upset and wanted to file a complaint, but after I informed them of your... standing with this business, they left instead."

He nodded. "Thanks." He wondered instantly if the couple was staying somewhere in town and if he would see them again before they left to go back to Miami. Then he realized he didn't really care. His father had made his opinion very clear.

"I assume things didn't go well?" Elle asked.

"Later," Scarlett told her. "We'll have a meeting after the party?" She touched his shoulder.

Elle nodded and quickly gave Liam a kiss before heading back out to help collect more glasses for Britt.

"Sorry, kid." Britt touched his arm. "I never knew my old man either. I heard he spent a few hard years in prison for robbing a bank. He died a year before he was due to be released." She shook her head. "Pissed off the wrong inmate. I think it was easier on me not having met him."

Levi chuckled. "Yeah." He glanced over to where Scarlett was washing dishes and watching him. "At least I know his name now." He gave Scarlett a weak smile.

For the rest of the evening, only one thing played over in his mind. The surprising news of his mother's death. He hadn't lied when he'd said he had wondered if her death hadn't been an accident.

After all, his grandmother had said that his mother had left him at her place so that she could go to work at her job as a hair stylist in town. If she was supposed to be at work, why had she ended up at her apartment with a needle in her arm instead?

The only thing he could think of was that she'd planned it all along.

When the party started to die down, he helped gather all the dishes and clean up. Before the last couple had left, the group of friends were already gathered around the bar.

He had a beer in his hand that Britt had given him, but he had only taken a sip or two. He didn't want to relax or let go of his problems. Not at the moment, anyway.

He was thankful that the talk hadn't turned to what had happened earlier. At least not yet.

"I think the cleanup crew can finish the rest," Hannah suggested with a yawn.

"The sergeant is off duty," Aubrey joked, causing Hannah to narrow her eyes towards her. "Hey, don't get me wrong. I'm glad you're the one bossing people around and not me." She motioned to the room. "Otherwise parties such as this wouldn't be so amazing."

Aubrey slung an arm over Hannah's shoulders as they started walking out.

"We need a meeting," Zoey said to everyone in the small group. "Upstairs, before you all go." Several people turned to her to complain, but she held up her hands to stop them. "It's important."

Several eyes turned towards him and they all nodded. Then they all made their way up to the apartment that he'd been sharing with Scarlett.

He hadn't really thought about it, but for the past week, he'd been practically living with her.

He and Scarlett had stopped off at his grandmother's place for dinner earlier that week. Since she wasn't back at work full time yet, their evenings had been free. He'd packed a small bag of clothes and had brought some necessities over to the small room they shared.

Now, the thought of returning to his grandmother's place full time was somehow depressing. But he feared that at some point he would have to go back.

Following Scarlett upstairs, he felt the weight on his chest deepen with each step he took. He didn't want to have to retell the horror that he'd gone through earlier. To replay the rejection once more for all to witness.

But he knew that this was how the Wildflowers rolled. They didn't do anything without the help of each other. Not that he wasn't grateful that they cared so much about him. He just wished he had a little time to himself to... process it all.

Sitting down on the sofa next to Scarlett, he was handed another beer by Dylan. The living room was way too small for all nine of them but, somehow, they all fit comfortably enough.

"Who wants to start?" Zoey asked him and Scarlett.

Thankfully, Scarlett took the reins and started explaining everything that had happened earlier. He sat there, looking into his beer, as she told the story. If the events had happened to any one of them, he would have felt instant sorrow, but now, instead, he just felt... dull.

By the time she was done telling the story, his beer was empty, and he knew the trip home he'd wanted to take that night to talk to his grandmother would have to wait until the morning.

"I can't believe it," Elle said after Scarlett finished talking. "That he would just turn his back so easily on you."

"He did it long ago. What difference does it make now?" he said with a shrug.

"That... ass wipe," Hannah added. "Sorry, I'm too tired to come up with something really horrible to call the man."

He held in a chuckle. "I'm fine, really," he said to the room. "I've gone my entire life not knowing who the guy was. It's not like I hadn't thought something like this would happen sooner or later."

Everyone was quiet.

"I didn't know who my father was until I was eight." Everyone turned to Aubrey. "Then when my mother died... I suddenly found myself living with this stranger, a really old man who lived in a different state, in a house bigger than I even knew homes could be." She glanced around. "Harold Smith is many things, but a loving and devoted father, he is not."

Zoey grabbed Aubrey's hand in her own and held onto it as Elle took Aubrey's other hand.

"I know what it's like to be rejected by family." Aubrey smiled suddenly. "But the ones that love you no matter what"—

she held up her linked fingers with her friends—"are all that really matters."

"You have us," Hannah said to him.

"Here, here." Several shouts echoed in the small room.

"Thanks, everyone." He held up his almost empty beer. "Here's to the family that matters."

CHAPTER TWENTY-THREE

The day after the reunion was Scarlett and Levi's first day off from work together. Shortly after breakfast, Levi drove them into town in his Jeep.

"If it's okay with you, I'm going to drop you off at your place and then swing by my gran's place for a... visit," he said as he drove.

"I can come with you, if you want?" she suggested.

"No." He reached over and took her hand. "I need to do this alone." He smiled over at her. "Thanks."

"If you need me, you know where I am." Part of her wanted to be there for Levi but the other part knew that it was a private moment between him and his grandmother.

"Thanks." He lifted her hand up and placed a kiss on her knuckles.

She held in a yawn, trying to hide the fact that she hadn't gotten a lot of sleep last night because she'd been worried about him. Even though he'd been sleeping peacefully next to her, her mind refused to shut down.

When he stopped in front of the big house, she climbed out

and leaned across the seat to give him a kiss. "I'll see you in a while?"

He nodded. "I'll be back soon," he promised her.

"Levi, don't be hard on your grandmother. She was just trying to protect you." His eyes softened.

"I'm not upset at her." He smiled. "I could never be mad at her. At least not for long."

"Good." She relaxed and then added, "I think I'm going to go up, take a bath, and maybe take a nap." She smiled. "Maybe I'll wake up to a kiss from my prince charming." She wiggled her eyebrows and had him laughing.

"I'll make sure to leave my horse outside." He waved as he drove away. Scarlett stood on the front porch for a few moments, looking around the small town. Besides her childhood home in Jacksonville, this was the only other place she'd felt fully accepted.

Sure, the camp was at the top of that list, but here, in this town, people liked her for who she was, not because she was one of the bosses.

Elle paid one of the kids on the street to maintain the yard and flowers around the house so that none of them would have to struggle with mowing a yard on their days off. Now, looking around the tidy fenced yard, she realized just how nice the place really was and how much she'd taken it for granted. Suddenly, she was energized and decided that she wanted to do something nice for Levi.

Lunch, she thought suddenly as she tossed her overnight bag down inside the doorway. She could walk to the store and grab a couple steaks and some vegetables and cook them up a nice lunch. Then she could set up a romantic area on the back patio for them.

Levi had never stayed there at the house with her. He'd slept on the sofa that one time, but for the next two days, it was going to seem like they were living together. Okay, they had been pretty much living together in her small room, but this felt different. This was an entire house, and Aubrey wasn't just down the hallway from them.

She grabbed her purse and walked down the sidewalk towards the small grocery store.

Two full days with no friends or family barging in or sharing meals with them, no distractions.

After spending that much time with Levi, she was sure she would know exactly how she felt about him. At least, that was the hope.

Stepping out of the heat into the small grocery store, she pushed a cart through the aisles and grabbed what she needed, mindful that she would have to carry it all back down the three blocks to the house.

"Scarlett?" Someone stopped her as she was making her way towards the steaks.

She looked over and stiffened when Rose Parker, one of Jenny's cronies, started walking down the aisle towards her. Rose had a small baby hanging in a pouch that was wrapped around her body and a little girl sitting in the shopping cart, swinging her legs and singing to herself.

"I thought that was you." Rose stopped besides Scarlett with a smile. "Gosh, you look amazing."

"Thanks." Scarlett glanced around, making sure Jenny wasn't anywhere near them. "You look—"

"Terrible." The woman chuckled and brushed a strand of dark hair out of her face. "Having a baby less than a month ago and caring for a two-year-old will do that to you." She smiled. "I've been meaning to come visit you and your sisters."

Scarlett's eyebrows shot up at that. Only people who cared for them knew how the Wildflowers thought of each other as family instead of just friends.

"Oh?" she asked, still a little on guard. She didn't think Rose would be in cahoots with Jenny, but then again, she hadn't believed Jenny would push her into a shallow pool on purpose either.

"Yes." Rose's smile slipped. "I heard what Jenny did to you. My husband works at the ER. He was one of the nurses that worked on you when you first came in. Anyway…" She shook her head, dislodging the strand of hair she'd pushed behind her ear. Then she ran a hand down her daughter's matching dark locks. "I lost track of her after that last year at camp. We all did." She sighed and shifted the baby. "I wanted to say that I am sorry. I know that Jenny and the rest of our gang used to torture you and your friends. For my role in your torment, I'm sorry. I wish I could go back and redo how I treated you and your friends."

"Thank you," Scarlett said slowly.

"I heard Jenny's still in town. My cousin owns a rental place along the beach and called me up to tell me that she rented the place from him, for a year."

Scarlett frowned. "I didn't know that she and her husband were sticking around."

"Oh, her husband didn't stay. He left that next day." Rose sighed. "Apparently, they had a huge fight in front of my cousin and her husband took off after calling his son."

"So, Jenny is still in town?" Scarlett glanced around again.

"Yes." Rose touched her arm. "But I'm sure she won't do anything crazy again." She shook her head. "I mean, I never would have guessed she would push you into a pool and almost kill you."

"Yeah." Scarlett nodded. "I… um." She glanced around, suddenly needing some fresh air. "I have to go."

"If you need anything," Rose said to her. "I really am sorry about… everything." Scarlett could tell that the woman was being sincere. Obviously, motherhood and time had changed her for the better.

"Thanks," she said before pushing her cart towards the meat aisle. Grabbing the first two steaks she saw, she made her way towards the checkout lane.

She kept darting her eyes around everywhere as she rushed home, as if waiting for Jenny to jump out of the bushes. Normally, she wouldn't have locked the front door of the house, but this time, she secured even the deadbolt.

Breathing heavy, a bead of sweat trickling down her back, she took a couple of deep breaths and tried to reassure herself that Jenny was not out for revenge. After all, she'd already done it. If you really looked at things, Scarlett had gotten the worse of things.

She pulled out her cell phone and shot a group text message off to her sister and friends.

-Just heard that Jenny rented a place in town. For a year!

Her sister and Elle replied immediately with the same comment.

-WHAT?

Hannah also responded quickly.

-You've got to be kidding

Aubrey didn't respond, and Scarlett realized that she was probably still teaching her Tai Chi class.

-Ran into Rose Parker at the store. She claims that Jenny is still in town, but her husband left.

A few seconds after hitting send, her phone rang.

"I couldn't do this over chat," Zoey said a little breathless when Scarlett answered. "I've got everyone here, except for Aubrey. She's in a class, so we'll fill her in later. What's up?"

Scarlett took a deep breath and then relayed what information she had as she moved around the kitchen putting the groceries away.

She desperately wanted a shower before she started making the food. She guessed she had at least another hour before Levi would be returning back.

"Lock all the doors," Elle suggested.

"Done." It was the first thing she'd done. She'd rushed around the large house and checked every window and door. "You guys keep an eye out there as well. There is no way she knows my schedule or that I'm off for the next two days." She shut the refrigerator door and leaned against the counter.

"True," Zoey added. "Still, we all feel so much better knowing Levi is staying there with you."

Scarlett decided not to mention that Levi was currently nowhere to be found. Instead, she made an excuse that she wanted a shower before making lunch and got off the phone.

Double checking the locks, she climbed the stairs, dragging her bag with her. There were, thankfully, five bedrooms and four bathrooms in the home, which meant they each had their own spaces.

Levi had been right. Although some of Scarlett's private things were in her room at the house, most of the things that mattered to her were at the camp.

Here she shared a Jack and Jill bathroom with her sister, but since Zoey's days off were two days after hers, they never ran into issues sharing the space.

Setting down her bag on her queen-sized bed, she moved into the large bathroom, wishing instantly that she had this bathroom in the apartment on the campgrounds as well. Turning on the water in the large glass shower, she pulled off her sweaty clothes and stepped under the cool water.

She couldn't stop thinking about the possibility of running into Jenny again. Why hadn't she taken more of Aubrey's self-defense classes? It wasn't as if she hadn't had the time over the last two years.

She'd even had to fill in for Aubrey once when Aubrey had the flu.

Zoey was more skilled at fighting back than Scarlett was. After all, her sister had had a few run-ins with their stepmother

Bridgette shortly after their father had died. Zoey hadn't let the woman push her around, at least not without pushing back. When Ryan had been holding a gun on Dylan, her sister had tackled her like a linebacker, according to Dylan, knocking them both down and saving Dylan from a deranged psychopath.

Scarlett sagged as she remembered that she'd stood there and taken the abuse from Jenny. She leaned her head under the spray, trying to relax.

Why was it that they were doomed to have to deal with crazy people? Before opening the camp, the worst she'd had to deal with was... well, Jenny. Back when they'd been teenagers.

She stayed in the shower until she felt every muscle in her body relax. As she stepped out and wrapped a towel around herself, she saw a flash of movement from Zoey's bedroom and froze.

Her body began to shake as she looked around for something, anything, to protect herself with. There was no way she was going to let Jenny get the upper hand with her again. This time, she was going to fight back.

Picking up a large can of hair spray, she tiptoed towards the door and glanced through the crack.

She held in a gasp as a shadow passed across the light from the window. With the towel securely wrapped around her body, she jumped out of the bathroom, screaming at the top of her lungs as she threw the can of hairspray towards the dark shadow standing in front of the window.

The heavy can hit Levi square in the chest. He jumped back and knocked over a lamp on her sister's desk.

Instead of being angry, he laughed at her as he rubbed the spot where the can had connected. Then, at that very moment, her towel slipped from her body and landed on the floor at her feet.

Levi's laughter died away as his eyes moved over her body.

"Damn, if this is how you treat all people you suspect as

burglars, we may have to change the locks on the house. I may have to sneak into your room more often." His voice was a little hoarse.

She picked up the towel and wrapped it around her body again. "I thought..." She noticed his bag sitting on her sister's bed and took a deep breath and tried to settle her heart. "This is my sister's room. Mine is next door." She nodded towards the bathroom door.

"Oh?" he said, not taking his eyes from her as he slowly moved forward. He almost tripped on the can of hair spray as he practically stalked her. "I think you missed a spot," he said as he reached for her.

She held her breath as his fingers ran over the edge of the towel. Closing her eyes, she swayed as he ran his hands over her skin.

"Sassy." He sighed and nudged the towel to the floor again. "My god," he groaned as he looked at her. Hunger filled his eyes as took a step closer.

"You have too many clothes on," she complained, reaching for his shirt. As she pulled it over his head, she watched those muscles bunch and move and felt her knees grow weak. "Levi." She licked her lips, wanting a taste of him, already daydreaming about exploring every inch of him. "I don't think I can wait..." She leaned up on her toes and kissed him.

"Me either." He hoisted her up against him. She wrapped her legs around his hips as he walked towards the bed.

"No, not in here." She nodded towards the door. "My sister would kill us." She chuckled as she took his earlobe into her mouth and sucked on it.

"I don't think I can make it..." he growled as she slid her tongue into his ear. Then he practically ran into her bedroom. When her body hit the mattress she laughed.

"Told you that you could make it." She sighed and watched

him slide his jeans off his hips, pulling on a condom as he kicked the denim aside.

When he slid into her this time, it felt as if she'd returned home. She couldn't explain it, but for the first time in her life, everything felt... perfect.

CHAPTER TWENTY-FOUR

"Who did you think I was?" Levi asked Scarlett as they lay naked on top of her bedspread. The midday sun was streaming in the window as their breathing leveled off.

She shrugged and then answered. "It doesn't matter, but I wasn't going to let anyone push me around this time without a fight."

He smiled against her skin and brushed a hand down her hip, enjoying the sound of her breath catching as he did so. "That's my Sassy."

"How did you get in?" she asked, shifting so she could look down at him.

"I saw you take out the hide-a-key last time." He shrugged.

She stiffened and then glanced towards the bedroom door.

"I locked the door behind me," he supplied. "The key is on the kitchen table." He felt her relax.

"Thanks." She sighed.

"What's going on?" he asked, knowing instantly that there was something she wasn't telling him.

"Jenny didn't go home," she said.

He sat up slightly.

"She is renting a place a few miles from here."

"What?" He sat up fully and looked down at her. "How did you find that out?"

"I ran into Rose," She reached for her shirt, but instead, picked his up and threw it over her head. "Her cousin is the one who rented the place to Jenny." She pulled on a pair of shorts. "She rented the place for a year."

He was silent as he thought, all the terrible possibilities rushing through his mind. "I think we should head back—"

"No." She shook her head and laid a hand on his shoulder, holding him in place. "Don't you dare say we should head back to the camp. There is no way she knows where I am. Besides, I'm not letting some crazy woman dictate my days off."

He opened his mouth to argue with her, but the determined look on Scarlett's face had him shutting it instead.

"Okay, what do you suggest we do instead?" he asked after a moment.

She smiled. "Well, I went to the store earlier and bought us a few steaks. I thought we could cook out and enjoy the beautiful day. We have a wonderful backyard here." She smiled as she wrapped her arms around his shoulders. "There's a large hammock that is big enough for two in the shade of the trees. There might even be some margarita mix left over from last week." She kissed him. "Then, when we've had our fun in the sun…" She ran her mouth over his ear, and he felt himself growing hard again. "We can come back in and…" She kissed him slowly. "Play Scrabble." He chuckled as he pulled her back down onto the bed.

A little over an hour later, they sat out on the patio furniture while their steaks finished cooking on the small grill. Scarlett had put together a quick salad and toasted some bread. Since she claimed she'd been too upset upon hearing the news about

Jenny to purchase any vegetables, they made do with chips and salsa that she found in the pantry.

"Do you think she's staying in town to torture us?" Scarlett asked after he'd pulled the steaks off the heat.

"No," he answered automatically. He'd thought about it while he'd cooked the steaks and had come up with an idea. "I think she's staying because she's afraid of her husband's family."

"What do you mean?" Scarlett asked before taking a bite of her steak.

He shrugged. "It's one of the reasons I went to see my gran." He took a bite of his own steak and smiled. "Great choice." He waved the next bite on his fork and shoved it in his mouth.

"Levi, what does your gran have to do with Jenny."

He set his fork down. "My gran is friends with her grandmother. It's funny, but I didn't even know that until she mentioned it the other day. Anyway, she told me that Jenny and her husband have been having issues. It's true what we heard. His son now runs the family business, and Jenny did empty out her husband's bank accounts. Well, for the most part. It's been a huge conflict between the old man and the rest of his family. Gran heard that the family has set up legal action to block Jenny from getting another dime of his. The word divorce was mentioned several times." He shrugged. "I think she took this last trip knowing she wouldn't return with her husband."

"That makes sense," Scarlett agreed. "We'd wondered why she chose now to come here. I mean, we've been open for two years now."

They ate in silence for a few minutes. "That explains why she was flirting with so many men at the pool. She was probably looking for husband number two," Scarlett said with a frown.

"There is no better place than around here to look for a rich husband?" He sighed. "Trust me, there are a lot of gold diggers around this area."

"Oh?" Her eyebrows shot up as she leaned slightly across the table. "And you would know this... how?"

He chuckled. "Because over the past few years, I've gone out with more than a handful. When they see my old Jeep pull up, they usually find some reason to call the date off."

She frowned. "Bitches." He chuckled. "I like your Jeep. It's perfect for around here. You can drive with the top and doors off most of the year. You don't have to worry if it rains, because it won't ruin your seats. You can drive in the sand." She ticked each item off on her fingers, then shrugged. "I'm building a list of possibilities, since I'm thinking of getting a Jeep for myself."

He laughed. "See, you get it, all my reasons for keeping the old gal around."

"You must not have been trying to date the right kind of women," she added.

He reached over and took her hand. "No, I wasn't." He lifted it to his lips and kissed her fingers. "I believe you mentioned something about a hammock?" he said once he was done eating.

"Yes." She motioned across the yard. There were several low live oak trees filling the backyard and, through their branches, he could see a blue hammock swaying in the breeze.

"Perfect." He stood up to take their empty dishes back into the house. "You make the drinks, I'll clean up."

They worked around one another in the kitchen, Scarlett mixing the cold drinks while he rinsed the dirty dishes and put them in the dishwasher.

They followed the small stone pathway out to the hanging hammock, and he helped her get in.

"Don't spill the drinks." She laughed as he sat on the edge of the hammock, holding both drinks. "Have you done this before?" she asked.

He laughed and almost tipped them both over, but finally got in. "Once," he answered and shifted until she settled in the crook of his arm. Handing her one of the drinks, he tapped his glass to hers. "To days off together."

She smiled. "This is nice," she said after taking a sip. "Normally I spend all my time inside, by myself, reading."

He sighed and relaxed back. "My gran has a list of things I try to fix each time I have a free day." He chuckled. "I could be cleaning out her gutters right now." He leaned down and kissed her. "Thank you for that."

She smiled up at him as she took another sip. When he saw her smile slip, he knew she was thinking about Jenny again.

Instead, she surprised him by asking.

"Did you say anything to your gran about your dad?" she asked.

"Yes." He sighed.

"And?"

"She was surprised. We Googled him together," he admitted, remembering all the information they had found.

Scarlett sat up slightly. "And?"

"He was surprisingly easy to find, now that I know his name and where he's from." He thought about all the details he'd read about the man he'd been searching for all his life. "He's from a powerful family in Copenhagen. He moved to the States with Leslie shortly after they were married. He took control of his family's furniture business in Miami shortly after that." He sent the hammock swaying by pushing his foot against a branch that hung over them.

"And?" she asked.

He chuckled and continued. "He and Leslie have no children. From an old article, I take it that they couldn't have kids." He frowned. "He actually said in the interview how he'd always wanted kids, but shortly after marrying Leslie they found out they couldn't have any."

She glanced up at him. "You've got to be kidding me?"

He shook his head. "No." He pulled her back down to his

side. "Like I said, he's heading up his family's furniture business."

"Which is?"

"Skrivbord Enterprises."

She sat up again. "As in... the major supplier for Ikea?"

He shrugged. "I'd never heard of it before."

"Levi, that's huge." She shook her head. "Yes, talk about a powerful family." She leaned back down against him. "Wow."

"Yeah, after reading up on things, I understand a little more."

"How did he and your mother meet? I mean, did your mother ever go overseas?" she asked.

"No. Michael Stiles was a foreign exchange student. He came over and lived in town with a family during my mother's sophomore year. When the year was up, he returned home. My guess is, it was after he found out about me and told my mother to..."

"Get rid of you," Scarlett finished for him.

"Yeah." He sighed.

"Then how did he and Leslie get together?"

"In another interview, he mentioned something about her traveling overseas to see him. Gran did some asking around about it. It appears that Leslie returned the favor and became a foreign exchange student, heading over to Denmark her senior year. My guess is they hooked up over there and, after she returned to the States for a few years, went back."

Scarlett leaned over and set her glass down on the small table next to the hammock and then took his and put it down as well. When she was done, she wrapped her arms around him.

"Do we know if he is still in town?" she asked with a yawn.

"No." He shook his head and realized he could enjoy a quick nap. It was so warm, but the breeze and the shade had cooled them off enough to be comfortable. The hammock was still swaying in the breeze and just feeling Scarlett against him had him relaxed.

"I'm sorry. That he was such a dick and you didn't get to know him better."

"So am I," he said and felt her drift off to sleep.

He never really drifted into a deep sleep, since so much was running through his mind, but he did enjoy shutting down physically for an hour.

When Scarlett shifted and woke, he held onto her as she yawned.

"You awake?" she asked.

"Yes. How'd you sleep?"

"Wonderful." She stretched. "I love sleeping outdoors. The fresh air is so... peaceful."

He nodded. "I take it you like camping then?"

She leaned up and smiled down at him. "It depends on what you call camping. If you mean hiking for hours and pitching a tent in the middle of nowhere..." She shook her head. "But pitching a tent on the edge of the beach..." She smiled. "I could get behind that."

"I'll make a note of it." He smiled and kissed her. "What do you want to do now?"

The way she was running her hands over his chest gave him plenty of ideas.

"How about a bike ride?" she suggested, sitting up. "There are bikes in the garage." She smiled down at him. "We can ride to the beach for an hour or two?"

"That sounds wonderful." He pulled her down again for a kiss, but overshifted and they both ended up on the grass underneath the hammock. He laughed as soon as his breath came back to him.

"That was smooth." She smiled down at him.

He groaned when her knee brushed against him, shrinking any possibility of heading upstairs for some fun before they went on that bike ride.

"Sorry." She gasped and moved quickly off him.

"It's okay, no permanent damage. This time." He sat up and brushed some grass from her shirt. "I'll pack us some drinks and snacks for the beach while you get ready."

"Thanks," she said as he helped her up from the ground. "Are your... jewels, okay?"

He took a cleansing breath and nodded. "Bruised, but I will overcome." He kissed her.

He found some cookies and sodas in the pantry and packed them in a beach bag that Scarlett gave him. Grabbing two beach towels from the laundry room, he opened the front door just as Scarlett came down the stairs.

"Ready?" he asked her.

"Yes, the bikes are in the garage." She smiled and set a sun hat on her head. She'd braided her hair and had changed into a swimsuit, shorts, and a large flowing tank top with flip flops.

Since he'd pulled on his board shorts before they'd come downstairs, he was already ready.

"Need anything else?" he asked as she stuffed a bottle of sunblock into the bag he carried.

"Nope, there are water bottles in the garage. We can grab two on our way out."

She turned and locked the door and then followed him out to the garage.

She used a code to get the door opened and stood back as he pulled out two bikes. He set the beach bag in the basket on the front of the bike that he chose for himself.

"Lead the way." He motioned ahead of them after she'd shut the garage door again.

They slowly rode their bikes to the entrance of the beach, which was less than a mile from the house. They had to pass the main part of town as they went, and he waved to several people he knew.

"You must know everyone in town," she said as they parked their bikes at the entrance of the beach.

He chuckled. "I have lived here all of my life," he pointed out.

"Right."

He threw the bag over his shoulder and took her hand.

"What's the farthest you've been from here?" she asked.

He thought about it. "Germany."

Her eyebrows shot up and he laughed. "I'm kidding. I've been to New York City but never outside the US. One summer Gran and I went to visit her family up there when I was fifteen."

"I haven't been to New York City yet." She frowned.

"We can go together. I still have an uncle and cousins up there." He laid their towels on the white sand.

"I'd like that." She pulled off her tank top and shorts, giving him a sexy view of her bright blue bikini. He felt his mouth water at the sight of her in the small suit.

Then he pulled his shirt off and saw her eyes heat.

"Here, let me." She held up the sunblock. He turned and let her slather the lotion on his skin.

"Your scratches are gone. Gosh, you only have a small scar." She moved her hands over him. "You're so light skinned. How do you keep from burning?" she asked. Her fingers running over him was pure torture.

"I use a lot of sunblock, but I still tan though. Just slowly." He shrugged. "Guess I know where I get the light Scandinavian skin from now. Gran and her family are Italian." He chuckled. "I used to think it was all a joke. That somehow I'd been switched at the hospital after birth." He sighed. "Now I know I just take after my father."

"Want to talk about it?" She handed the bottle to him and turned her back so he could smear the lotion into her skin.

"I think I've pretty much said it all," he said, making sure he covered every inch of her skin. He didn't want her to get burned.

"Except how you feel about all of this." She glanced over her shoulder.

He thought about it, then said. "I'm hurt and pissed." He shrugged. "That pretty much sums it up."

"Hurt at what? And pissed at what?"

"Hurt that he didn't want me and pissed that he didn't own me."

She laughed and turned towards him, taking his hands in her own. "Why is it men can't talk about their feelings?"

"I'm talking about them." He frowned out at the clear water, then glanced at her.

She was giving him a look that told him she wasn't buying it. Then she shifted until they were facing each other and took his hands in hers.

"You know, after my father left us, I was mad. Madder than I'd ever been. He hurt my mother. He hurt Zoey and me. It felt as if he chose some stranger over us. Like we weren't good enough anymore. Then Jenny sent me that picture and all of my hurt feelings were doubled. I decided right then and there that no man would break my heart. Just like I decided that Jenny would never get the upper hand on me again."

"Is that why I got the hairspray can to my chest earlier?" he joked.

"Hey, it was the only thing handy." She smiled. "But yes. I'm not going to let anyone push me around."

He pulled her into his arms. "I won't let anything like that happen ever again. She will never get close to you again."

She sighed and held onto him. "Talk to me." She pulled back.

"For as long as I can remember, I've dreamed of the day I would meet my father," he began. "Hundreds of different scenarios played in my mind. None of them came close to what happened. I'm hurt that I mean so little to a man who six years earlier said in an interview that his greatest regret was not having children." He looked down at their joined fingers. "And I'm pissed that I allowed a stranger's opinion to hurt me so badly. Especially when I know that I was raised by the most wonderful woman, who sacrificed everything for me." He smiled. "So, after further reflection, just like you, I've decided not to allow him to hurt me like that again. Next time I see him, I won't let him get the better of me."

She smiled. "I have a hairspray can that you can toss at him," she suggested.

He laughed and wrapped his arms around her. "Thanks, I'll keep that in mind. How about we head into the water for a swim? I need to cool off."

"Thank you," she said after he kissed her. "For opening up to me."

"Any time."

CHAPTER TWENTY-FIVE

Scarlett never imagined that spending two days with Levi would be so wonderful. The man was more attentive than anyone else she'd ever been with.

From stopping at a local diner for dinner after a few hours at the beach to the flowers and breakfast in bed he'd delivered to her the following morning.

She'd never had a man treat her with such... love, before. She knew she had to keep her heart shielded, but the more he opened up to her, the more the shield she'd built up around her heart melted.

By the time they drove back to the camp, she was pretty sure she was fully in love with Levi. Of course, that meant she was in desperate need of counsel from her mother. So during her first break of the day, she rushed across campus to her mother's cabin. Since her mother had started dating Reed, Scarlett no longer barged into the cabin unannounced.

"Scarlett." Her mother straightened her shirt after answering the door. Instantly, Scarlett knew that Reed was somewhere in the house.

"Sorry, I didn't mean to bother you." She started to back up.

"Honey, you're never a bother." Her mother pulled her into the house. Sure enough, Reed was standing in the kitchen, looking smug and horny.

"Mom, I can come back…"

"I was just heading out." Reed smiled at her, then swooped down and kissed her mother. "I've got a tennis game that I'm late for." He smiled at Scarlett. "We'll be joining you for a sunset ride tonight. See you later."

"Sure." She waited until the man had left the cabin. "I'm so sorry. I should have texted you." She groaned.

Her mother chuckled "It wouldn't have mattered. I didn't know he was stopping by. He swung by on his way to the courts." She sighed. "He does that all the time."

"What? Kiss you silly?" Scarlett joked.

"Yes, that too," her mother said easily. "Want something to drink? Cookies?" She pulled out a plate full of chocolate chip cookies that were still warm.

"Did you just bake these?" she asked after taking a bite.

"Yes, Zoey is supposed to be—"

"Mom!" Zoey called out from the front of the cabin.

Without a word, their mother held up the plate as Zoey rushed in.

"Thank god. This kid loves his cookies," her sister said, taking two of them from the plate. "What are you doing here?"

"I was here to talk," Scarlett said, leaning against the counter.

"About?" Her sister leaned next to her as she shoved another cookie in her mouth.

"It's nothing." Scarlett shrugged and started walking towards the door.

"No." Her mother took her by the shoulders and stopped her. "Talk," she said, pushing her lightly into a chair.

Scarlett knew better than to try and get out of it at this point. There was no way she could escape her mother and Zoey at the same time.

"Fine." She sighed. "But I need some chocolate milk first."

Her sister sat beside her as their mother poured three glasses of chocolate milk and set them down in front of them.

"I think I'm in love," she started.

Zoey almost spewed her milk out her nose as she laughed. "Duh," she said after she swallowed the drink of milk. "We've all known that for, like, weeks."

Her mother took her hand. "Sweetie, that's wonderful. Does Levi know?"

"No," she answered her mother as she glared at her sister. "I'm not sure. I guess I've locked myself away for so long, I'm not really positive how it feels."

"How do you feel?" her mother asked.

"Sick," she answered after a while.

"Yup, that's love," Zoey said with a smile. "The truth sucks." She shrugged when their mother glanced at her quickly.

"Love isn't easy," her mother added. "It's complicated and messy and sometimes makes you feel sick." She smiled. "But it's also the most wonderful feeling in the world." She hugged her. "And when you're in love, you won't question if you are. You'll know it instantly." She kissed her cheek.

"Are you in love with Reed?" Scarlett asked her and her mother's smile grew.

"Yes," she answered immediately. "Now, if I could just convince him that he's not just in lust with me." She chuckled. "Time. Sometimes it takes a little more time for one partner than the other to come to terms with how they feel."

Scarlett thought about her mother's words for the next few days. It was basically the only thing she thought about, except for the whole Jenny situation and the business with Levi's dad.

Security had been tightened around the campgrounds again since they had officially confirmed that Jenny was living just a few miles from there. They had learned their lesson with Ryan about how to deal with crazy.

JILL SANDERS

Dinner parties continued to pack the house, which meant extra security. Levi normally had a few evenings off each week, but since he'd moved in with her, he'd ended up helping out each night.

She knew it was because he hadn't wanted to leave her vulnerable again.

Actually, everyone was watching out for her more than normal. She couldn't even go on an evening ride with a group of guests without someone tagging along.

Tonight, it was her sister that rode Lady next to her. Scarlett loved all the horses they'd adopted from the local shelter, Alaqua Refuge. Carter, one of the vets that worked at the refuge, had picked ten of the best animals for them and was constantly keeping an eye out for more that would fit at the camp.

Scarlett was riding Butter, one of their newest adoptions, since the horse was still a little skittish. But Scarlett knew that Butter would come around once she knew she was safe and in a permanent home.

"Did you hear anything more from Levi's dad?" Zoey asked as they made their way up the trail towards the small bonfire area where the group would stop to watch the sunset for s'mores and drinks.

"No," she said as she made sure the small group of riders were all okay. "We're not even sure he's still in town. He could have gone back to Miami."

"Is that where he's from?" Zoey asked.

"That's where he and his wife currently live. I guess his wife was best friends with Levi's mother in high school."

"And she knew about Levi?" she asked.

"She had to have." Scarlett shifted in the saddle. "I mean, his mother was just sixteen when she had him. She went on to graduate with the woman. From what I understand, Leslie—that's her name—left shortly after Levi's mother's death."

Zoey was silent for a while. "Do you really think she committed suicide?"

Scarlett sighed. "I don't know. Levi's grandmother seems to think she didn't. When he asked her, she said she knew about the rumors that had been going around for years but didn't believe any of them."

"Rumors? As in plural? What else was going around?" Zoey asked.

Scarlett remembered what Levi had found out from his grandmother.

"That Levi's dad was someone with power and he'd had her murdered. Then there was one rumor that she'd been raped and beaten, and Levi's father was in prison and had escaped and killed her."

Scarlett shivered. "Like Elle's dad?"

"Yeah." Scarlett frowned. "I think that's where that one came from. A mix of the two stories." She shrugged.

"What does Levi think?" Zoey asked as they entered the small clearing where employees were waiting with the treats and drinks.

"He doesn't know." She nodded. "Later."

Her sister stopped her horse beside her.

"We'll dismount here for some treats and drinks so we can all enjoy the sunset," she told the guests. "There are restrooms..." She motioned towards the small hut that had recently been finished with bathroom stalls. "Feel free to roam about. We'll head back to the stable in an hour. If you need help dismounting... let one of us know."

For the next few minutes, they helped guests get settled and secured the animals to the posts. They handed out the fixings for s'mores and poured drinks as everyone gathered around the fire pit.

The pathway back to the barn was lit, so the horses wouldn't stumble in the darkness, and guests wouldn't lose their way. She would have never thought that nighttime rides could be so fulfilling.

"This was a fantastic addition." Zoey sighed, sipping her own mug of hot chocolate. She turned to Scarlett. "Great idea."

"Thanks," Scarlett laughed. "I got hungry during a ride and thought, hey, why not add food to the fun?" She sat in the chair next to her sister. She skipped out on the treat tonight, since she'd had a large dinner earlier with Levi.

"We've come a long way," Zoey said, tucking her feet up to her chest. "The wedding is just over a month away. I'm having a baby. The camp." Her sister's voice rose slightly with excitement. "Everything that has happened in the past few years. Three of us are engaged."

"To brothers no less," Scarlett added with a chuckle.

"Who would have thought." Zoey smiled. "We're going to be real family soon. I can't wait to help Elle and Hannah plan their spring and summer weddings after we're done focusing on mine and Dylan's." Zoey leaned her head back and looked up at the sky.

Scarlett did the same and enjoyed watching the colors change as the sky darkened.

Scarlett had to admit to herself that she was a little jealous of that fact, even though technically, they would be part of her family too. She liked the Costa men, all of them, including their father Leo, who stopped by the camp more often now that his sons were so involved in it. The man had even rekindled the relationship with Elle, his goddaughter.

"Then it will be baby showers," Scarlett said with a sigh. "Yours and god knows who else is going to be popping out a tiny Costa soon." She glanced over at her sister. "Or are you keeping the Rowlett name?"

Zoey laughed. "Nope. Would you?"

Scarlett thought about the last time she'd seen her father and instantly shook her head. "Hell no."

"I think the only one who would want to keep her name between all of us is Elle, and it's not even her birth name. She got rid of her father's name long before we all met."

Scarlett remembered when her friend had told them that she'd changed her last name after her father had killed her mother. When she'd moved to live with her grandfather, the change had been suggested to protect the young girl from all the town's gossip. After all, murder didn't happen very often in Pelican Point.

"Yeah. Giving up that last hold on Grandpa Joe will be hard."

"He was a great man. Probably the only father figure any of us had growing up," Zoey added.

"Agreed." She thought about the older man who had shown them nothing but kindness and love when they'd been five scrappy girls full of hormones and distrust.

"I need to…" Scarlett stood suddenly as she nodded towards the bathrooms.

"Sure." Zoey stood as well. "I'm going to snag another s'more before we head back."

Scarlett laughed. "You know, when they have to roll you into the delivery room, I'll remind you that it was the extra s'more that did it."

Zoey laughed as she moved away. Instead of stepping into the bathroom, Scarlett pulled out her phone and called Levi.

He had taken a group of guests out for an evening hike and should have been back by then, since the hike ended on the beach with champagne at sunset.

"Hey," he answered on the second ring.

"Hi." She smiled and hugged the phone to her ear.

"Are you almost done?" he asked her.

"No, another hour. We're about to head back after s'mores." She glanced around at the group. "You?"

"Yeah, I just finished up. I'm heading back now." She could hear him walking. "Want me to meet you at the barn?"

"No." She thought of the long day she'd had and knew that he'd started an hour before her. "Go get some rest. I'll meet you back in our room."

"Are you sure?"

"Yes." She smiled. "Zoey is here with me. I have to go pry the box of candy bars from her fingers before she stuffs them in her saddle bag."

Levi laughed. "I'll see you soon."

"Okay," she said and hung up.

She couldn't deny it from herself much longer. She was completely in love with the man. He'd changed everything about her. How she thought of not only him, but even herself.

For the past two years, she'd looked forward to each day, because she loved her job and wanted their business to succeed. Now, that wasn't the only reason she was happy to wake up each day. Having Levi sleep next to her, being there when she opened her eyes and when she fell asleep, had changed everything.

She couldn't imagine life without him now. He'd ruined her. Spoiled her. Loved her. And it was about time she let him know just how she felt.

CHAPTER TWENTY-SIX

Levi hung up his phone and tucked it in his back pocket as he continued down the path. The small group he'd led out on the evening hike had decided to stay at the beach.

When his phone rang again, he frowned down at the number. Normally, he wouldn't have answered the call from an unknown number, but he figured he had time to discourage whatever salesperson was calling him this late.

"Hello?" He stopped under one of the lights and listened.

"Levi?" The man's voice was instantly familiar.

"Yeah." Levi glanced around, unsure what to say to his father. He hadn't expected the man to call him. How had he even gotten Levi's number?

"This is Michael Stiles. Your... father," the man said uncomfortably.

"Yeah." Levi sat on one of the benches along the path, instantly enjoying getting off his feet, since he'd been on them for hours. "I surmised. What can I do for you?"

"I... wanted to see if we could meet sometime?" Michael asked.

Levi realized the man was nervous, which shocked him a little. The last time they'd talked, the guy had made it very clear that he wanted nothing to do with Levi. Actually, he'd acted pissed that Levi was even around.

"Why?" Levi asked, needing to know before he agreed to seeing him again.

His father was quiet for a moment, and Levi thought for a second that they'd been disconnected.

"I know this may come as a surprise to you, but I was a little in shock myself the other night. I had no clue you even existed. Until you were there. Standing in front of me. If possible, I'd like a chance to get to know you."

Bullshit, Levi thought, but kept his mouth shut.

"I'm still in town. We could meet tomorrow somewhere for lunch?" he suggested. "Please?" he added. Levi slumped slightly in the bench.

"There's a burger diner in town," Levi started.

"Sunset Café?" his father asked, surprising him.

"Yeah." Levi frowned. "Noon." Before he could change his mind, he hung up.

He must have sat there thinking for fifteen minutes before his phone rang again in his hands. Without looking, he answered.

"Hello?"

"Levi?" He practically groaned at hearing Jenny's voice on the line.

"Yes." He laid his head in his hand and held in the desire to kick himself for not screening his calls. How the hell had she gotten his number?

"I wanted to call and apologize for the other day. I know you think I pushed Scarlett on purpose, but I didn't. I was upset. That woman got between us once before all those years ago. I just didn't want her to do it again." Jenny's speech was slurred again.

"There is no us. You're married," Levi reminded her.

"No. I mean, yes, I am, but it's been over for a while now. I'd really like a chance to see you again."

"I'm seeing Scarlett," he growled. "And not interested."

She laughed, a high-pitched cackle. "I know, well, I heard about it at any rate. I think we both know there's something stronger between us. We felt it all those years ago and again just last week."

It was then that he realized that she must be extremely drunk again.

He knew that the only way to get through to her was to be direct. So he chose his words carefully to make sure she understood.

"Jenny, there has never been and will never be anything between us." He hung up.

When the phone rang again immediately, he answered it, ready to block her number if he needed to.

"You think this is over?" the muffled voice hissed in his ear. "I won't let you ruin everything. I got rid of you once, I'll do it again." When the phone chimed that the call had ended, he rolled his eyes at Jenny's tactics. Just as long as her anger was aimed at him and not Scarlett.

The woman was deranged.

Standing up, he strolled back to the main building and meet Zoey and Scarlett in the lobby. They were talking with Julie, one of the main employees, who worked at the front desk.

"Hey," Scarlett said when he walked up to her and wrapped his arms around her.

"Hey. Got a sec?"

"Sure." She frowned. "Thanks, Julie, I'll let them know." She waved as they stepped away. Instead of heading up the stairs towards the apartment and their room on the third floor, he took her hand and pulled her towards the back door, needing some fresh air again.

"What's up?" she asked once they were outside.

"My dad called," he said, dropping her hand to run his fingers through his hair.

"What?" She watched him.

"And Jenny called right after I hung up with him. Not sure how they both got my number, but I'm thinking I need to change it."

"Seriously?" She blinked a few times. "How the hell did they get your number?"

"I guess my home number is in the phone directory, but my cell..." He shook his head. "I'm not sure."

"Double whammy," she said softly as she strolled towards the back stairs and sat down. He moved over and sat next to her.

"Yeah. After I told Jenny I wasn't interested..." She glanced over at him quickly. "Long story, she thinks we have a... connection." He rolled his eyes. "Anyway, I discouraged her and hung up. Then she called back and..." He shrugged, unsure exactly what to call it. "She threatened me, I guess."

"What did she say?" she asked, concerned.

"That she wouldn't let me ruin everything." He wrapped an arm around her shoulders and pulled her close. "She's crazy and not the one I'm worried about currently. I'm meeting my dad tomorrow for lunch." He felt his gut twist at the thought of what he would say to the man.

"You are?" She glanced up at him. "Want me to—"

"No." He shook his head. "I need to do this alone."

"If you are sure." She bit her bottom lip and the slight unconscious move had his mind moving away from his father and his problems to kissing her again.

"I am." He smiled. "Now, help me get my mind off things. How was your ride?" He brushed a strand of her hair that had come loose from her long braid.

"Fine." She smiled and cupped his face. "I... have thought about things."

250

"And?" His heart skipped.

She paused a moment. "I think we should officially move in together."

He laughed immediately and hugged her. "Okay." He enjoyed the soft scent of her mixed with horse. He couldn't explain it, but it turned him on even more knowing she loved being outdoors so much.

"I know my room is small, but—"

"It doesn't matter. Most of my things are already here." He bent down and kissed her.

"They are?" she asked after he pulled back.

"The ones that matter," he said softly. He didn't want to think about anything besides her anymore. He was exhausted and still wanted to be able to make love to her that night. "I'm tired." He smiled at her. "What do you say we head up."

She jumped up and pulled him to his feet as he laughed. She was still so full of energy, something that always amazed him at the end of the day.

There was nothing better than holding Scarlett in his arms as they fell asleep after using up the rest of his energy to make love to her. When his mind continued to return to the call with his father, he focused on her breathing and the feel of her next to him and drifted off.

The following morning, he had to rush around the grounds to find someone to fill in for him for lunch. He had a hike and a zip-line tour scheduled that he was supposed to help out with. In the end, he got Dean to cover for him.

He felt nervous as he drove into town and parked in front of the Sunset Café to meet his father.

When Levi walked inside, the man wasn't there yet. Choosing an empty booth near the front, he sat and waited. He ordered an iced tea and tried to calm his nerves as he watched the door.

The man walked in ten minutes later dressed in a very

expensive grey suit. Instantly, every eye turned towards the door, then back at him as they grew large with curiosity.

Levi hadn't thought about everyone knowing him in town and the fact that seeing his double walk in would cause awareness to spread like wildfire through the town.

Holding in a groan, he waved the man over.

"Hi," his father said and sat down.

"Hi," Levi said and waited for the man to make the first move.

"This place hasn't changed." He looked around. Then he frowned. "I think we've drawn some attention."

"Yeah, sorry. I didn't think about that when I suggested meeting here."

The waitress, Brenda, a girl he'd gone to school with, walked over and smiled down at him.

"Levi, you didn't tell me that you'd found your father." Brenda smiled at his father.

"I just found out myself," Levi said dryly.

"Oh, well, how... exciting," Brenda said softly. "What can I get you?" She turned to his father with the same smile.

"I'll have the same, some tea." He nodded to Levi's glass.

When Brenda left to go get their drinks, Levi asked, "Why did you want to meet with me? I think you made your thoughts about me perfectly clear the other night."

Michael sighed and leaned back in the booth. "I was in shock." He shook his head. "I honestly didn't know about you until you were standing in front of me." He leaned closer. "My wife and I argued over it. Over her not telling me... earlier."

Levi watched sadness fill the man's eyes, and he knew he was sincere, since he was practically staring at his own face.

"How did you not know? Your wife was my mother's best friend."

Michael shrugged. "We never talked about Mary."

Something nagged at Levi. He thought whether he and Scarlett would keep secrets from one another like that. Could he go so long while withholding something so important?

He remembered that for the past two years, Scarlett had kept the reason behind her hurt from him. But that was different. Wasn't it? She'd opened up to him now. There was no doubt she'd been truthful about the entire situation with him once she'd finally told him what had happened.

"Why meet with me?" Levi asked.

Michael took a deep breath, his eyes running over Levi's face. "I have a son," he said, a slight smile turning his lips up. "Do you know how long I've dreamed..." He shook his head as he choked on his words. "A long time."

"I read your interviews," Levi broke in. "I know you don't have any other children. I know what you do. What your family does," he corrected.

Michael nodded, then waited until Brenda set his tea down.

"What can I get you for lunch?" she asked them both.

"Burger, you know how I like it," Levi said without taking his eyes from his father.

"I'll have the same," Michael said with a nod.

When Brenda left them, his father turned back to him.

"So, you know all about me. If you'd let me, I'd like to get the chance to know all about you," the man said nervously. Levi suddenly understood that he had the upper hand with the man.

He wasn't the one wanting something from their relationship. He'd had the benefit of knowing the man was out there, somewhere, for years. But his father had only known Levi existed for a few days now.

Levi relaxed slightly and decided that opening up a little to the man wouldn't hurt. And for the rest of the time they sat at the diner, Levi filled the man in on his somewhat boring life, making a point to explain how much his grandmother had done and how much she meant to him.

How she had sacrificed so much to raise Levi after his mother's death.

When they finished eating, Levi tried to pay for his own food, but Michael had insisted, and Levi didn't feel like arguing. Instead, he'd added a few extra bills to the table for Brenda and followed the man outside. "If possible," Michael said when they stood in the parking lot, "I'd like to see you again."

Levi nodded. He'd known it was coming. After all, the man had been glued to every word Levi had said. He'd even asked him more questions than Levi had come up with for him.

"You know where to find me." Levi shook the man's hand and, when he turned to go, he saw his grandmother standing on the sidewalk a few feet away from him with her book club group.

"Levi?" She recovered from the shock and smiled at him and then moved closer. "I didn't know you were meeting… here… today."

Shit, he thought. He hadn't called her and told her about the meeting with his father. What had he been thinking?

"Michael Stiles, this is my grandmother, Mary Lynn Grant. Gran, this is… my father." He stood there as his grandmother moved forward. Instead of shaking the man's hand, she wrapped her arms around him.

"You don't know how long Levi has been looking for you. I know I can speak for him when I say that he is excited to finally meet you." She looked between them and nodded. "I can see that your lunch went well." She reached up and touched his face, a move he'd grown up with his entire life.

Michael nodded and glanced towards him. "I… Whatever you may have heard, I had no idea Levi existed until the other night." He ran his hands through his hair. "I behaved badly, but I'm going to make things right between me and my son. I can't thank you enough for stepping up and taking Levi into your life. He's told me all about the sacrifices that you've made in order to raise him."

"It wasn't a sacrifice," his gran said easily. "He's family. He's mine." She reached over and took his hand. "I'd do anything for him." Her eyes moved to his father's as her smile slipped slightly. "And if anyone set out to hurt him, I'd do everything in my power to stop them and to protect him."

Levi felt his love for his gran spread even more.

"I understand," Michael said smoothly, taking the threat easily. He turned to Levi. "Thank you for meeting me today. As I mentioned, I'd like to meet again. Soon. I'll call you." He turned to go, then stopped. "If you want..." He pulled out a business card from his pocket and then took out a pen and wrote something on the back. "My private number. Call me if you want or need anything... to talk or whatever." He smiled and then Levi stood still as he moved closer and wrapped his arms around him in a hug. "Thanks," he said again softly next to Levi's ear. "You don't know how much this meant to me." He turned around and walked across the parking lot and climbed behind the wheel of a shiny silver BMW.

"That was... interesting," his gran said when they were alone. "Are you okay?" She turned to him.

"Yes," he said automatically. "You?"

"Yes." She chuckled. "I didn't believe you when you said he could be your twin." She touched his face again. "If I'd run into that man alone, I'd have known instantly that he was your father. I might even have assumed it was you."

"Yeah, that's what happened with Scarlett." He chuckled. "I think the news is out." He motioned towards the diner. "The entire town will be talking about it now."

"Good." She smiled at him and kissed his cheek. "Wonderful news should spread as fast as possible."

CHAPTER TWENTY-SEVEN

Scarlett waited for Levi in the parking lot. When she spotted his Jeep, she waved and moved over to the parking spot he took.

"So?" she asked as he stepped out and wrapped his arms around her. "How did it go?"

"Good." He kissed her. "Gran even got a chance to meet him." He groaned slightly. "I should have called her and told her that I was meeting him."

"Yeah," she agreed. "We should have let her know. But how did it go?" she asked again, needing more details.

"I believe him when he says he didn't know about me. He wanted to know everything about me."

"Did you tell him?"

"I did." He took her hand as they started walking towards the bar area, where she knew he was supposed to help Britt out for the afternoon rush.

She was supposed to be there, helping out with another water volleyball game before dinner. Which meant she could hang out with him a little longer.

"And?" she asked again.

He smiled over at her. "He seems pretty cool."

She stopped him and waited until he looked down at her. "Are you okay?"

"I am." He smiled down at her. "Really. It was actually pretty good."

"If you're sure." She tried to assess his emotions and realized he was lighthearted and totally back to himself.

"I am." He rubbed her arms and then kissed her.

"I'm happy for you," she said as they started walking again. She held his hand as they went down the pathway towards the larger pool area.

"Scarlett." Ruth, one of the other counselors, rushed down the pathway towards them. "Elle said she needed you to make sure Eli showed up today." Ruth smiled at Levi. "Hey." She waved to him before jogging off again.

"Hey." He laughed. "That was like a hit and run."

"Ugh." Scarlett sighed. "I love my job, but I hate being a boss."

He chuckled and pulled her into his arms. "But you're so good at it."

"I think that's why Elle sends me to fire people. Eli has been late for work all week long." She rolled her eyes. "No doubt she sent Ruth to tell me instead of calling me on the walkie talkie so I couldn't argue with her." She motioned to the small device hanging on her hip.

He chuckled and kissed her. "Go, be a boss. I don't want to be late for my shift either." He motioned towards the bar area.

"Later," she said and kissed him. She rushed across the grounds and stopped a few feet from the beach. Eli was talking with an older man, showing him how to put on the snorkeling gear.

Relaxing slightly, she slowly walked towards the little hut.

"Afternoon," she said easily when the guest left.

"Hey," Eli said with a shrug. "Checking up on me?"

She smiled easily. "Just passing by."

"I'm here." He tossed down a scuba mask in frustration.

"And I'm thankful you are. Otherwise I was going to have to cancel my own schedule to fill in for you." She moved closer and leaned on the counter to watch him. "Are you doing okay?" she asked, seeing the young man struggling with his attitude.

He turned and was about to say something when she noticed the worry in his eyes.

"What's going on?" she asked him, her tone changing to concern instead of annoyance. "Is everything okay at home?"

He deflated instantly. His eyes moved around, landing anywhere but on her. "My mom's sick."

Scarlett quickly scanned her memory and remembered that Eli lived alone with his mother.

"Is it serious?" she asked.

"They say it's stage four." He almost cried.

"Oh my god." She moved around the counter and touched his arm. "I'm so sorry. Is there anything we can do to help out?"

She hadn't expected the boy to burst into tears and wrap his arms around her as he told her all about watching his mother's health deteriorate. She held onto the teenager and, when he was done crying, called for backup.

"Hi, Dylan," she said when he showed up less than five minutes later. "Thanks for filling in for Eli."

"Sure thing." Dylan smiled at the kid. "You doing okay?"

"Yeah." The boy wiped his nose on his arm and looked embarrassed that he'd cried.

"Eli, one thing that's really great about this job is it comes with perks. Such as working with five women bosses who care more about our employees than most. Go home, be with your mom when you need to. Your job is going to be here. Your pay is going to stay the same no matter what during this hard time." She touched his arm. "Don't worry. We're going to do everything we can to help you through this. Okay?"

The kid looked between her and Dylan, then nodded. "Thanks Miss…"

"Oh god, don't call me that. Scarlett." She pointed to her chest. "You should know that by now." She hugged him. "Keep us posted on your mother's health."

"Okay," he said and wiped his eyes. "She's at the hospital in Pensacola. Which is why I've been late the last couple days."

"Don't worry about it." She smiled. "If you need anything, give us a call. We are here for you. When you want to work, just come on in. We will find something for you to do." She touched his arm.

"Thanks, Miss…. Scarlett." Eli glanced over at Dylan. "Thanks."

"Sure thing, bud." Dylan nodded.

When Eli left, Scarlett turned to Dylan. "Thanks for filling in so quickly."

"Sure." He nodded. "That's rough. No kid should have to go through something like that. Does he have a dad? Any other family?"

She thought about it. "No dad. I think he has a younger sister."

Dylan nodded. "If it's okay, I'd like to step up and make sure he's taken care of financially. Owen can…"

She stopped him by walking over and wrapping her arms around him. "I think it's wonderful," she said and kissed his cheek. "I know why my sister loves you so much." She smiled up at him. "Do what you can. I'll make sure we do the same."

Dylan nodded. "Now, want to show me what it is I need to do here? I haven't worked this job before."

She laughed and, for the next few minutes, filled him in on his job.

When she was done, she made her way back towards the pool area. Her water volleyball game wasn't supposed to start for another half an hour. But when she stepped into the bar area, she didn't see Levi.

"Where's Levi?" she asked Britt, who was rushing around, trying to stay on top of the orders.

"I don't know, he didn't show up." She shrugged and moved to fill a beer.

"What?" She frowned. "I left him a few feet from here." She glanced back at the pathway where she'd left him almost half an hour ago. "He was on his way here."

Britt shrugged. "Guess he got distracted," she said as she took another order.

Scarlett pulled out her phone and called his but it went to voicemail instantly.

"Problem?" Britt asked.

Pulling out her walkie talkie, she asked if anyone had seen Levi in the last half hour.

"No," Zoey answered immediately.

Elle, Hannah, and Aubrey all answered shortly after, followed by Aiden, Dylan, and Liam.

"Someone check the kitchen," she asked as she scanned the crowded pool deck.

"Not here," Zoey answered. "I'm in the dining hall."

"Big surprise there," Elle joked into the walkie talkie.

"Could he still be having lunch with his dad?" Zoey asked.

"No, I met him and left him a few feet from the pool bar. Britt said he never showed up."

Everyone was silent. "Heading your way," Zoey said.

"Me too," Elle added. "Liam, Aub, and I are just around the corner."

By the time that her friends arrived, she'd worked herself into a full-blown panic attack.

"Sit." Britt shoved her into a chair.

"What's going on?" her sister asked.

"I left him..." Scarlett said between deep breaths and

drinking a glass of water. "Right there." She pointed to the pathway. "He was only fifteen feet from here. He was going to come in and help Britt." She glanced around at the faces. "He had a good lunch with his dad and was upbeat about working."

"We'll find him," her sister said. "I'm sure he just had to… maybe change clothes?"

"No." She shut her eyes. "He was wearing his camp shirt and slacks."

"Okay, then maybe…" Zoey glanced around then pulled out her cell phone and called the front desk. "Julie, did you send out a notice for Levi?" Her sister was silent as she listened. "And no one has seen him since?" She waited again. "Okay, keep me posted." She hung up.

"What?" Scarlett asked.

"Someone saw him walking with a woman, heading towards the boat dock."

Before her sister was done talking, Scarlett jumped up and rushed down the pathway. She heard footsteps behind her and watched Liam passed her. She pushed herself harder and caught up with him, not willing to let him overtake her and find Levi first.

They stopped in front of the boat house at the same time.

"You check inside, I'll check around on the pathways," he said and disappeared. Scarlett could hear the rest of the group on the pathway and rushed into the boathouse, knowing instantly that the place was empty.

"He's not here," she called out and moved to step out the door. She stopped when she noticed something on the ground.

Bending over, she picked up the small card and frowned down at Levi's dad's business card.

"What's that?" Zoey asked, a little breathless as she stopped next to her.

"Levi must have gotten this at lunch." She scanned the boat house. "He was here." She tucked the card in her pocket and rushed around the space. "He's not here now." She turned to her sister.

"Maybe he took a boat out?" Zoey motioned to the spot where one of the smaller motorboats usually sat.

Without thinking, Scarlett jumped in the boat in the next slip and started it.

"I'm coming with," Zoey said, but before she could jump in, Aubrey was there.

"No, you are not. You got motion sick the other night in the rowboat. I'll go with her. You stay here and keep us posted." Aubrey pushed the boat away after Zoey released the ropes.

"He has to be here," Scarlett said, pushing the boat to full throttle, unsure which direction to take.

"There," Aubrey motioned. "The water is still rippling."

Scarlett saw it then, the ripples in the small calm river area that was filled with tall sea grass and headed away from the open waters of the bay and the gulf.

"Reed's house is this way," Aubrey pointed out.

"Right." Scarlett nodded.

"He could have gone to visit him?" she suggested.

"No." She shook her head. "He was a few steps away from helping Britt. He wouldn't have just decided to leave. Not without telling me." She scanned the water.

"What's that?" Aubrey asked and Scarlett glanced back to see where Aubrey was pointing. "Is that a... shoe?"

Scarlett cut the motor, and the boat drifted until she could bend down and pick Levi's flip flop from the water.

"It's Levi's." She scanned the horizon then called out several times.

"Are you sure?" Aubrey asked.

"Yes, he was wearing..." She gasped suddenly and then turned her eyes towards the water. She screamed out. Without saying anything, she tossed her phone down and jumped over the edge of the boat.

Her lungs screamed at her as she made her way towards the bottom of the sandy bank. If she hadn't been looking for him, she would never have spotted Levi struggling under the water.

She didn't know what to expect, but the thick rope wrapped around his chest and arms hadn't been part of the plan.

When he noticed her, he stilled for a split second, then they worked together to free his arms.

She lost count of the moments, but when Levi stopped moving, she stopped herself from crying out. They hadn't even removed a single rope from around him and now it was so twisted, she doubted she would ever be able to break him free. Not in time.

Then a hand shoved at her, pushing her up towards the surface. Aubrey pointed to the surface and motioned towards Levi. Scarlett rushed to the surface and gulped in a large breath before heading back down. This time, however, as Aubrey worked on the ropes, she took Levi's face in her hands and blew all of the breath she'd taken into his lungs. Most of it spewed back out at her, but she prayed some of the oxygen reached his lungs. She repeated that twice before Aubrey had to surface for a breath.

It took way too long for the rope to loosen around him. Too long for them to drag his lifeless body up and into the small boat. They almost tipped it over as she gripped him and tugged him over the edge of the boat until he lay in the hull.

"You do CPR," Aubrey said a little breathless. "I'll drive. I called it in before jumping in the water."

Scarlett started chest compressions, making sure to check his airway often and clearing as much water as she could each time.

"Please," she begged as she pushed on his chest. "Don't leave me," she cried over and over again.

When the boat bumped into the dock, the EMTs were waiting for them.

"Help," Scarlett cried, totally drained of energy.

Levi was lifted and one of the EMTs took over with the chest compressions.

"I can't lose him," she said to her sister, who wrapped her arms around her along with Aubrey, Elle, and Hannah. A jacket was pushed around her shoulders as they followed the ambulance workers.

"You won't," her friends assured her.

She watched as they rolled him away and knew that, if he survived this, she was never going to question her love for Levi again. No matter what happened, nothing could ever hurt as bad as this moment. Even if he broke her heart, she could never hurt as much as seeing him fight for his life at the bottom of the river.

CHAPTER TWENTY-EIGHT

*D*ying didn't hurt as much as coming back to life did. Drifting away while looking at the woman he loved was peaceful. Sure, it pained him, knowing that she would hurt for a time. But after a brief moment, he knew she would recover and continue to live life thanks to the support of her friends and loved ones.

He thought briefly about his grandmother and felt sorrow for her. After all, the woman had lost her husband and daughter. Would it break her? Losing him?

Then he'd been consumed by the blackness. Sweet peacefulness. Until he hadn't. Pins and needles jabbed him all at once, all over his body. His lungs felt like they were on fire; his throat burned and felt constricted.

His toes and fingers ached and it spread up to the rest of his body.

He moved to push away the pain, only to be held in place.

"Easy," someone said above him. "We've got you."

Who the hell? He tried to remember where he was. What had happened? The only thing he could remember was that he wanted to see Scarlett and his grandmother one last time.

"Levi," Scarlett's voice cried out. "Please," she begged him. He was just about to pass back into the darkness, but upon hearing her voice, he fought it and tried to open his eyes. His eyelids felt like they weighed a million pounds.

He managed to crack them enough to see dark grey shadows hovering above him.

"Levi, I'm here," Scarlett said over and over. "Don't leave me. Please," she cried. He tried to reach out for her, but his entire body was weighed down now.

"Levi?" His grandmother's voice hovered somewhere in the background. "Come back to us."

"Sassy?" He tried to fight the darkness. "Gran?" He shook his head, confused, the women and what each of them meant to him blurring. His grandmother was his life. She'd been the only one he had really loved, until recently. "Help me," he wanted to shout. "I can't break free." The darkness overtook him again. This time when he surfaced, he blinked a few times and realized he was looking down at himself.

When he blinked again, the face hovering above him didn't. He opened his mouth to talk and the reflection did the same only it said his name instead of what he'd been trying to say.

Then, his reflection was replaced by Scarlett, and Levi smiled as she moved closer to him.

"You're back." She smiled down at him. "Your grandmother and dad are here." She nodded behind her.

His eyes never left her face as he reached up, hindered slightly by the tubes taped to his arm. When his fingers touched her face, he sighed.

"You're real." He groaned.

"Yes." She smiled down at him. "I'm real." She leaned down and placed a soft kiss on his lips as a tear fell from her eyes and landed on his cheek. "And I love you." She reached over and quickly wiped the tear away. "I love you," she said again with a smile.

"I love you." He took a deep breath, and instantly regretted it as his chest tightened, causing him to cough.

"Easy," she said and reached for a glass of water with a straw hanging out of it. "Here." She tried to get him to drink but he pushed it away.

"I've..." —he took a deep breath—"had enough water for a while."

She paused, then chuckled as more tears slipped down her face. Then she buried her face into his shoulder and cried as he held onto her.

"Gran?" he asked, holding onto Scarlett.

"I'm here, Levi." His grandmother's face came into view. She too had tears flowing from her eyes.

He reached for her and took her offered hand. "I'm sorry."

She shook her head quickly. "For what, boy?"

He smiled. "I didn't want to leave you. I know everyone else has, but I didn't want to."

"I know, son." She smiled down at him as she wiped her eyes. "I know."

"I love you," he said as Scarlett sat up again and wiped her eyes dry.

"I love you too," his grandmother said, then she glanced over her shoulder. "I think your dad would like a moment with you."

"Dad?" He frowned and then just as it had been uploaded to his memory like the Matrix, the last meeting with the man played in his head and he remembered. "Michael's here?"

"Right here." His father stepped into his view.

Levi realized then that he hadn't been looking down at himself earlier. It had been his father leaning over him.

"Hey," he said softly. He reached to shake the man's hand.

"You don't know how happy I am to know that you're okay," his father said.

"Me too," he agreed.

"I'll let you get some rest. When you're up to it, I'd like to have a chat with you," Michael said, soberly.

"Sure thing." He turned his attention back to Scarlett.

"What happened?" he asked when he heard a door shut.

"You don't remember?" she asked.

"I'm going to tell everyone that he's awake," his grandmother said from somewhere in the room.

"See you later?" he asked.

"Count on it," she agreed and, again, he heard a door shut.

"Well?" he asked when they were alone.

Scarlett brushed her hand over his face slowly, then after taking a deep breath, said, "Someone tied an anchor around you and threw you in the bottom of the river."

He frowned, trying to remember anything. Closing his eyes, he listened to Scarlett tell him how Aubrey and she had saved him.

It was strange. The last thing he could remember was walking down the path with Scarlett, talking about his lunch with his dad.

"I can't remember anything," he said after she was done.

"The doctor... she said that the drugs she'd given you would mess with your memory. That it would come back in time." She lifted his hand to her lips. "You're alive." She rested her head in his hand. "I don't know what I would have done if..." She glanced up at him. "They did CPR on you for almost fifteen minutes." Another tear slipped from her eyes and he reached up to catch it.

"I don't remember anything," he reassured her. "My chest and throat hurt."

"You swallowed a lot of water and well... chest compressions and them zapping you with the paddles." She closed her eyes as if she was remembering it all.

"Hey." He touched her face. "I'm here now." He sighed,

feeling the stiffness in his entire body. "I think I need a nap though."

"She laughed. "Sleep. I'll be right here." She kissed him again. "Sassy?"

"Yes." She smiled at his nickname.

"Whoever did this to me, I'll remember," he assured her.

"I know you will," she agreed as he closed his eyes and once again drifted into the darkness.

When he opened his eyes the next time, it was to the annoying sound of Zoey and Aubrey arguing.

"I don't care what the man says. He's not coming in. This is about family now. Not blood family, but family," Zoey was saying.

"He is family. Just because he married crazy doesn't mean he doesn't care as much about Levi as we do," Aubrey replied.

"Really?" he said, getting everyone's attention. "Is this the best way to wake a man up from the dead?"

"Levi." Scarlett smiled at him as he reached for the bed controls and slowly raised his bed so he could see the rest of the small crowd in his room.

"Why wasn't I invited to the party?" he asked as he looked around. There were even balloons and flowers. "Where's the cake?" he asked dryly.

"Sorry," Zoey and Aubrey said together.

"What's going on?" he asked Scarlett.

"You remember... our last conversation?" She bit her bottom lip.

"Yes." He nodded slowly, testing the soreness in his body.

"Well, you don't have to remember anything that happened to you. We checked the video and well..."

"It was Leslie," Zoey blurted out. "She approached you after Scarlett left you on the pathway. She had a gun and forced you walk to the boathouse. We assume she tied the anchor to you and knocked you over the head, since there's a large bump on your forehead." Zoey motioned to his head.

He hadn't even felt that pain until she'd mentioned it.

"Thanks, I was unaware until you said something." He touched the bandage slowly.

"She dumped the boat near the road," Aubrey finished.

"They have her in custody," Elle supplied.

"Your dad," Aubrey started again. "He's outside. The police don't think he had anything to do with any of this. Well, he wants to talk to you. If you want."

"I don't think you should," Zoey added. "He could have known about her plans." She crossed her arms over her chest. "We're all the family you need." Her eyes narrowed. "Us and your grandmother."

"Where is Gran?" he asked Scarlett.

"Home, resting," she assured him. "It's a little past nine in the morning. She'll be here soon."

He nodded. "I'll talk to him," he said to the room. "Thank you, everyone, for your concern. But I'd like to hear what he has to say."

Zoey frowned but then nodded.

"I'll go let him in. Would you like us to leave?" Aubrey asked.

"No, as you all pointed out, you are family too. Whatever he has to say, he can say in front of my family."

Scarlett took his hand and smiled down at him.

When Michael stepped into the room, Levi realized how different he looked from the last time he'd seen him.

Gone was the suave sophisticated man. He'd been replaced by a man in jeans and a wrinkled T-shirt. The man looked tired and a little lost.

"Son, I had no idea…" he started only to stop and shake his head and close his eyes. "I swear."

"Here," Scarlett said, holding out a chair for him. "Why don't you sit and tell us everything you know."

His father sat just as his grandmother stepped into the room with a huge container from the bakery.

"Donuts." She motioned. "What's going on?"

Zoey grabbed the container from her and whispered. "Michael's going to tell us everything he knows about his deranged wife who tried to kill your grandson."

Every eye turned to Michael as they all waited.

His father took another deep breath. "I had no idea Leslie had even gone to the camp." He looked around the room. "I mentioned, during our lunch, that we had fought about me contacting you."

Levi nodded in agreement. "You did." He remembered that part.

"Well, what I didn't mention was that she had given me an ultimatum. Her or you." He took a deep breath. "Things haven't been great between us for a few years now. And, after knowing how she'd hidden you from me for all these years... Well, I chose to meet you for lunch. I had no idea she would do something like this." He shook his head as sadness filled his blue eyes. "I just found you. I want a chance to get to know you. To have you in my life. I can't imagine losing you now."

"I believe you," Levi said, reaching out for the man's hand. "After all, you're wearing my face. I know when I'm lying." He chuckled and then groaned at the pain it caused him.

His father let a breath of relief out and nodded.

"I think you are the one wearing his face," Aubrey said softly. "He is your father, after all."

Levi smiled, then glanced around. "Why?" he asked. "Why would she do this?"

"When they woke us up to arrest her at our rental, she kept screaming that she'd gotten rid of you before. That you and your mother had gotten in between us before, and that she'd taken care of you both before." His father sobered. He glanced around the room, then his eyes zoned in on his grandmother's eyes. "I think Leslie had something to do with your daughter's death."

Levi stiffened and jerked his head around to his grandmother.

"They're interviewing her about it now," his father added. "But some of the things she was saying when they arrested her..." He closed his eyes and shook his head. "She's not the woman I married." His eyes flew open. "If I had known about you, that you existed, I would have tried to reach out. I'd always wondered why she was dead set against coming back home or to the reunion." He looked down at his hands.

Levi watched his grandmother move across the room and wrap her arms around the man. "You couldn't have known," she said softly. "What's in the past is done. Now you have to look forward to time with your son." She smiled over at him. "And trust me when I say, Levi has been looking forward to spending time with you his entire life."

EPILOGUE

"So," Levi said as he settled on the sofa in the house in Pelican Point, "you love me?"

She laughed and would have playfully slapped his shoulder, but then she remembered how bruised he was under his shirt and touched his cheek instead.

"Yes, you idiot." She leaned over and kissed him. "I do."

"Do what?" he asked with a wicked smile.

"How many times are you going to make me say it?" she asked.

He chuckled, then hissed and held his ribs. "Forever," he answered once he'd recovered.

"Don't overdo it," she warned him.

"Never." He pulled her closer to his side. "What time is everyone coming over?" he asked after he'd kissed her.

"Soon." She pulled him back down to her lips, but was interrupted by the front door of the house swinging open as everyone crowded into the living room.

"Not enough time." He sighed and let her go as she moved to help carry in the food and drinks.

"This is the first bachelorette party I've ever been to," he joked as everyone moved around him.

"You are not really here," Elle said. "In fact..." She removed something from a bag she'd been carrying and then laughed. "You are officially Lisa tonight." She set a hat on his head. A big, pink hat full of ribbons and bows. "There." Elle nodded. "That suits you."

Scarlett laughed while Aubrey snapped a picture quickly of him before he had a chance to remove it.

"Sorry," Aubrey said softly as she looked down at her phone.

"Don't you dare post that," he warned.

"Too late," Aubrey said, moving out of the room. "I wouldn't post it if you could catch me, but seeing as you're on bed rest..." She stuck out her tongue at him as she moved into the kitchen.

"You owe me," he said to Scarlett when she came back into the room.

"Here." She handed him a large slice of chocolate cake and set a glass of milk down next to him. "My first payment," she said with a kiss. "The rest will come later." She wiggled her eyebrows.

When she stepped into the next room, her sister and friends were gathered around the kitchen table talking in low tones.

"What's up?" She frowned, instantly worried.

They parted and sitting there, on the kitchen table, sat a small box. Scarlett's heart jumped.

"What... is that..." She shook her head.

"It's your turn," Zoey said with a smile.

Scarlett moved forward and gently flipped the lid of the box open. The ugly unicorn ring sat nestled inside it as if it was the rarest of gems.

She remembered when the five friends had pooled their money together to purchase the thing years ago. They had all promised, after a fight of who would wear it, that the first one of them to fall in love would get the ring. Thus far the ring had been passed from Zoey to Elle to Hannah. And now, it appears it was her turn to wear it.

Scarlett couldn't stop herself from laughing.

"That is so ugly." She covered her mouth with her hand as tears started falling from her eyes.

"Yes, it is, but it's yours for now." Hannah moved forward and lifted the box towards her.

"And, until another ring is on that finger, it will stay there," Elle said, slipping it onto her finger for her.

Scarlett looked down through tear-filled eyes at the silly unicorn staring back up at her.

"It's the most beautiful thing I've ever seen," she said to her friends as they surrounded her in a hug.

ALSO BY JILL SANDERS

The Pride Series

Finding Pride

Discovering Pride

Returning Pride

Lasting Pride

Serving Pride

Red Hot Christmas

My Sweet Valentine

Return To Me

Rescue Me

A Pride Christmas

The Secret Series

Secret Seduction

Secret Pleasure

Secret Guardian

Secret Passions

Secret Identity

Secret Sauce

The West Series

Loving Lauren

Taming Alex

Holding Haley

Missy's Moment

Breaking Travis

Roping Ryan

Wild Bride

Corey's Catch

Tessa's Turn

Saving Trace

The Grayton Series

Last Resort

Someday Beach

Rip Current

In Too Deep

Swept Away

High Tide

Lucky Series

Unlucky In Love

Sweet Resolve

Best of Luck

A Little Luck

Silver Cove Series

Silver Lining

French Kiss

Happy Accident

Hidden Charm

A Silver Cove Christmas

Sweet Surrender

Entangled Series – Paranormal Romance

The Awakening
The Beckoning
The Ascension
The Presence

Haven, Montana Series
Closer to You
Never Let Go
Holding On
Coming Home

Pride Oregon Series
A Dash of Love
My Kind of Love
Season of Love
Tis the Season
Dare to Love
Where I Belong

Wildflowers Series
Summer Nights
Summer Heat
Summer Secrets
Summer Fling
Summer's End

Distracted Series
Wake Me
Tame Me

Stand Alone Books

Twisted Rock

Hope Harbor

For a complete list of books:

http://JillSanders.com

ABOUT THE AUTHOR

Jill Sanders is a New York Times, USA Today, and international bestselling author of Sweet Contemporary Romance, Romantic Suspense, Western Romance, and Paranormal Romance novels. With over 55 books in eleven series, translations into several different languages, and audiobooks there's plenty to choose from. Look for Jill's bestselling stories wherever romance books are sold or visit her at jillsanders.com

Jill comes from a large family with six siblings, including an identical twin. She was raised in the Pacific Northwest and later relocated to Colorado for college and a successful IT career before discovering her talent for writing sweet and sexy page-turners. After Colorado, she decided to move south, living in Texas and now making her home along the Emerald Coast of Florida. You will find that the settings of several of her series are inspired by her time spent living in these areas. She has two sons and off-set the testosterone in her house by adopting three furry little ladies that provide her company while she's locked in her writing cave. She enjoys heading to the beach, hiking, swimming, wine-tasting, and pickleball with her husband, and of course writing. If you have read any of her books, you may also notice that there is a love of food, especially sweets! She has been blamed for a few added pounds by her assistant, editor, and fans... donuts or pie anyone?

facebook.com/JillSandersBooks
twitter.com/JillMSanders
bookbub.com/authors/jill-sanders

Made in the USA
Las Vegas, NV
15 May 2021

23097034R00173